I Plight Thee My Troth

To Have and Be Told
In Sickness and in Stealth
'Til the Ranch Do Us Part

JULANE HIEBERT

Wings of Hope

EST. 2013

Published by Wings of Hope Publishing Group
Established 2013
www.wingsofhopepublishing.com
Find us on Facebook: Search "Wings of Hope"

Printed in the United States of America

Hiebert, Julane
I Plight Thee My Throth / Julane Hiebert

    To Have and Be Told / Julane Hiebert
    In Sickness and In Stealth / Julane Hiebert
    'Til the Ranch Do Us Part / Julane Hiebert

Wings of Hope Publishing Group
ISBN-13: 978-1-944309-25-1

This is a work of fiction. Names, characters, incidents, and dialogues are products of the author's imagination and are not to be construed as real. Any resemblance to actual events or people, living or dead, is entirely coincidental.

Cover artwork by Kim Vogel Sawyer and David Vogel.
Typesetting by Vogel Design in Hillsboro, Kansas.

Cover photo: "Church near Junction City, Kansas," Library of Congress Prints and Photographs Division Washington, D.C., Farm Security Administration - Office of War Information color slides and transparencies collection, LC-DIG-fsac-1a34277 (digital reproduction; slides, color).

To Have and Be Told

Whoso findeth a wife findeth a good thing,
and obtaineth favour of the LORD.

Proverbs 18:22 KJV

To *Kathy and James Terral,* my cousin and her preacher husband,
whose love story would make a great novella of its own.
May God continue to bless your lives,
as you have blessed mine and others.

ONE

Cedar Bluff, Kansas
August, 1879

" *W*hoso findeth a wife findeth a good thing, and obtaineth favour of the Lord."

Obed Mason rested his head against the back of the chair and took a long, deep suck of air in an attempt to silence the heartbeat pulsing in his ears like a bass drum. As was his daily habit, he'd read the chapter in Proverbs corresponding with the day of the month. He'd prayed, as he always did, that the Lord would give him a special message through the reading. And there it was—Proverbs chapter eighteen, verse twenty-two.

He shut his eyes. But his closed eyes didn't keep the image of Henrietta Harvey from parading into his vision, plain as day. But this time… This time she was also the one beating the drum. If he didn't know better, he'd think she and God were in cahoots.

Not that he doubted the Lord. Truth was, he'd seriously considered asking Henrietta for her hand. The bigger question was would he—or could he—ever get past comparing her to his first love? His Clara. His quiet, steady, never-uttered-a-disparaging-word Clara, God rest her soul.

Popping open his eyes, he rubbed his chin. It was wrong to compare, and Clara would be the first to tell him. After all, he wouldn't be Henrietta's first love, either, and he didn't relish the thought of being likened to another man. He'd never met Herman Harvey, but from all accounts he was an outstanding citizen, one who never offered an opinion until asked, a man of wisdom and integrity, and—others were quick to add—a man of extreme patience. He smiled. Though those who reported it never elaborated about the need for patience, the nod of their head and wink of their eye spoke volumes.

Maybe it was the nod and the wink that endeared Henrietta to him. No one seemed to think ill of her. She was just known to be a bit...well, perhaps impulsive and unpredictable. And maybe, just maybe, those were the qualities he liked best. Being fully aware of all her idiosyncrasies, yet never knowing which one would manifest itself at any given moment or under any given situation, made life around Henrietta...hmm...

"Exciting."

There! He'd said it. Mercy, what would his congregation think if they knew he'd labeled Henrietta Harvey exciting? And did the description fit the expected temperament of a preacher's wife?

He laid his Bible on the side table and leaned forward to rest his forearms on his thighs. "Lord, I asked for a message, and then I read that I would obtain favor if I were to find a wife. I've never doubted Your Word, and I won't question it now. But I need wisdom. You know my heart and my feelings toward Henrietta. If I'm getting ahead of You, please make it very clear. I don't want to go one step ahead of, nor lag one step behind You. And I do want to obtain Your favor. So I'm asking You to open my eyes that I might recognize the help meet You have prepared for me. I pray this in the name of Your Son, Jesus. Amen."

He stood and stretched his arms above his head. While the drum no longer beat in his ears, a tingle of anticipation tightened his chest. Morning visits awaited him. The shut-ins who missed Sunday service looked forward to him coming by. He would get to them. First, though, he'd venture to Emma's Mercantile. Candy wasn't a normal temptation, but this morning a sugarcoated gumdrop or two sounded real good.

Bright morning sun filtered through the curtains in the parlor of Henrietta Harvey's boardinghouse and cast lacy shadows across her open Bible. She lifted the book from her lap and turned a bit to take better advantage of the light to make sure she hadn't misread it the first time.

"Whoso findeth a wife, findeth a good thing…"

She wriggled in glee, and it took all the decorum she could muster to keep from squealing right out loud. She stole a furtive glance toward Tillie Rogers and prayed that her friend and business partner would be too busy with her own reading to ask questions. Tillie remained the picture of concentration.

Henrietta sighed with relief. She hugged the Bible to her chest. Proverbs chapter eighteen verse twenty-two made it quite clear Reverend Obed Mason would obtain favor of the Lord if he were to choose a wife. And of course he'd choose her. Why, she had all the attributes required of a preacher's wife—kind, generous, talented, humble. She'd not mention beauty as that would be vain. Hadn't he come close to asking her several times? Oh, not in words. Outside of the pulpit, words didn't seem to come easily for Obed, but his actions certainly left no question.

Why, only last night when he escorted her home after church, he'd stolen a kiss. She furrowed her brow. *Stolen* might not be the right term. It was more like he asked and received all in one breath. But that's when she knew he loved her, although she couldn't be sure he was aware of it yet.

She pulled a lace handkerchief from her sleeve and fanned her face with the memory. Goodness, but it was warm.

Tillie closed her Bible. "You're smiling like you've just been given the prize, my friend. And I bet I know the reason for your happy mood this morning."

Henrietta flicked her wrist in her friend's direction. "Why, Tillie Rogers. I'm always in a happy mood." She set her Bible on the cushion beside her. "It's a lovely Monday morning, don't you agree?"

"It was a lovelier Sunday night, wasn't it?" Tillie grinned and tilted her head. "And the moon was so bright it was almost like daylight."

Henrietta gasped. "You were watching?"

"I wasn't spying, if that's what you mean. We were sitting on the porch swing. I guess we were in the shadows so you didn't see us."

Henrietta puffed out a breath. "We? Us? You mean you weren't alone?"

"Abe was with me."

"Oh, now we'll be the talk of the town." Henrietta covered her face with her hands. Would she ever live this down?

"You'll be no such thing." Tillie joined Henrietta on the settee. "You know I won't tell a soul, and Abe promised he'd not say a word." She giggled. "Though he did say it gave him ideas of his own."

Henrietta tilted her head and peeked through her fingers. "Doc Mercer kissed you?"

"Oh, heavens no. He just said it gave him ideas. That man doesn't have an impulsive bone in his body."

"And you're sure he won't tell?

"As sure as I *can* be. But you have to know that Reverend Mason and Henrietta Harvey sneaking a kiss on the porch wouldn't be all that much of a surprise to the townsfolk, except maybe to those too young to notice how you goggle at one another."

"We do not goggle. That's sounds crude."

"What would you call it, then?"

Henrietta lifted her chin. "We admire each another."

"Well, you *admire* each another with rolled eyes, fluttering eyelids, and pink faces. Goggle may sound crude, but it's an apt description." Tillie stood and brushed at her skirt. "I believe I'll make a batch of biscuits before the kitchen gets much hotter. I'll debone what's left of the chicken from yesterday and put it in the leftover gravy for our dinner."

"Then I'm going to the post office and will stop at Emma's." The mercantile owner was the best advice-giver in town. She'd know whether Henrietta should tell Obed what the Bible spoke so clearly. "I won't be long."

"If you stop at Emma's you'll be gone all morning. Don't forget to wear a bonnet. That sun is already hot."

Tillie left the room, and Henrietta straightened the antimacassars on the settee then shook the dust from the peacock feathers filling the vase on the marble topped table in the hallway. She didn't like to leave the boardinghouse without everything in its place. After spending so many years in four tiny rooms behind the post office, the fact that she could now welcome guests into her very own boardinghouse was more than she could ever have dreamed.

She took one last look around and nodded with satisfaction. The room would pass inspection from even the pickiest of guests. She slipped her bonnet from its hook and stood in front of the long mirror in the hallway while she tied the strings under her chin. If only they were wide satin ribbons she could fluff against her cheek instead of the flimsy strips of fabric that somehow managed to roll into the crevice between her two chins. But no proper lady, no matter how fancy, would go out in the Kansas heat without a bonnet to protect her face from the sun, and few bonnets had wide satin ribbons. She sighed and gave her cheeks a quick pinch, then hung her reticule over her wrist. Would it be wrong to pray no one would interrupt her visit with Emma?

At least she needn't worry about running into Reverend Mason. He'd be out on his usual Monday morning calls to the shut-ins. By the time he arrived back in town, she'd have her answer. Oh, she hoped Emma agreed that Obed should be told right away.

TWO

A blanket of anxiety tied with threads of guilt lay across Obed's shoulders and added to the morning's heat. Other than the sharp ring of iron against iron from the blacksmith shop and a dog barking in the distance, the streets of Cedar Bluff seemed abnormally quiet. But then, what did he know about a normal Monday morning in town? His usual Monday morning activity did not include a visit to Emma's Mercantile to ask for wisdom concerning God's Word for the day.

He liked Mondays, and he looked forward to his visits with those who were unable to be out and about. It put feet to the words he often spoke on Sunday about *doing unto others,* and *loving your neighbors.* While still in the hills of Missouri, it meant a horseback ride through shallow branches of water or across hollows thick with timber to tiny cabins tucked so far back in the hills one could have easily overlooked them had it not been for the usual bevy of hounds baying at his appearance like he was a treed coon. Clara would pack him a lunch, and she always included a loaf of bread or a small crock of apple butter to let the shut-in know she was thinking of them. She'd kiss him goodbye, assure him her prayers traveled with him, and stand on the porch waving her apron until he'd lose sight of her once beyond the clearing.

Things were different here in these hills of Kansas. Not hills like his Missouri hills, but hills nonetheless. He'd learned to love them and the undulating prairie that cradled them. It was a different land, a different people, but God formed both. For Obed, that was good enough.

But he missed the ritual of the kiss, the assurance of prayers, and turning back for one last look at the apron waving him onward. He wouldn't admit it to just anyone, but he missed the hand on the shoulder in passing, the cold feet at night, and the fragrance of cinnamon and taste of sugar when he kissed Clara. He ran his hand between his collar and his neck in the heat of remembrance. Clara would be embarrassed if she knew his thoughts.

At the door of Emma's Mercantile he paused and took a deep breath. In his hurry to get to his destination, he'd failed to come up with a reason for being in the store. What if another customer was already there? Emma's usual greeting to anyone entering was, *"What can I do for you today?"* He couldn't answer, *"What do you think about me asking Henrietta Harvey to become my wife?"*

"What're you doing in town, Reverend?"

Obed turned and spotted Doc Mercer advancing toward him, his hand extended and a smile plastered across his face.

"I thought you'd be long gone on your visitation rounds by now, what with the heat and all. 'Course, you might be a bit tired after that full moon last night." He winked.

Obed grasped his friend's hand. "What does a full moon have to do with my energy level, may I ask?"

Doc tilted his head and batted his eyelashes. "Oooh, Obed. What if someone sees us?" He mimicked Henrietta's voice.

"You saw us?" Obed groaned. "We didn't do anything wrong. And where were you, anyway? I don't like the idea of you spying on us."

"No need to spy. You stood right in front of me and Tillie like two moonstruck school kids. I never said you kissing Henrietta was wrong. Fact is, it doesn't surprise me. You staying in town this morning to ask Emma's advice?"

"Why would I need Emma's advice?" He rubbed the back of his

neck. Was it his imagination, or had the temperature just shot up several degrees? "I, um, actually I was going to get a can of peaches to take to Oscar Wylie. He wasn't in church yesterday. I'm thinking he must be under the weather."

Doc plucked the head of a wilted geranium from the bucket of plants in front of Emma's Mercantile and handed it to Obed. "Here. This posy is about as dead as that excuse. Never thought I'd hear Reverend Obed Mason tell an out and out fib." He bumped shoulders with Obed. "But you needn't worry. Tillie swore me to secrecy, and I don't aim to get that little woman riled up. Besides that, everyone around here knows Emma Ledbetter is the knowingest person in these parts. If I was courting Henrietta Harvey, I reckon I'd be asking Emma some questions myself."

Obed leaned one shoulder against the side of the mercantile. Two could play this game. "So, what is it you're needing from Emma's so early this morning? Got a question about Tillie, do you? You know, wouldn't come as a surprise if you were to tell me you and Tillie were courting."

Doc's face turned as red as a geranium bloom. "Don't reckon that's any of your business."

Obed tipped his head back and laughed. "Maybe we should draw straws to see who gets to be first to glean from Emma's advice."

"Here we are, two old men acting like schoolboys." Doc chuckled. "I'll let you go first, my friend. After all, you're older so it stands to reason you don't have as much time left as I do. Gotta make the most of every minute, you know."

Obed pulled his shoulders back and puffed out his chest. "In this case it's experience, not age, that trumps youth. But I'll step aside. You have a whole lot more to learn, so maybe you should go first."

"No, no." Doc opened the door and motioned for Obed to go ahead of him. "If all you want from Emma's is a can of peaches, I've plenty of time after you leave."

There was that temperature hike again. Obed shrugged. He could only hope Oscar Wylie liked peaches.

Henrietta moved away from the window inside the post office. The last person she expected to see this morning was Obed. But there he was, entering the mercantile with Doc Mercer on his heels.

What was he doing at Emma's? He shouldn't even be in town. It was Monday, after all. How could she ask Emma's advice with Obed in the store, too? Should she wait until he left, or should she go in and feign interest in something so he wouldn't suspect her reason for being there? She tapped her lips with her finger. What could she examine? Fabric, perhaps? Yes, she could choose something blue. Obed's favorite color was blue. She smoothed the skirt of her green print dress. She much preferred green, but for Obed she'd choose blue. Maybe a nice taffeta. She might even ask Emma if such a choice would make a nice wedding dress.

She took a deep breath, pursed her lips, and let it escape with a *whoosh*. Why did she feel so twitchy down deep in her tummy? He'd kissed her last night, God's Word this morning made it clear he should seek a wife, and who else would he consider? Her heart fluttered as she turned to peer at her reflection in the window. If only her bonnet had a wide ribbon she could fluff. A preacher's wife should be modest, but who could find fault with wide ribbon? Or even a pretty straw hat? Obed didn't have a fancy bone in his body— at least she'd not observed such—and she couldn't imagine he'd want his wife to put on airs. But a blue taffeta dress and a pretty hat would hardly be putting on airs, would it?

She steepled her hands beneath her chin and gathered her courage to enter the mercantile. Then she remembered who else was in the store. Doc Mercer! Given the conversation with Tillie, she had no desire to face Abe Mercer. Her shoulders sagged with disappointment, but the present situation didn't leave her much choice. She'd go back to the boardinghouse and perhaps later make another trek to Emma's.

To avoid being observed as she passed the mercantile, Henrietta stepped from the boardwalk to cross the street. She stopped, allowing an unfamiliar horse and buggy to roll past her. The woman holding the reins smiled and nodded, and Henrietta gaped. Not only was the driver a stranger to Cedar Bluff but judging by her head covering, she must also be new to Kansas. The woman wore a blue taffeta dress, and perched on her head was the prettiest yellow straw hat adorned with bright red cherries and tied with a wide blue and yellow plaid taffeta ribbon, fluffed against her cheek.

Henrietta fingered the limp strings of her own bonnet and swiveled on her heels. One thing for sure, no matter if Doc was in Emma's Mercantile, if this woman stopped at the hitching rail and entered the store, Henrietta would be right behind her. And if Obed so much as twitched his eye at the one putting on such airs, she'd ask him if he'd read the Proverb for the day.

THREE

Obed lingered at the shelf of canned goods, repeatedly taking down and putting back a can of peaches, while Emma filled Doc's lengthy order. The aroma of new leather shoes, lamp oil, and spices mingled and permeated every nook and cranny of the mercantile, and he pulled in one slow breath after another. He hadn't planned to stay in town so long, but he couldn't talk to Emma with Doc in the store. Doc was a good friend, and Obed had never known him to gossip, but he wasn't about to divulge his feelings for Henrietta Harvey with the doc present. No, sir. There were some things a man didn't do, especially a preacher, and discussing his attraction to a woman of his congregation was at the top of the list.

Finally Emma pushed the crate of purchases across the counter to Doc, so Obed hurried from his hiding spot, eager to speak to the mercantile owner.

"I was going to ask what I could do to help you, Obed, but looks like you've made a decision without my service." Emma pointed to the can of fruit. "Anything else?"

Doc snickered. "You have any salve for chapped lips?"

Emma smiled at him. "You have chapped lips, Doc?"

"More like a big mouth." Obed scowled. Seemed Doc wasn't in any hurry to leave. He'd have to come back later and hope to catch Emma alone. "What do I owe you, Emma?"

The jangle of the bell above the door interrupted Emma's response. The trio turned to see who'd entered, and Obed nearly swallowed his tongue. Few strangers came through Cedar Bluff, and even fewer were attractive, mature women. Doc's exaggerated cough communicated his shock, too.

"I'm so sorry to interrupt."

The woman's musical voice made Obed's ears tingle with heat. He hoped it didn't show.

Doc stepped in front of Obed. "Not at all, not at all. What can I do for you today?"

Obed leaned to Doc's ear. "That's Emma's line, you know."

"Just being friendly," Doc muttered. He took another step forward.

"Oh, are you the proprietor of this fine establishment?" The woman's skirts rustled as she slid in front of Doc. "I'm so very glad to make your acquaintance." She took Doc's hand in both of hers. "My name is Evangeline Moore, and as you most certainly already know, I'm new to the area. But I must say, it's very nice to be welcomed so graciously."

Doc placed his free hand on top of hers. "We're a friendly town. Do you plan to stay long?"

She pulled her hands from Doc's and brushed at a stray strand of hair. "As a matter of fact, my desire is to establish residence here."

Doc coughed again, and Obed patted him on the back. "You better see a doctor about that cough, Abe. Seems to be getting worse."

Emma moved from behind the counter. "Actually, I'm the proprietor. Welcome to Cedar Bluff." She pointed to Abe. "This impersonator is really Doctor Abe Mercer." She nodded toward Obed. "And this is—"

The woman fluttered her hands. "Oh, don't tell me. Let me guess." Her brow furrowed as her gaze traveled from Obed's eyes past his suit to his feet then to his eyes again. He involuntarily checked the buttons on his shirt to make sure they were closed. She smiled. "I don't know your name, but I would say you're a preacher, and you're not married. Am I right?"

Obed gulped, and the temperature shot up another notch, straight to the top of his head. "How did you know that?" He groaned. His voice cracked with the last word, and he feared he was blushing like a girl.

She leaned his direction. "The can of peaches you're holding. You see, if you had a wife, she'd be making the purchase. And it's Monday morning. I would say you were getting ready to go visit a member of your congregation who wasn't able to make it to church yesterday."

Emma put her arm around the woman's shoulders. "My goodness, dear. How did you ever come to that conclusion?"

Obed wondered the same thing. It was one thing to have Emma seem to know so much, but quite another to have a stranger making such guesses. If either of them could sense what was going on in his mind, he'd be in big trouble.

Evangeline gave a little shrug. "My late husband, God rest his soul, was a preacher. I know the routine well."

The clang of the bell above the door, and a *whoosh* of clove scented air hit Obed's senses. Henrietta bustled in his direction, her smile unnaturally bright.

"Oh, there you are Obed, I was—"

Evangeline grabbed his hand. "Your name is Obed? Reverend Obed Mason?"

Obed gulped and nodded. Good sense told him he should at least acknowledge Henrietta, maybe even take her hand, but how when Evangeline had one of his hands gripped so tight it would be an obvious tug to pull it free and the other one still held the can of peaches?

"Do I know you?" *Careful, Obed. A lady doesn't like to be forgotten.*

Henrietta pulled a handkerchief from her sleeve and fanned her face, sending a waft of cloves like a cloud around them. "Yes, please tell us. Does he know you?" She took the can of peaches from Obed's hand and hooked her elbow through his bent arm. He didn't miss the smirk on Doc's face, nor Emma's pursed lips.

Evangeline's eyebrows arched. "Oh, I'm so sorry. I forgot that we'd never actually been introduced. My husband—that is, my late husband, Thornton Moore—was sent to pastor the church you left in Missouri." She released her hold on Obed's hand. "But I've heard so much about you, it's as though we're already well acquainted."

Obed patted Henrietta's hand, hoping she'd quit pinching his arm. He should've visited Oscar Wylie, that's for sure. "I'm sorry, Mrs. Thornton. I never was introduced to your husband. I knew that a younger man replaced me, but I left before he arrived."

"Yes, well, you left quite an impression on the poor people of that God-forsaken place, I'm afraid. Thornton was never regarded as one of them, you know, no matter how many Monday mornings were spent away from me so he could visit the good folk."

Obed stifled a response. Surely she hadn't meant to be unkind, but that so-called forsaken place had been his home since childhood—until he traveled to Cedar Bluff to find his daughter—and those good folk were his people. Oh, not all blood relatives, but still they were good people. Honest, hardworking, God fearing…

"You say you're thinking of residing here, Mrs. Moore?" Emma grasped Evangeline's elbow.

Obed took a deep breath. Bless Emma's heart. He could only surmise her *knowing* caused her to intervene in the conversation.

"I am, as a matter of fact. But only if I can find a place to live and a building in which I might open my milliner shop. Now that Thornton is no longer here, I must find a way to support myself."

"And how is it you chose Cedar Bluff?" Henrietta gripped Obed's arm even tighter. Now he understood how it felt to be caught in the grips of a vise. Yet, for some strange reason, her possessiveness pleased him.

Evangeline swiped her hand across her eyes. "I would like to believe that Cedar Bluff chose me." She smiled at Henrietta. "I got off the train, rented a horse and buggy, and was going to journey until I found a suitable place for my business. But when I took a good look at this sweet little town, I thought to myself, 'Evangline, perhaps the fine ladies around here would like a new hat now and again.' I'm also a seamstress, and I specialize in dressing a woman from top to bottom. I call my business The Virtuous Woman, after the woman in Proverbs thirty-one. It's my habit to read a Proverb daily, and I've found it to be such a blessing. Have you tried it, Reverend? You must, you know."

Henrietta jutted her chin. "And are your prices above that of rubies?"

Emma stepped between Henrietta and Evangeline. "Your shop would be a wonderful addition to our town, Mrs. Moore. I'd be most happy to rearrange a corner of the mercantile to accommodate your business until you're able to find something more suitable. If you need a place to stay, Henrietta Harvey's boardinghouse is most delightful. I'm quite sure Henrietta and her business partner, Tillie Rogers, would be more than happy to have you as their guest."

Evangeline beamed. "Oh, now I know for certain I've made the right choice. Where might I find this wonderful place you suggested. Harrietta Harvey, you say?"

Obed winced. He didn't think his arm could stand another pinch, but to be called the wrong name would certainly elicit some kind of response that would incur injury to someone, and right now he was the most likely recipient .

Henrietta lifted her chin. "It's Henrietta, and I'm the owner."

Evangeline's gaze swept Henrietta from top to bottom then up again. Obed knew how the perusal felt, but he didn't dare check to see if Henrietta's buttons were closed.

"I had no idea I was in the company of someone so important as the proprietress of her very own boardinghouse. This confirms my decision again. To show my appreciation for such a generous welcome, I would like for you, Harrietta, to be my very first client—at my expense, of course. I'm thinking a lovely brown fabric would bring out the once-red in your hair and make you appear slimmer at the same time."

"My name is Henrietta. *Hen*-ri-etta."

Obed groaned inwardly and withdrew his arm from Henrietta's clutches to avoid further pain. If only he'd gone to visit Oscar Wylie.

FOUR

Henrietta's heart hit bottom. Not only did Obed pull away from her, but did anyone else notice how this woman had insulted her in every way possible? To draw attention to her graying hair and ample size was bad enough. But to do it in mixed company was humiliating and indiscreet. Then she couldn't even remember her name. Harrietta, of all things. She sensed she'd already shown too much agitation, a demeanor particularly unworthy of a preacher's wife, so she swallowed the lump in her throat and the words fighting to escape, and smiled instead.

"How nice, Mrs. Moore. I'm flattered you deemed me worthy of such attention. I'm sure when the ladies of Cedar Bluff see what an improvement you've made in my appearance, they will flock to you for help."

Evangeline's face crumbled. "Oh, my. I'm afraid I was quite careless in the choice of my words." She gripped Henrietta's arms. "Forgive me, my dear. I only meant to portray my relief and excitement at the kindness of you all."

Emma wiggled between the two women and put her arms around their waists. "I'm sure you meant no harm, and you will find Henrietta the most charming hostess you've ever encountered." She nodded toward the two men, who stood meek as lambs on the other side of her. "Doc, why don't you show Mrs. Moore the way to Henrietta's boardinghouse. Obed, you accompany Henrietta and make sure she gets in out of this heat."

Henrietta bit her tongue. She could very well find her own way home, and it only made sense that she arrive ahead of the rest of them so she could forewarn Tillie. But to argue the point would cause a scene, and goodness knows she didn't need anything more.

She did, however, want to tell Obed about the message she gleaned from today's reading from Proverbs. But what if this Evangeline Moore had read the same passage? She was, after all, the widow of a preacher. And she even had the nerve to suggest such a habit to Obed.

With no argument left, Henrietta chose to go along with Emma's plan. She waved the can of peaches in the air. "Put these on my ticket, Emma. Tillie might need them for dessert since we'll have a guest." She nodded toward the door. "Are you ready, Obed? I'm sure Tillie will want to know as soon as possible how many will be present around our table." She turned to Emma. "As a matter of fact, why don't you come, too, Emma? And you, Obed. I'm sure we won't have to persuade you, will we, Abe?"

Doc seemed to find something interesting to observe on the toe of his shoe. "Uh, why, no." He coughed. "I...I always enjoy Tillie's cooking." He coughed again.

"Well, then, why don't you and Mrs. Moore scurry on over to our place, and Obed and I will be along shortly. We'll eat at half past eleven, Emma, so you can keep your usual midday break."

Henrietta stood in the hallway and plunked her hands on her hips, then quickly reconsidered the stance. No doubt it would cause her to look even more *ample,* so she folded her hands across her middle. Well, that wouldn't do, either. The pose made her appear thicker. What was a lady to do? What she wanted to do was talk to Emma. As soon as she could find a good reason, she'd make her way back to the mercantile.

In the meantime, as hostess, she'd endure the antics of those around her. Tillie giggled and hung onto every word their guest uttered, while Doc and Obed scurried back and forth from the buggy to Evangeline's upstairs room, hauling her various trunks and boxes. They were like silly boys, pushing and shoving each another to get through the door first, balancing the trunks on their shoulders, and climbing the steps as though they carried mere toys. It was enough to make a grown woman sputter, though it did give her satisfaction to see them both whip out their handkerchiefs and wipe their brows when Evangeline was out of sight. Did they have any idea how foolish they appeared? Why, they'd be the first ones to poke fun of any other man in Cedar Bluff who displayed such behavior merely because there was an attractive woman in their midst.

She turned and entered the kitchen. Good manners required her to offer everyone a cool drink. On second thought, perhaps this would be a good time to make her escape. They were all so preoccupied, they probably wouldn't even miss her. She'd sneak out the kitchen door and be gone and back in no time. She grabbed her garden bonnet from the hook by the back door. It wasn't the least bit stylish, but it would suffice.

By the time she reached Emma's Mercantile, Henrietta wished she'd given more thought to her hasty departure. Late morning, the sun beat down on Cedar Bluff with a vengeance. It seemed to even drain the color from the sky, while no doubt painting her cheeks a bright red. Tillie would scold, but she could endure Tillie's rebuke easier than the insult she'd received from Mrs. Moore—whether or not the woman meant to be unkind.

Emma was dusting shelves when Henrietta entered the mercantile. "I wondered how long it would take you to come back here, Henrietta." She laid her feather duster on the counter and looked at the gold watch pinned to her blouse. "Thirty minutes. I gave you an hour, tops."

"Can you blame me?" Henrietta puffed.

"Blame is the last thing on my mind, my friend. Here…" She led Henrietta to a chair behind the counter. "Sit, and I'll get us something cool to drink. You need to simmer down before you get all het up again. If someone comes in, you can slip behind the curtain if you wish. No need for anyone else to know you're upset."

After Henrietta finished a glass of cool water, Emma sat on a stool nearby. "Now, let's hear what you have on your mind."

Henrietta pulled in a deep breath. "I read Proverbs this morning, like I always do—like Obed encouraged me to do. One chapter a day for each day of the month. And this morning God told me that Obed should take a wife, and I was so sure it would be me, but then this... this woman, who claims she was a preacher's wife and is a milliner and a seamstress, who insulted me in front of everyone arrived, and... and...and you even offered her a place for her business. I thought we were friends, Emma." She wiped her face with her handkerchief and hung her head. "Doc and Obed are over there right now, falling all over themselves trying to get her attention, and Tillie just giggles and—"

"And you're jealous, Henrietta Harvey. You should know that while I may have other friends, old and new, no one will ever take your place in my heart. You do know that, don't you?" She leaned toward Henrietta. "Look at me, and tell me you know that's true."

Henrietta looked and caught a glimmer of tears in Emma's eyes. "I know. But what about Obed?"

"Obed Mason? You're worried about the preacher?"

"Shouldn't I be worried? You saw him. He and Doc both are clearly enthralled with that woman. And here I am, turning gray and as plump as a Christmas goose." She could no longer hold her tears in check. "I was on my way here earlier to tell you what God said. Now it's too late."

Emma patted Henrietta's cheek. "Oh, my dear friend, it's never too late. Way down deep inside my heart, I believe Obed Mason came here this morning for the very same reason."

"You think so?" Henrietta sniffed. "Why?"

"Why do I think so? Think about it. Have you ever known Obed Mason to stay in town on a Monday morning? He's as faithful on Monday to those who weren't in church on Sunday as he is to those who graced the pews on the Lord's day."

"And he did have a can of peaches. Maybe that Evangeline woman was right. Could be he was going to take them to someone. It was that...that preacher's widow who stopped him, that's who."

"No, no. The newcomer had nothing to do with him not divulging his reason for being here. You did see Abe Mercer in here, didn't you?"

Henrietta nodded.

"Would you be talking to me like this if Tillie or any other woman in Cedar Bluff, were present?"

"No, but—"

The jangle of the bell above the door alerted them to a new arrival. "Emma, have you— Oh, there you are, Henrietta."

Obed. Henrietta swiped her hands across her face. She didn't want him to catch her crying.

"Tillie thought you might be here. She sent me to find you and give you this list of things she'll need for the rest of the week. Guess you weren't expecting a paying guest, were you? Evangeline graciously allowed me to use her buggy so you needn't carry things back to the boardinghouse." He handed her the list. "I let Doc off at his place, and I'll mosey on home, but we'll be there for lunch. I believe you said 11:30, is that correct?" He turned back to the door. "See you then. Thank you for the invitation. Oh, and don't worry. That's one of Pederson's old mares from the livery pulling the buggy. You'll have no trouble handling her." He turned and whistled his way out of the store.

Emma looked at Henrietta, a scowl so deep her eyebrows nearly touched in the middle. "Well! I never would have—"

"What are you feeling way down deep in your heart now, Emma?" Tears rolled freely, and Henrietta made no attempt to wipe them away.

FIVE

Obed walked a few steps away from the mercantile, then leaned against the side of the building. Henrietta had been crying. Oh, she tried to hide it, but he knew all the signs. Clara's nose turned red, too, when she shed tears. But as much as he could know for sure, he'd never been the cause of her weeping. Clara had spilled tears over injustice, she wept with those who wept—freely and unashamedly—and shared tears of joy with those who rejoiced. But seldom, if ever, had he known her to cry because of personal slights or rejection.

"They're only words," Clara would remind him.

"But they're hurled like stones," he'd argue.

"Then we have a choice, dear husband. We build walls, or we lay a beautiful path that will lead those who cast such hurtful utterances straight to the cross."

In the end, he would always agree to pave the way to the Savior.

But now what? Whether Evangeline's actions were purposeful or not remained to be seen, but she had definitely thrown stones—pebbles, perhaps—but hurtful nonetheless. And he might as well have been the one handing her the weapons, because he'd done nothing to shield Henrietta from the bruising.

He shouldered away from the building and with heavy steps made his way home. He'd read Proverbs eighteen again, just to make sure he wasn't missing something, and pray there'd be an opportunity tonight to talk with Emma...alone.

Henrietta stood in front of the open doors of her clothespress, hands on hips. She'd gone through her entire wardrobe several times but still couldn't find one blue dress. Not one. It was Herman's fault. When she was still young and thin, and her hair still had all its color, Herman insisted she wear green.

"Henny, my sweet, you have no idea how beautiful you are in green."

She dabbed at her eyes. Herman was the only person she'd ever allowed to call her Henny. From his lips, it was a name of endearment. But for the naughty schoolboys of her past, it'd been a way to poke fun... *Here henny-henny, here chick-chick.*

She plopped onto the side of her bed. What would those boys have done if her name was Harrietta, as declared by Evangeline Moore? She rubbed her temples. All these years later she could still remember running home crying and begging her parents to give her a different name. Now this new lady came to town, and—

"Henrietta? Are you in there?" The door flung open and Tillie barged into the room. "What is taking you so long? Don't you know we have company, and a paying guest, no less? And here you sit in your...your... Oh, for goodness' sake, Henrietta. Would you put on some clothes and come help me?"

"I can't." Henrietta sniffed.

"You can't? Why? Are you ill?" Tillie pressed her hand against Henrietta's forehead. "You don't have a fever. Should I send Doc in when he gets here?"

"No."

"No, what? Henrietta Harvey, what is the matter with you?"

"I don't have anything blue to wea-a-ar." She covered her face and sobbed.

"You don't have anything blue?" Tillie stomped her foot. "Well, guess what? I don't have anything yellow, but I can't let that stop me. We have guests coming, and not a single one of them even cares what color dress you don't have." She marched to Henrietta's wardrobe and pulled out a green and white gingham. "Here, put this on and come help me. Please!"

"Do you have anything blue?"

Tillie tilted her head. "Blue? Why?"

"Could I borrow something blue to wear today?"

Tillie rolled her eyes. "My dear friend, I know this will sound very rude, but do you really think you could—"

Henrietta jumped to her feet and put her fingers across Tillie's lips. "Don't you dare say it. That Evangeline woman has already called it to the attention of Doc, Obed, and Emma that I'm ample. Perhaps I am a bit fluffier than you, but you bring me the dress and I'll find a way to wear it. But it must be blue. Please, Tillie. I'll explain tonight, after our guests are gone, but please let me borrow something blue."

It took both of them to tuck, roll, and adjust all of Henrietta to fit into Tillie's dress.

"You're stuffed in there tight as a sausage. Can you still breathe?" Tillie's frown mirrored Henrietta's own concern. She could breathe if she took shallow breaths, but how in the world would she be able to eat and still manage that one small, necessary detail?

"I can, but do you think it might be possible to leave the two middle buttons undone?"

Tillie laid her hand on Henrietta's forehead. "I checked once, and you didn't have fever. But I'm beginning to think you're a bit off in the head. You do remember Abe and Obed will be present at our table?"

"Of course I remember." Henrietta unbuttoned the middle two buttons and took a deep breath of relief. "There. That's better."

"And where do you propose I seat the two gentlemen so they will not be aware of your impropriety? Whatever will you do should all we have tucked behind you decides to make an escape?" She held two fingers over her mouth.

"You laugh and I'll just die, Tillie Rogers."

"I can guarantee that if you go down to greet our guests looking as though you forgot to dress, I'll not laugh alone."

"No one will ever know. Hand me the fichu from the top drawer, please."

Tillie stepped to the dresser and pulled the triangular shawl from the drawer. "The ends aren't long enough to cover all of you."

"I know, but watch this." She flipped the fichu so the pointed edge was in front. "See, I've started a new style." She handed Tillie a pearl brooch. "Pin the ends in back, below my shoulders. I'll look fine from any angle and won't have to fear a thing."

"Henrietta, I do believe you've gone daft."

Henrietta patted Tillie's cheek. "Proverbs thirty-one, verse twenty-two. 'She maketh herself coverings of tapestry.'"

"It's not tapestry, and it looks like you're wearing a bib. Not to mention you'll probably get heat exhaustion with the extra layer covering you."

Henrietta peered into the mirror above her washstand. "I think it's rather stylish. Trust me, Tillie. That virtuous woman has nothing on me."

Obed took a deep breath and prayed for wisdom. Whatever was Tillie thinking? She'd seated him directly across from Evangeline Moore. Then she declared Henrietta's chair at the far end of the table the seat of honor—since she was, after all, the proprietress of this fine establishment—where she was able to preside over the meal.

Not only could Henrietta preside, but she could also observe every move. And it was more than obvious Mrs. Moore's moves were going to be difficult to ignore.

Dressed in a green and white checkered dress that exposed more neck and shoulders than any woman in Cedar Bluff would dare reveal, she seemed to find it necessary to lean forward to take part in the trivial attempts at conversation.

"My, hasn't it been hot?"

"Some say it's the hottest summer they can remember."

"Do you think it will rain?"

"Has to, some day."

And all the time this was going on, Mrs. Moore patted her pink cheeks and long, slender, very white neck with a lace-edged handkerchief. While in contrast, Henrietta sat at the end of the table, wrapped in a shawl like it was the dead of winter. Did anyone else notice how very quiet Henrietta was? What happened to her normal chatter?

Evangeline tapped her spoon against her water glass and turned sideways in her chair. "I'm sorry to interrupt this fine conversation but, Harrietta, my dear, are you feeling well?"

Henrietta smiled. "I'm just fine, *Eunice*. But thank you for asking."

"It's Evangeline, but if that's difficult for you to remember, my good friends call me Angie. And I was concerned that perhaps you were too warm. Your cheeks are so red."

Henrietta stood and crossed to the nearest window. "Not at all, Annie. In fact, I've been worried that perhaps you were chilly, what with so much skin exposed." She closed the window with a flourish. "There. I would so hate for you to catch a summer cold."

Obed winced. If he weren't mistaken, things were about to become very—

Emma scooted her chair from the table and stood. "Tillie, might I help you serve dessert?"

"Well, I was thinking that perhaps we could adjourn to the parlor for dessert, where—"

Evangeline clapped her hands. "What a wonderful idea. Perhaps we could be entertained?"

Henrietta beamed. "Why, yes, I—"

"I was so hoping I would have the opportunity to perform." Evangeline stood and smoothed her dress. "Thornton insisted I only sing hymns, you know." She batted her eyelashes at Obed. "I'm sure you wouldn't be so stuffy if *your* wife possessed such talent, would you?"

"You...you sing?" Henrietta's voice wavered.

"Oh, my dear, I studied for years. Why, some say I could have been on stage had I not chosen to follow my late husband to his so-called mission field."

Obed choked back a reply. As though the hills of Missouri were some faraway land populated by heathens. Mission field, indeed.

"Henrietta plays the piano," Tillie volunteered. "I'm sure she'd be happy to accompany you."

"Oh, really?" Evangeline's brow wrinkled as she faced Henrietta. "I don't suppose you might know 'Beautiful Dreamer'?"

Obed's heart lurched. Of course Henrietta knew the song. Hadn't he heard her sing it time and again when she entertained with voice and piano? He'd often requested it himself. "I'm sure she—"

"No, I'm not familiar with that one." Henrietta's cheeks pinked. "But I'd very much like to hear you sing and play. My, how talented you are."

What just happened? Obed wished, more than ever, he could talk with Emma. While there was definitely a battle brewing, it seemed an all-out war had just been averted—and by Henrietta, no less. This woman, who liked nothing more than to entertain her guests with voice and piano had just graciously relinquished the opportunity. Would he ever understand the ways of a woman?

SIX

Heat crept through Henrietta's whole body, and it had nothing to do with the fichu draped across her front. Of course she knew the song, but to accompany Evangeline she'd have to use her arms. And that was out of the question. Had anyone noticed she'd kept her arms clamped to her sides since the chicken was passed?

With the first plate of biscuits she'd passed to the right, the sleeve of Tillie's dress ripped. She knew by the rush of cooler air that hit her underarm. Using the other arm to pass the chicken gravy resulted in a tear on that side also. What might happen if she were to use both arms at the same time at the piano?

What bothered her more than the torn apparel was the out-and-out lie she told. Her friends had to be aware she'd hidden the truth. But if she explained why, then Obed would know she tried to impress him by wearing something blue. And to top it all off, Evangeline had worn green and white, the very thing Tillie suggested for her in the first place. *Oh, what a tangled web we weave...*

Emma nodded to Henrietta. "Why don't you and I clean up the table while Tillie and the guests enjoy dessert in the parlor?"

Tillie's hands fluttered. "Oh, no, I—"

Bless Emma's heart. At least she'd maintain some of her dignity. Henrietta clamped her arms tight to her sides as she stood. "Don't argue, Tillie. You always do the cleaning up while I do the entertaining.

Today it's my turn to return the favor."

"If you insist." Tillie beamed.

"I insist." Henrietta gathered her plate and moved to the kitchen. Unable to reach without revealing the ever-widening gap under her arms, she'd at least be able to breathe a sigh of relief once in the kitchen and out of sight.

When all the guests were settled in the parlor and she and Emma were alone, Henrietta took a long, deep breath.

Emma put her arm around Henrietta's shoulders. "What's made you most uncomfortable, my dear Henrietta? Tillie's dress, the rips under the arms, or the fact that you just lied your way out of sight?"

"I knew I couldn't hide anything from you. Oh, Emma, what have I done?" She lifted an apron from the hook by the stove and handed it to her friend. "Here, you'll have to tie this. Goodness knows, if the sleeves rip any more they'll fall clear off."

Emma took the apron and tied it around Henrietta's waist. "There, that will keep it on. Now, you asked me what you did. Well, for starters, you tried to be someone you aren't. That seldom works."

"'Beautiful dreamer, wake unto me...'" Evangeline Moore's rich voice floated under the closed door of the kitchen.

"Well, that was appropriate, wasn't it?" Henrietta laughed. "I am a dreamer to think I could fool Obed. But I so wanted to impress him."

Emma poured hot water into the dishpan. "Believe me, my dear friend, you impressed him."

Henrietta took a towel from the hook beside the sink. "But not the right way. A preacher's wife would never try to deceive, would she? Do you think he recognized Tillie's dress? I'll just die if you say yes."

"I don't know about Obed, but Abe did." Emma shaved soap into the hot water. "At least he opened his mouth, but Tillie kicked his ankle before he could utter one word."

"You're sure?"

"I'm sure. She kicked mine first." She swished her hand in the dishwater and added the water glasses. "Now, I think we need to—"

Frantic pounding on the outside kitchen door interrupted.

Henrietta frowned, dishtowel in hand. "Who could that be?"

"We won't know until you open the door, and you'll have to do it because my hands are wet."

Henrietta threw the towel over her shoulder and opened the door. She found the son of one of the nearby ranchers on her stoop. "Why, Frankie Kearn, what are you doing here all alone?"

"Is Doc Mercer here? I found a note on his door. Ma, she said to fetch help."

Emma grabbed the towel from Henrietta's shoulder and dried her hands. "Is it your mama's time, Frankie?"

The young boy's freckles faded with his blush. "Yes, ma'am. I stopped by Oscar Wylie's first, 'cause he's closest, but couldn't get him to answer the door. So I came on to town. I think we better hurry."

"I'll get Doc, Henrietta. You get this young man a nice cool drink."

Henrietta ushered him across the floor and handed him a glass of water. "Here, you sit over at the table, and Doc will be here shortly. Where's your pa?"

He took the water and plunked onto the nearest chair. "Pa left this mornin' for to help Uncle Eugene over Elmira way. He's to be home tomorrow long about supper."

Within moments, Tillie, Doc, Abe, Obed, and even Mrs. Moore crowded into the kitchen.

Doc bent to the boy's eye level. "You've been there before, Frankie, so tell me—is your mama's babe coming?"

The boy gave a lopsided grin. "Yes, sir. Only she said it were too soon. But I don't know how she knows."

Henrietta touched Doc's shoulder. "Abe, Frankie says he stopped at Oscar Wylie's house first but couldn't get him to come to the door."

Doc straightened. "Emma, you come with me. Obed, you best be making that house call on Oscar like you started out to do this morning. Frankie, you got your horse?"

"Yes, sir. I rid him awful fast coming in, but he's had a little rest."

"Good. Ride on ahead and let your mama know I'm coming right behind you. Then you take your brothers and sisters somewhere out of the way. You understand?"

Frankie nodded. "I done it before, reckon I can do it again." He turned and ran through the still open doorway.

"My buggy is already out front, Emma. We best be on our way. Obed, you know where to find me if there's trouble at Oscar's."

"Wait!" Henrietta rushed to the cupboard where the can of peaches was still unopened. No doubt everyone present observed the air vents under her arms but this task was more important. "Here, Obed. Take this along. Maybe Oscar didn't hear the knock. He's hard of hearing, you know."

Obed's hand closed around hers when he took the can. "Thank you for thinking of him. I better hurry."

"Wait, you mean you have to leave? Now? Why?" Evangeline plopped her hands on her hips. "Couldn't the doctor look in on this Mr. Willie? I mean, if he's ill or injured, he'll need the doctor. And if he's…well, if he's dead, what good can you do?"

"I'll tell you what he can do!" Henrietta put herself between Obed and Mrs. Moore. "First of all, he can take those peaches and go see about Oscar Wylie—that's Wylie, not Willie. If he's hurt, Obed will know what to do until Doc can get to him. If he's no longer living, then Obed will stay right there, weep over a friend lost, pray his passing was gentle, and wait for Doc to come back by to check on him. Obed is a shepherd, Mrs. Moore, and a shepherd looks after his sheep."

She turned to Obed. "And you, Obed Mason, while you're driving out to the Wylie place, you be thinking about that Proverb you read this morning. And then, after this is all over, you and me are going to sit down with Emma and have us a good, long talk." She stood on tiptoe and brushed her lips across his cheek. "Now go, and God go with you. I'll be praying."

Obed's mouth opened, but he didn't say a word. And Evangeline Moore turned red as a Kansas sunrise when it warned of an oncoming storm.

Like as not, Henrietta told herself, she'd have words with Mrs.

Moore before the night was over. And hard telling what Obed had going around in his mind. But at least he knew that she read a Proverb a day, just like he suggested. And if it took her telling him what he read, then so be it.

She followed the still-silent, mouth-gaping man out to the porch then whipped off her apron and waved it until he rounded the corner. He might not have noticed, but no matter. She did it anyway.

Obed cast a quick glance back over his shoulder as he drove away. Henrietta stood—like somehow he knew she would—on the back stoop, her white apron waving like a beam from a lighthouse. He brushed his knuckles against the cheek that still held the warmth of her lips. He could've saved himself a whole lot of trouble if he'd gone to see Oscar this morning, instead of thinking he needed advice from Emma. Fact is, he didn't need another woman telling him what to do about Henrietta, did he?

Think it through, Obed. Mrs. Moore is attractive, and if the first strains of "Beautiful Dreamer" were any indication, she's also quite talented. She's also given to flattery and a lot of eyelash batting. But it doesn't seem she has much heart for God's people. Given a choice between a beautiful face and a beautiful heart, well, it's pretty clear what choice you need to make.

On the other hand, as a shepherd, there could be times an attractive lamb of the fold needs attention. How will Henrietta handle that? Jealousy is as unattractive as pride and a stony heart.

The buggy wheel hit a bump and jolted Obed back to the task on hand. First things first. If he found Oscar alive and well, he'd hie it on to the Kearns's place. If not—like Henrietta said—he'd most likely weep and pray and wait for Abe and Emma.

Proverbs chapter eighteen, verse twenty-two would have to come later.

SEVEN

Oscar Wylie rubbed the stubble of whiskers on his chin. "So, what you're a tellin' me, Preacher-man, is you drove a buggy all the way out here 'cause you was thinkin' I was dead or somethin'?"

Obed pulled a chair from the table, brushed crumbs off the seat, and straddled it. "You weren't in church yesterday, and the Kearn boy said you didn't answer the door when he came by earlier today. We were worried about you."

"Phooey. Who's the we in this sad tale? Ain't had nobody worry about me since I started wearin' britches 'stead of shifts."

"Doc, Emma, Henrietta Harvey, Tillie Rogers, and then there's a new—"

Oscar raised his hand. "Whoa, there. You say Henrietta Harvey was worried? About me?" He scratched the side of his whiskery face. "Who'd ever a-thunk the likes of someone like her would ever have the worrisomes over me." He winked at Obed. "Always did think she was right comely, you know. Never figgered she'd have feelin's for anybody but Herman. O' course, him bein' dead and all might jist be the boot I need to get in the door. Leastwise prop it open a bit."

There were times when Obed lamented his calling as a preacher. Preachers weren't supposed to be jealous. But there envy went, racing down his spine like a bead of sweat on a hot day. Surely this man didn't think he'd have a chance with Henrietta.

"Uh, you've known Henrietta for a while, I take it?" *Of course he has, Obed. You're the relative newcomer to these parts, you know.*

"Knowed her?" Oscar snapped his fingers and slapped his thigh. "Why, we was just like this." He crossed his fingers and waggled them in Obed's face. "'Course, we was right young. But I'll tell ya this, and it's the truth sure as shootin', I's the one who kissed her first...on the cheek. She done turned her head or I'd a put one right on her lips." He walked to the cupboard and picked up the can of peaches and held it close to his chest. "You say it were Henrietta what wanted me to have these here peaches?" He sniffed.

As much as Obed hated to even think about it, evidence was mounting fast that indeed Oscar and Henrietta were more than mere acquaintances. "Yes." He clenched his fist. "Yes, as a matter of fact, she did." At the risk of sounding bitter, he'd not mention the peaches were his idea in the first place. Of course, he'd only thought of them as an excuse to keep Doc from asking too many questions. *Oh, what a tangled web we weave—*

Oscar sniffed again. "Doggone if she don't be rememberin' they's my favorite. I'm thinkin' it sure 'nough is a sign." He plunked the can of peaches down on the table. "Wait just a cat's whisker minute." He shook his finger in the air. "I done thought of somethin' and I reckon I'll be askin' ya, seein' how ya is the preacher and knows about such things and all."

He shuffled to another room and came back carrying his Bible. "I done read me somethin' this mornin', and I'm thinkin' hard-like right now that it was the Good Lord fixin' to tell me somethin'." He adjusted his glasses and flipped through the pages. "Here 'tis, Proverbs chapter eighteen, verse twenty-two. You want I should read it to you?"

Obed crossed his arms on the table and hung his head. "No need, Oscar. I'm familiar with the verse."

"You don't say. Now if that ain't a for sure go-ahead, my name ain't Oscar Wylie. What I'm a hearin' ya tellin' me is it were the Lord sayin' I might should be talkin' to Henrietta about this. Did I get it right?" He wiped his hand across his mouth.

Obed shrugged. Hadn't he had the same questions? To tell this man yes was to give him first chance with Henrietta. To tell him no was to say he didn't believe God spoke to man through His Word. Would the Lord give the same message to more than one man at a time? And about the same woman? Well, Obed Mason wouldn't give up so easily. "I suppose only time will tell, Oscar."

"Doggone, Preacher. I rightly am obliged you come a-callin'. Don't reckon I'd ever got up my man-nerve to be thinkin' about gettin' hitched at my age without you a- tellin' me it was Henrietta who had a worry and a can of my fav-oh-rite sweet fruit for me."

"Uh, you know what, Oscar? Now that I know you aren't sick or injured, I think I'll go on to the Kearns's ranch and see if I can help Doc and Emma." He extended his hand. "Hope to see you in church next Sunday."

"Well, don't you be gettin' in such an all-fired hurry. The reason I weren't in church was I broke a wheel on my buggy, an' the buckle on my saddle cinch done fell off. I ain't so young as to try to bounce all the way to town bareback. I'm thinkin' maybe I'll just ride along, if ya don't mind."

"To the Kearns's?"

Oscar made a face. "No, to town. You'll be a-goin' there after a peek-in at the Kearns's place, won't ya?"

"I... I..."

"I see that there wrinkle runnin' across your forehead. Thinkin' Oscar Wylie would up and go to town on a weekday leaves ya plumb without words, don't it? Just give me a minute to get all cleaned up and all." He slapped his knee. "Doggone, this is like havin' Christmas in August. And I bet I know what you've got swimmin' in that head of your'n."

If he wasn't a preacher, Obed would be tempted to tell him.

"I reckon you're a-thinkin' you're gonna be askin' me an' Henrietta to be sayin' our I-do's right soon, ain't ya?"

Obed straightened his shoulders. "That isn't at all what I'm thinking, Oscar. Not even close."

"Preacher? You still here?"

Obed clenched his teeth. "I'm here. What do you need this time?"

"This here water is a mite cool. Was wonderin' if you might wanna help an old man get all spiffed up and bring me some more hot water. I wanna be smellin' like one of them flowers when next I see my Henrietta."

"Oscar, I've brought you hot water three different times, handed you the soap you dropped on the floor more times than I can count, and if you don't get out and get dressed you're not going to be ready by the time Doc and Emma are finished at the Kearns's ranch."

Obed took a deep breath. One more reference from Oscar about Henrietta being *his,* and he'd disavow his position as shepherd of the flock and let the old man soak until he shriveled into obscurity. Oscar wouldn't stand a chance with Henrietta, would he? Oh, the man was nice enough. Had a good reputation. Money enough to be comfortable—though one would never know it by the way he lived. But he wasn't Henrietta's type. Not at all.

And what type is that, Obed?

Well, you know—the more...more...

Preacher type?

Well, at least when I talk, people listen.

Oh! Big man, are you? They listen because they're a captive audience. Face it, Obed, you're no different than Oscar.

Huh? Of course I'm different.

No. You spend your evenings alone. You eat alone, unless someone from your congregation invites you to partake with them. You spend hours reminiscing about a cabin full of laughter and shrieks and giggles and what it was like to have a wife waiting for you at the end of the day. Oscar Wylie is a lonely old man, Obed. And so are you.

"Well, Preacher. How do I look?"

Obed jolted. There stood Oscar. Clean shaven. His hair was parted in the middle and plastered down close to his head. He wore what looked like a brand new pair of Levi blue jeans, white shirt, string tie, and a gray jacket buttoned across his middle. His black boots were so shiny Obed could almost see his face in them. He held a black Stetson hat.

Obed cleared his throat. "Well, I must say, you've made quite a change, Oscar."

Oscar grinned, his toothless gums pink as a baby's. "Ain't that the truth? You think Henrietta might notice?" He stepped closer. "Take a sniff. You think I smell like one of them purty flowers? I want Henrietta to be drunk with love when I give her a big hug." He chuckled. "I read that in a book once, the part about bein' drunk in love."

The being drunk part might not be so far out of the question, though Obed didn't want to think about it. The man smelled like straight-out-of-the-bottle rum—not the kind the barber splashed on a fresh-shaved face either.

"Uh, where did you get that smelly stuff for your face, Oscar?"

He tipped his head to one side and screwed up his mouth, like he was thinking. "Hmm. Don't rightly recall. Seems like it was somethin' I picked up in Kansas City some years back. Been sittin' on my shelf all this time. Never sawed no need for it, not havin' me a woman and all. But now"—he snapped his fingers and slapped his leg with his Stetson—"that's gonna change just soon as we can get to town. I'm a tellin' you. Preacher, I done got me a real good feelin' about this."

Obed clenched his teeth so tight he felt them crunch. He had a feeling, too, but it wasn't at all good. But he did have a plan. It wouldn't be something he'd want his congregation to witness, but he fully intended to race Oscar to the boardinghouse once they reined to a stop. And if questioned, he'd quote First Corinthians chapter nine, verse twenty-four—"*Know ye not that they which run in a race run all, but one receiveth the prize? So run that ye may obtain.*"

He intended to *receiveth* and *obtain*.

EIGHT

Henrietta pulled back the lace curtain and laid her forehead against the window. Supper had come and gone a half hour ago, and still no sign of Obed. If he'd gone to the Kearns's ranch, he might not return until after dark, but she intended to greet him on his return. She'd had time to rethink her actions earlier in the day and now was sorry she insisted he think about the Proverbs reading. Had she really gone so far as to inform him they'd discuss it with Emma? What must he think? A bossy preacher's wife would not do.

"Any sign of them yet?" Evangeline swept past Henrietta and seated herself on the settee. "I thought sure they'd be back by now. Do you think there's been trouble?"

Henrietta turned from the window and shrugged. "It always seems longer when you're on the waiting end."

"I've been on the waiting end, as you call it, far too many times to take any kind of comfort from that remark." Evangeline straightened the lace on her cuffs. "Thornton would take off every Monday morning to visit his 'good folk' and leave me much like we are today—pacing and watching for his safe return."

"You never accompanied him?" Henrietta smoothed the collar of her simple day dress. If Mrs. Moore's fancy lace-edged blouse was any indication of her normal everyday attire, she could understand her hesitancy to ride horseback through the timber.

Evangeline rolled her eyes. "You've never been to Missouri, have you? He went places like Buzzard Hollow, Coon Gap Flats, and the best of all—three coves and a branch west of the old Dickerson cabin. Hardly a leisurely ride through the tangle of timber and brush."

Henrietta shrugged. "You're right—I've never been to Missouri." But would it have made a difference if the terrain had been friendlier? Maybe a preacher's wife wasn't expected to tag along. Had Obed's wife followed him through the hills? Would that be his expectation? Obed's usual mode of transportation was his horse and buggy. That gave her some measure of relief.

"I hated those Monday visits." Evangeline's mouth twisted. "Yes, I do know that sounds selfish. You mentioned that Obed was a shepherd. Well, that's exactly how Thornton saw himself. He was quick to remind me that a good shepherd puts the well-being of his flock first. He was a very, very good shepherd. He just seemed to forget that I was also one of those sheep." She gave a wan smile that never reached her eyes.

Henrietta frowned. "I recall you said you chose to follow him to his so-called mission field."

"I recall I had just discovered that Obed Mason was the man my husband replaced. To divulge that Thornton had to drag me kicking and screaming to such an ungodly place would not be appropriate for a preacher's wife, now would it? The truth is, I had no choice in the matter whatsoever."

"None?"

"None. Thornton insisted God called him." Evangeline shifted in her chair to face Henrietta. "Tell me, does God only speak to one person about something that ultimately includes two lives? Don't you think if God truly called Thornton, He would have at least talked to me about it, too?"

"Thornton didn't discuss it with you?"

"*Pfft.*" She waved her hand in the air. "Thornton talked about it all the time. It was God who remained quiet on the subject. I asked Him. Over and over I asked Him to give me a sign, or speak to me, or whatever it was He did to get my husband's attention. But He never saw fit to reply."

"God speaks through his Word, Evangeline."

Evangeline jumped to her feet. "Then you show me, Harrietta. Show me where in His Word He tells a husband to leave a fine church, a beautiful home, and good friends, and go traipsing off to rocky hills and flimsy cabins, bugs and snakes, and people who live by superstition. Then you show me where it says God need only speak to one when the decision involves two. Can you do that? Does God keep secrets?" She plunked down into her chair again and folded her hands on her lap.

Henrietta gripped Evangeline's hands. She couldn't answer her questions because they were hers also. But perhaps it would help to change the subject. "Thornton had another church first? Where?"

"Saint Louis. A large church. I loved it there. I had friends. There were brick streets and fine shops and wonderful entertainment— though Thornton was quite adamant about what kind of entertainment was appropriate for a preacher and his wife. Can you understand how difficult it was for me to leave there, and go...go..." She pulled her hands from Henrietta's and walked to the front door. "Oh, never mind. I still find it most difficult to discuss without becoming angry. If you'll excuse me, I think I could use a bit of fresh air."

She opened the door, then turned back to Henrietta. "You know, dear, since you wear your heart on your sleeve, I think it only fair to warn you."

"Warn me about what?"

"I choose to answer that with a quote from the poet John Lyly, 'The rules of fair play do not apply in love or war.' You see, I read Proverbs eighteen also. I detested being the wife of a backwoods shepherd. But I did not hate being a preacher's wife. I think you understand."

The click of the door as Evangeline exited to the porch echoed in Henrietta's ears. One minute the woman spun a tale so sad she'd gained Henrietta's sympathy. But now the real Evangeline Moore emerged. Henrietta had no idea who John Lyly was. But if she wasn't mistaken, the newcomer had just declared war. And again, if she wasn't mistaken, Obed Mason was the spoil.

Obed rubbed the back of his neck. Thank goodness the Doc hadn't needed him for anything more than offering a prayer for the mother and newly arrived babe. He was tired, hungry, and more irritated than he'd been in a good long while. Now it seemed as though someone had stretched the road between the Kearns's place and Cedar Bluff.

Maybe it was Oscar's constant chatter. The man was convinced he had Obed's blessing to claim Henrietta as his bride before the week was over. Or maybe it was because he hadn't yet come up with a foolproof way to beat Oscar to the boardinghouse to ask—beg, if needed—Henrietta to not make any decisions until they could talk. Obed clutched the reins in one hand and ran the other hand down the leg of his britches. There had to be a way to beat this man. If he drove right to the boardinghouse hitching rail, the way Doc and Emma were sure to do, Oscar could be out and running before he had a chance to get out of the buggy.

What if…

Obed smiled to himself. Of course. He wouldn't go to the boardinghouse. He'd take his horse and buggy home, and they'd be forced to walk to Henrietta's. He stood a good six inches taller than Oscar. He was almost certain he could out-stride the shorter legged, wiry man. As a last resort, surely he could outrun him.

"Ya done look right happy, Preacher." Oscar punched him in the shoulder. "Bet your innards aren't a jumpin' 'round like mine, though. I swan, this takin' on a wife is more excitin' than tippin' outhouses."

Obed grimaced. What would Henrietta say if she knew marrying her rated right alongside upsetting a necessary? As much as he never wanted to see or hear of such a thing, it would give him a very unpreacherly satisfaction to see the look on Oscar Wylie's face when she got through with him.

46

He glanced at the little man out of the corner of his eye. "You mind if we walk to Henrietta's? I'm thinking my horse would like a rest."

Oscar let go of the can of peaches and snapped his fingers. "I'd be mighty obliged to stretch my legs a fair bit. Missed my walk this evenin' you know. Fact is, I musta been out for my mornin' hike when that Kearn boy came by. Never gave it a thought before now. Yes, sir. That's where I were."

Obed swallowed. "You…hike often, do you?"

Oscar wiped his chin. "Reckon often enough, since I can't use my saddle."

"Far? Do you go far?" The idea of out-striding him was becoming less and less attractive.

"Nah. Not far. It's near on to two mile to check on my south fence. One way, that is. Don't rightly know how far 'tis to get back home."

Obed frowned. Wouldn't it be the same distance? But he wouldn't confuse the man by asking. Four miles didn't seem all that far.

"Course, I check my east and west fences, too. Figger while I'm out and about it won't hurt none."

This was getting worse all the time. "So, you could have walked to church without any problem."

Oscar stretched his legs in front of him and pointed to his boots. "Ain't never put that much ground underneath these here walkin' bottoms. Been savin' 'em for special doings. And they do pinch my toes a bit. But if Henrietta takes a fancy for a stroll, I reckon we'll meander real slow-like and say our howdies to the folks a-watchin' us. Won't be like chasin' cows. I'll wear 'em for my weddin' day."

No, it wouldn't be like chasing cows. And he'd never known Henrietta to meander anywhere. Just walking from one room to another, she strode out like she was running a race. As for his predicted "weddin' day," well, that remained to be seen.

By the time they reached his barn, Obed was convinced he needed to beat the man to Henrietta's side. "I tell you what, Oscar. I'll let you out here at the hitching post. You do know the way to the Henrietta's, don't you?"

Oscar beamed. "I could take ya right there with my eyes shut."

"That's good. So, you go ahead and get started. I might have to run, but I'll catch up with you." *I gave you warning, my friend. So don't be surprised when I pass you along the way, because I'm going to get a good running start at this prize.*

Obed was confident Oscar couldn't get too far ahead of him with new boots pinching his toes. But when he stepped out of the barn, the man was nowhere in sight.

NINE

Henrietta stopped in the hallway long enough to peek into the mirror, pinch her cheeks, and re-pin a loose strand of hair. She would not go into battle appearing disheveled in the eyes of the enemy. If Tillie saw her, she would scold her for not wearing a bonnet. But a bonnet would obscure her peripheral vision, and she intended to be the first to see Obed when he turned the corner. One last swipe of her eyebrows with her fingers, and she joined Evangeline just as Doc's buggy turned the corner and advanced to the hitching rail in front of the boardinghouse. But where was Obed's wagon?

Evangeline descended the first step, and Henrietta did the same. She didn't relish jumping down stairs but if that's what the Moore woman did, she'd do her best to leap right along with her.

Evangeline put her hand above her eyes and peered down the street.

Henrietta took one more step down and mirrored the other woman's actions.

Doc climbed out of the buggy and helped Emma disembark. Emma waved.

"Reverend Mason is not with you?" Evangeline sounded worried.

Doc shook his head. "He was following us until we got to his corner, then he turned off toward his house. I imagine he'll be along shortly. Uh...where's Tillie?"

Henrietta took her eyes off the street long enough to smile at him. "She's in the kitchen. You can surprise her."

He turned pink. "Guess that might not be such a bad idea. Was hoping she might have something we could eat. Been a long time since lunch, and all we had for supper was a slice of bread and a cup of coffee at the Kearns's ranch."

Henrietta gave a glance toward Emma. "Did everything go well?"

Emma stopped at the bottom of the wide porch steps. "They have another boy. He's small, but he's healthy. "

Evangeline descended two steps so she was a step below Henrietta. "What about that man? That Willie or whatever his name is?"

Henrietta went down two and joined Emma at the bottom. "His name is Wylie, Oscar Wylie." What was it about this woman and not bothering to learn a person's correct name? She was rude, that's what. Plain and simple rude.

Emma's gaze darted between the two women and Henrietta held her breath. There was no hiding anything from Emma Ledbetter, so sooner or later she'd for sure be questioned. But for now, she was not about to let the Moore woman be the first to get to Obed. She skirted around Emma and took several steps down the walkway toward the street. If Obed was coming from home, he should turn the corner from her left. But as to not give away her advantage of knowing from whence Obed might arrive, she turned to the right and shaded her eyes, hoping Evangeline would do the same.

"I see him! I see him!" Evangeline squealed.

"I see him, too." Why was he coming from that direction? Well, no time to argue. If she wanted to get to him first she best hurry. Henrietta gathered her skirts to free her ankles and strode to meet him. She wouldn't run. That would be a bit too obvious. But she would walk fast. Very fast.

She threw a quick look over her shoulder to make sure she was ahead of Evangeline, only to witness the woman striding the other direction toward— Obed? Her heart plunged. And Obed was running toward Evangeline. So who was…?

Little silver specks danced in front of her eyes, and her breath came in gasps. She fought to stay upright, but had no choice but to meet head-on the person yelling her name like a banshee. Oscar Wylie.

No matter how hard she tried, she couldn't stop the flow of tears. If she'd played by the rules, she'd have seen Obed turn the corner, just as she predicted, and it would be her waist encircled by his arm instead of Evangeline Moore's.

Not until Obed observed Oscar running toward Henrietta from the other direction did he realize what happened. The sneaky little man took a shortcut. Why hadn't he thought of that maneuver? Because he was a preacher, that's why. He played by the rules, and taking a shortcut during a race was cheating in any man's game.

There was little time to give more thought to his situation. Evangeline Moore reached him and threw herself into his arms before he could object. He saw her coming but thought she would stop when he did. But no, not only were her arms around his neck, he'd flung his arms around her waist to keep them both from tumbling. However, he doubted few would believe it.

To make it even worse, over Evangeline's shoulder he had a clear view of Oscar Wylie, and he had one arm around Henrietta's shoulders while the free hand still clutched the can of peaches.

"Oh, Obed. I'm so glad you're back safe and sound. I've been pacing all day, I was so worried." Evangeline's words were muffled against his neck.

He attempted to draw away from her, but she tightened her hold.

"I'm sorry we worried you, but you knew where we were going."

She whimpered. "I'm new here, and you can't expect me to know where you went or how long it would take. Did you find that Willie person alive? What did you do? Why were you gone so long?"

He reached behind his neck and grabbed her wrists to loosen her grip. "I appreciate you concern, Mrs. Moore, but surely you realize this behavior is...is...a bit unseemly."

She pulled away, her face pale with a frown etched deep across her forehead. "Of course. Oh, my, I do hope you didn't get the wrong impression. I wasn't... I didn't mean... It's just that I am so very relieved. You see, my late husband left and never came back. This just brought back so many very bad memories. Please forgive me." She turned to Emma. "Perhaps you can tell him, Mrs. Ledbetter. I meant no harm. Thornton always told me I was too free with affection. But you see, I read Proverbs eighteen yesterday, before I met any of you dear people, and my spirit has been troubled ever since. I think God gave me a message, but I... Oh, I did so want to ask you first." She swiped at her eyes, but Obed didn't detect any tears.

Emma moved to her side and put her arm around her shoulders. "I'm sure he'll take time to visit with you later, dear. Come. Let's you and me go in and see if we can help Tillie with a late dinner. We are all quite hungry, and if you've been so distraught I can imagine you might need to rest." She turned and scowled at Obed. *Be careful. Very careful,* she mouthed.

He wiped both hands down his face. *Please, Lord. Don't let it be verse twenty-two. I have more questions than answers about that one myself.*

"Oscar Wylie, what is the meaning of this?" Henrietta wiggled away from his arm. "You can't put your arm around me like that. And in front of the preacher, too." Though she doubted he even noticed, what with Evangeline's arms around his neck like a noose. At least they'd finally separated. She couldn't wait to corner him and have her say.

"Why, Henrietta, my sweet, that preacher man knows all about us. Gave me his blessing, he did."

"His blessing for what, Mr. Wylie?"

"Why, for me and you to get hitched. That's what."

She folded her arms across her stomach in an attempt to keep its contents from erupting.

"See, I done read in Proverbs that the Lord would favor me if I was to up and get me a wife. All them years alone, and I never thunk on what I was a missin'. All along it was you, Henrietta." He snapped his fingers. "Can you believe it?"

Her knees shook and the back of her throat hurt so bad she could hardly swallow. No, she couldn't believe it. Didn't want to believe it. What was Obed thinking? "Did Obed specifically say the verse you read was meant for the two of us?"

Oscar handed her a can of peaches. "He didn't use them words. But he said he knowed the verse, and when he told me it was your idea to send me the peaches, I knew for sure."

"The peaches? The peaches?" She wanted to scream and would have except her throat was too tight to get out more than a squeak. She pushed the peaches into his hand. "Did Reverend Mason tell you that he—"

Oscar patted her shoulder. "That preacher didn't have no need to tell me nothin' 'cause I knowed it. I knowed it was a secret message. Why, see here, you're so outright up and happy it shows all over." He leaned closer. "Just plumb flubberbusted, ain't ya? Them's tears of joy or my name ain't Oscar Wylie. I can tell by your eyes a sparklin' kinda wet-like. Had me an old hound dog used to look at me the same way long about the time he'd get a good sniff of a coon trail." He pounced his finger against his temple. "Smarts is what I got."

Henrietta yanked the peaches from Oscar's hand, turned on her heel, and fled as fast as she could. It'd been a long time since she'd tried to run, and no doubt she'd regret it later, but she had to get away from this man.

Obed and Emma were seated at the dining room table when she entered. There was no sign of Evangeline Moore, which pleased her more than she cared to admit. She had no desire whatsoever to see or converse with the woman. But she did have something to say to Obed Mason. The nerve of him. The absolute raw nerve of him to think he could give Oscar Wylie his blessing. And it hurt. It hurt way down deep where she couldn't rub it and make it go away. She was mortified to think she'd told him to read Proverbs eighteen. Even more embarrassed that she'd allowed herself to think maybe, just maybe, the message of verse twenty-two was meant for her and Obed.

Head low, she aimed herself for the stairs.

"There you are, Henrietta." Emma grabbed her arm and drew her to the dining room. "Come sit with us. Obed has something—"

"I'll tell you what Obed has." Henrietta plunked the can down in front of him. "You have a can of peaches—the same can you purchased to take to Oscar Wylie, who now thinks I sent them as some sort of secret love message. Fix it, Reverend Mason. And take back your blessing while you're at it."

She ran around the corner to her room and slammed the door behind her. She'd never been so miserable in all her life.

TEN

"*It is better to dwell in the wilderness, than with a contentious and an angry woman.*"

Obed laid his open Bible on the table beside his parlor chair. Proverbs twenty-one, verse nineteen—how relevant. Right now, living in the wilderness seemed like a reasonable solution to his problems. Not only would it take him away from Evangeline and Henrietta, but it would also relieve him from having to hear Oscar Wylie's infernal snoring from the sofa across the room. It was no wonder he didn't have a tooth in his head. He probably puffed them out and didn't even realize they were gone.

Still convinced Henrietta Harvey was his intended bride—and vowing to stay in Cedar Bluff until "the little darlin' sets the hitchin' date"—the man refused to return to his ranch "'til I can pick her up and carry my beloved across the doorsill." He'd been camped in Obed's parlor for going on his third day, an unwelcome and seemingly permanent guest.

If Henrietta wasn't the *little darlin'* or the *beloved* Oscar referred to, the whole idea would be funny. But there was nothing about this situation that made Obed smile. In some ways, he—the good preacher man—was responsible for the fiasco. However, guilt wouldn't solve the mess. And he'd run out of ideas.

He closed his Bible and leaned forward, elbows resting on his thighs. Three days ago he couldn't wait to talk with Emma. Maybe today he'd have more luck. He pushed himself to his feet, grabbed his hat, and closed the door behind him before Oscar woke up. Let the man snore. *Please, Lord, let the man snore until I get through talking with Emma.*

The minute he entered Emma's Mercantile, he realized he'd made a mistake. At the counter with Emma was Evangeline Moore. He had no desire to talk with her...again. He'd gone to Henrietta's Boarding House several times yesterday, and Evangeline met him at the door each time. Not only met him, but with each meeting reiterated how timely the Proverbs passage from Monday had been...and to think how God led her to Cedar Bluff on that very day.

There was no escaping. The jangle of the bell above the door had announced his entrance, and both women turned their gazes on him at the same time. Emma shot him a warning glance, while Evangeline blushed and batted her eyes. "Ladies." He tipped his hat.

"Reverend Mason." They answered as one.

He couldn't turn around and leave. So he scuffed to the counter with as much enthusiasm as a man approaching the gallows.

Evangeline put her arm through the handle of her reticule and picked up a package. "I really must be going. I'm sure Obed has an important matter to discuss with you." She put her hand on his arm. "Wait until you see the lovely fabric I've chosen for a special occasion." She tilted her head to one side. "Oh, silly me. Emma, quick hide the bolt. I want it to be a surprise." She slid her hand down his arm and allowed her fingers to linger on his. "Tillie baked fresh muffins this morning if you care to join me for a cup of tea...later."

He hiked one shoulder. "Thank you, Mrs. Moore, but I have quite a full day. Perhaps another time."

"I shall look forward to many *other times*." She gave his fingers a gentle squeeze then brushed past him, a bit too close for his comfort, as she left.

He closed his eyes and sucked in a deep breath. "You wouldn't happen to have a cup of very strong coffee would you, Emma?"

"Oh my dear man." She patted his arm in passing. "Sit over there by the cracker barrel, and I'll bring it to you. Are you sure you want something hot with this heat? You can't sweat your way out of trouble, you know."

Obed sank into the rocking chair next to the barrel as Emma bustled into her living quarters. Within minutes she returned.

"I know you normally take sugar, but I have a feeling it will do more good to skip that this time." She sat his cup on the barrel then pulled a chair from behind the counter for herself. "Now, tell me what's bothering you. I've heard rumors, but I want to hear it from you."

He took a sip of coffee and grimaced. Strong enough to remove rust. "It's a long story, and I haven't slept since Sunday night. Oscar Wylie snores like a locomotive from the minute his head hits a pillow, plus I can't seem to find my way through this maze of trouble I've managed to create. I'm not sure it will make sense—goodness knows I've been trying to decipher the saga myself—but I'll try."

To his great relief, no one entered while he poured out his story. When he finished, Obed set his coffee cup on the cracker barrel and put his hands behind his head. "What should I do, now, Emma? Evangeline thinks the passage in Proverbs was meant for the two of us. Henrietta won't talk to me. Oscar is convinced the same passage is a direct sign from God that he's to take Henrietta as his bride, and I thought the message was for me. Well, me with Henrietta to be exact."

She set her cup beside his. "First of all, I think you're giving yourself too much credit, taking responsibility for this entire situation."

"I was the one who encouraged the church to read a Proverb a day. I did the same thing when I was still in Missouri. Those dear people took it so much to heart that they stopped saying their 'howdies,' as they would put it. Rather, they quoted a verse. Oh, not always from a certain day, but one they felt held a special message for them. Though I don't recall ever being greeted with one quite so personal as the one that seems to be the center of this debacle."

"You weren't an eligible man at that time, either. Tell me… Monday morning, when you came in with Doc, did you really come in for a can of peaches?"

"Those peaches!" He rolled his head from side to side. "No. I was coming to ask your advice, but I didn't want Doc in on the conversation. Then when Oscar thought the peaches were a special gift from Henrietta, well, I let him think that very thing."

"I see. Perhaps I was too hasty to say you were taking too much credit." She chuckled. "It does seem you held the match that lit the fire. You know, Obed, anything less than truth, no matter how innocent it may seem, or what good reasons you might have, is a lie. And a lie is like a snake—it can slither its way through the smallest of openings and lie in wait, coiled and ready to strike. You do know how to kill that reptile, don't you?"

He nodded. "Chop off its head?"

"Exactly."

"Shall I get you a hoe?"

Emma stood and retrieved the coffee pot. "You want more? It's no longer hot, but it's liquid. Probably still carries the same punch."

He held his cup to be filled. "You didn't answer my question."

"I don't think you need my answer. You know what to do, Obed. It just won't be easy. This situation isn't the result of reading God's Word. It's the result of you not being honest to begin with."

Obed hung his head. Emma was right..

"Not telling Oscar the peaches were your idea instead of Henrietta's was wrong. The Bible says if you know the right thing to do and don't do it, it is sin. You could have corrected him right from the start."

"It would have broken his heart, Emma. You weren't there to see his eyes light up, or witness the way he clutched that can of peaches to his chest. I…I just couldn't do it."

"You think it's going to be easier now? The man is positive Henrietta is his intended bride. He was in here yesterday telling everyone who would listen that Henrietta has shut herself in her room to 'get all purtied up for their preacher-blessed nup-tu-als.' A can of peaches would have been much easier to explain, don't you think?"

He leaned his head back, clamped his hands on top of his forehead, and groaned.

"And Evangeline Moore. Well, now, that's a different story. You want to hear it?"

Obed grimaced. "It would have been easier for you to grab a hoe rather than a hammer. At least a hoe would make a clean cut, rather than to be pounded to death."

"Sin hurts, Obed. Maybe not at first, but it can only bring pain in the end. Evangeline Moore is on the hunt for a husband, or I'll disavow my so-called *knowing* ability. And you, my dear man, are right proud she sees you as the prey." She shrugged. "I suppose I can't blame you. She's a very attractive and talented woman. The kind of woman any preacher might see as a worthy help meet."

"I'm not any preacher, Emma. Yes, she is very attractive and quite talented. But nothing she's done thus far has endeared her to me quite as much as that can of peaches Henrietta asked me to take to Oscar."

"The same fruit Oscar claims is a sure sign from above."

He stood and paced from the cracker barrel to the counter and back. "A sign. The verse is a sign. The peaches are a sign. You sure I can't just hand you a hoe?"

Emma stood and gripped his hand. "I think you will find confession a much better tool to kill this snake. You must go to each one of them and tell the truth—whatever it is. Confess, and ask for forgiveness."

"What if they won't forgive me?"

Emma slapped her forehead with the palm of her hand. "For land's sake, Obed Mason, do you or don't you want to get this mess straightened out?"

"I do. Of course I do."

"Then why are you standing here? And for the record, whether or not they forgive you is not the issue. You started the deception, and I agree with Henrietta. Fix it."

Fix it. He'd try. But the whole wilderness decree seemed a more desirable option.

ELEVEN

"**H**enrietta, I know you're in there. Open the door please. I have your breakfast."

"Go away, Tillie. I'm not hungry." Henrietta crooked her elbow on the arm of the chair and rested her head on her hand. She'd not slept well since Obed arrived back in town, and she was near exhaustion. But each time she closed her eyes, the image of Oscar Wylie running toward her popped them back open again. It was enough to kill any woman's appetite.

"I went away yesterday, but I'll not do it again. Fine if you don't want to eat. But you need to hear me out, and I'm not standing in the hallway to talk."

"There's nothing to talk about." That wasn't true. There was so much to talk about she didn't know where to start. If only she'd had a chance to visit with Emma. Emma had been present to observe both Oscar Wylie's antics and Obed embracing the fair Mrs. Moore.

The doorknob jiggled and before Henrietta could react Tillie entered the room.

Henrietta sat up and gaped. "How—"

"Did you forget I have a key to every room in this boardinghouse?" Tillie set a tray of food on the table beside Henrietta's chair and plopped herself down on the edge of the bed. "Now, I'm going to stay here while you eat this, then you're going to get dressed and get out of this room."

"You can't make me." Why couldn't Tillie understand? How would she like it if Oscar Wylie chose her to be his bride...and the man she wanted to marry gave his blessing on the union?

"You sound like a spoiled child, and for two cents I'd do what my parents did when I displayed such an attitude."

"What's that?" Henrietta's nose twitched. She was hungrier than she wanted to admit to Tillie, and the biscuits smothered in sausage gravy smelled heavenly.

"A willow switch, that's what. Please, Henrietta. Stop this nonsense. Have you read the Proverb for today?"

She shook her head. "Reading a Proverb a day is what started this whole thing. I read it Monday. Evangeline read it and Oscar Wylie read it, and now look what a mess we're in."

"You focused on one verse, Henrietta. Verse twenty-two. I say you should read the chapter again, and this time pay special attention to verse thirteen. You took Oscar Wylie's word, but you won't hear Obed's side of the story." She lifted Henrietta's Bible from the table beside the tray of food. "Here. Read it."

Henrietta turned to Proverbs eighteen and found the verse. She read aloud, "'*He that answereth a matter before he heareth it, it is folly and shame unto him.*'" Shame flooded her. "Oh, Tillie. You're right. I've reacted to one side of a story, haven't I?"

"Obed was here yesterday, several times, hoping he could talk with you. Instead, he was waylaid each time by the Moore woman. It's as if she sat and watched for him. He wanted to see you, but you were angry and stubborn and wouldn't come out of your room."

"Thus the spoiled child." Henrietta clasped her hands together. "I was afraid if I went out of this room, Oscar Wylie would be waiting for me. I don't want to talk to him."

Tillie moved to Henrietta's side and put her arm around her shoulders. "I understand. Oscar thinks you're holed up in here preparing for your wedding. Obed thinks you're angry."

"He thinks I'm angry? Why?"

"Well, for starters, from what I heard, you threw a can of peaches at him and told him to fix it, then left in a huff. I'd say he has good reason to think you're angry. Face it, my good friend, you are. What you have to decide is who you're angry with—Obed, Oscar, or Evangeline Moore? Now, while you have your Bible in your lap, you best read the Proverb for today. I'll not tell you what message you'll receive, but I guarantee there will be one. God's Word never returns void, you know." She gave Henrietta's hand a brisk pat. "I'm going to bring you some warm water so you can freshen up a bit. If you're not down in an hour, I'm sending Doc in here. And remember, I have a key." She departed.

Henrietta scanned the passage in Proverbs twenty-two. She gave a jolt when she read verse nineteen. She read it, then reread it. What if Obed decided to dwell in the wilderness?

Tillie returned shortly and poured fresh water in the bowl on Henrietta's washstand, then went to her clothespress. "This time, my fair lady, you'll wear one of your dresses. It won't be blue, but at least you won't have to fear falling out of it." She pulled a green skirt and a green and white striped blouse from the wardrobe. "Here, this will do. You want me to brush your hair for you?"

Henrietta snorted. "I may act like a spoiled child, but I can fix my own hair."

"Well, do it then. And don't forget to pinch your cheeks and dab on a bit of rosewater."

Henrietta smiled at her friend. "Tillie, whatever would I do without you?"

Tillie giggled. "That's a question for another day. My question is—whatever am I going to do with you? Now, I'll leave you to your toilette."

Henrietta had just finished pinning her hair when she heard footsteps and voices in the hallway outside her room.

"Oh, Obed. You did come. Would you care to join me in the parlor? I'll ask Tillie to bring us some of her fresh muffins."

Obed came for tea with Evangeline? Defeat slumped Henrietta into her chair. She covered her ears with her hands. She didn't want to hear one more word. Neither could she bring herself to leave her room. How could she face the two of them together? She couldn't. That's all there was to it. She just couldn't.

Obed fisted his hands at his side. He'd been about to knock on Henrietta's door. As improper as it might seem on any other occasion, Tillie assured him it would afford them both the most privacy. How Evangeline knew he was in the house remained a mystery. He'd even come in the kitchen entrance, but somehow she'd detected his presence. And now, right outside Henrietta's door, where she was sure to hear every word, Mrs. Moore had once again claimed his company.

So what to do about her? Should he sit and have tea and a muffin with her? Allow her to think he had feelings for her? Allow Henrietta to think he had feelings for Evangeline? He was the preacher. Others brought problems like this to him to solve. Hadn't he always had a solution? Had they been platitudes—pat answers? He knew what the Bible said about knowing what to do and not doing it. But knowing and doing were two different things, and it was obvious he was much better at knowing.

Evangeline hooked her arm with his and drew him toward the parlor.

It was time for doing. "Wait, Evangeline." He dug in his heels and pulled his arm free. "We need to talk."

Her eyes widened. "You sound so serious, Obed. Is something wrong?"

He rubbed his forehead. "There is, but it's all my fault. You see—"

"There you are, Preacher-man." Oscar Wylie strode toward them.

Where had he come from? What was it about this place that seemed to produce people out of nowhere?

"Woke up an' ya was plumb gone. I was a hopin' I'd find ya here. Been thinkin' on the weddin' for me an' Henrietta. What say we do it after Sunday service? People're already there an' all. An' I be needin' to get back to my ranch. Got lots of work what needs a-doin'. I could use Henrietta's help."

Obed gritted his teeth. "Oscar, that isn't something for you and me to decide. Have you even asked her to marry you?"

"Didn't need to ask. Done told her ya gave your blessing an' she was so flubberbusted tears of joy went runnin' down her purty cheeks."

Evangeline took his arm again. "You know, Obed, I think it's romantic how Mr. Willie is so eager to plan their wedding. Since you've already blessed the arrangement, how could she refuse?"

"Why, thank ya." Oscar leaned closer to Evangeline. "What'd ya call me?"

"Mr. Willie."

"Wylie. The name's Wylie. But I think I be knowin' ya from somewheres." He scratched his head. "Have you an' me said howdy before?"

"I can't possibly think where that could have been."

Oscar walked around her, eyeing her from top to bottom, much like a buyer at a horse auction. "What is it they call ya?"

Evangeline paled. "You mean my name?"

"Front and back, ma'am. If ya don't mind."

She looked like she was going to faint. "Evangeline. Evangeline Moore."

Oscar's fingers rasped against his unshaven chin. "Moore. Moore. Hmm. Don't recall no Evangeline Moore. But recollect a sweet little gal name of Angie Carter up in Kansas City long about twenty year ago or so. Whooeee, but that little darlin' could sing. She never could get my name to come out right, though. Called me Oswald Willie."

Evangeline's face turned crimson. "I...I'm sorry, Obed. I've a sudden onset of a headache. I'm afraid I need to excuse myself." She rushed around the corner and pounded up the stairs.

Oscar snapped his fingers and slapped his thigh. "Doggone, Preacher, she sure 'nough do remind me of that sweet little Carter gal, Angie. She done had lots of headaches, too. All come on her real sudden like that. 'Specially if I got to talkin' about her comin' home with me."

Obed's heartbeat thrummed in his ears. Surely Evangeline and Angie weren't the same person. No, that couldn't be. Wouldn't she recognize Oscar? But then, a person could change a lot in twenty years. Oscar didn't say where he heard Angie sing...except in Kansas City. It could have been church, couldn't it? After all, she was a preacher's wife. Did he dare ask? And did he really want to know?

TWELVE

Obed grabbed Oscar's arm. "Come on. You and I are going to go have a visit with Emma."

Oscar jerked loose. "Just a cat's whisker minute there, Preacher. I'm right glad I got to see ya an' all, but I'm wantin' to have a sit-down with my sweetheart. That purty little darlin' has been so busy plannin' our weddin' day, I'm thinkin' she'll be right down happy to know I done got it all thunk out. A woman likes to be told them things, you know."

Obed wiped both hands down his face. This entire situation was enough to make him quit the pulpit. "No, Oscar, there are some things we men don't get to decide on our own, and a wedding is one of them."

But isn't that what you were going to do, Obed? Isn't that why you wanted to visit with Emma in the first place?

No, I was only going to ask her advice.

And you needed that because…?

Because I, well, I wanted to know what Emma thought about me asking Henrietta to be my wife.

Before you asked Henrietta, am I correct? You could have asked Me, you know. We are on speaking terms, aren't we?

I thought we were, Lord. Monday I thought You were telling me to take a wife—Henrietta, to be exact. And today I think You told me to go live in the wilderness.

"Preacher, are you all right? Ya done look all white an' sweaty." Oscar gripped Obed's shoulders and shook him like a dog killing a snake.

Obed squirmed free. "I'm fine. On second thought, it won't be necessary for you to come with me to Emma's. You proceed with your plans. Oh..., you have prayed about this, haven't you? You're sure this is what God wants you to do?"

The little man jammed his hands into the pockets of his britches. "Me an' the Lord, we've done talked my hankerin' to have me a wife near to pieces. Then you showed up with them peaches from Henrietta the very day I read that verse. And on top of that, you done pulled up to your barn an' gave me a head start a-runnin' to her. I reckon that's straight from heaven, and I'll say my thank-you to ya for makin' it real plain."

Obed rotated his head. His neck joints crackled. He'd have to go read it again, but he was fairly certain that today's chapter in Proverbs contained a verse about man's plan seeming right, but it was God himself who considers that man's heart.

"You know, Oscar, my friend." He gripped the man's bony shoulder. "I think the best thing for you to do is have a good long talk with Henrietta. But if you don't mind, I'd like to visit with her first."

Oscar's pink gums chomped a couple of times. "Why, I reckon that be a right fine idea. Mayhaps Miz Rogers might have a cup of coffee handy. You go right ahead an' have your say-so with my little darlin'."

"Good. Let's you and me go see if we can find Tillie. I think I smell the aroma of fresh muffins, and I could use a cup of coffee myself."

They met Tillie at the kitchen door. She carried a plate of muffins. "I didn't know Oscar was here. I didn't hear the door."

"I never called out my name or nothin'. The door was open, so I figgered I was growed enough to step right in."

"I see." She cocked one eyebrow at Obed. "Have you already... done what you came to do?"

"No, but Oscar has agreed to let me talk with Henrietta before he tells her his wedding plans." He bit the side of his cheek and hoped Tillie would get the message.

"Well, that sounds like a fine idea to me. Oscar, have a seat in the parlor. I'll be right in with coffee to go along with these muffins." She handed him the plate of baked goods.

Oscar sniffed the muffins and then winked at Obed. "Never had me a sit-down coffee in a parlor. Take your time, Preacher. I got me a whole lot of goodies to gnaw through."

Obed turned toward the hallway.

Tillie caught his arm. "Wait," she whispered. "Don't barge into Henrietta's room. Go to the kitchen. I'll take Oscar's coffee to him, then I'll excuse myself long enough to let Henrietta know you want to speak with her."

"What if she refuses?"

"She won't. I won't let her. But she needs to prepare herself." Tillie shrugged and giggled. "It's important to a woman that she be prepared, you know."

He didn't know. But if it was important to Henrietta, then it was important to him, too.

"I left a muffin for you in the kitchen, and there's coffee on the stove. Make yourself at home, and I'll let you know when Henrietta is ready to receive you. While you talk to her, I'll keep Oscar Wylie entertained." She shuddered. "I do wish that man would get some teeth. I don't care to watch him chaw on a muffin."

Obed laughed. Dear Tillie. He poured himself a cup of coffee and sat at the table. As he took the first sip, he detected movement out of the corner of his eye. He turned to the back staircase opening and met the gaze of Evangeline Moore. His heart plunged. How did this woman always manage to find him alone?

"Obed, may I join you?"

He forced a nod. "Have you recovered from your headache?"

She swept into the room and touched his shoulder with her fingertips. "Yes, and we must talk. Please."

He motioned to a chair across the table. "You care for a cup of coffee?"

"No, not here. Somewhere private."

"Where, then? Oscar is in the parlor and—"

"My room?"

He agreed they needed to talk, but he also needed to proceed with caution. Much caution. "No."

She raised both hands. "All right. Always the proper preacher. I understand. We can walk then. Outside where all of Cedar Bluff can observe. Is that better?"

He sighed. "Much better. Though I'm sure Tillie would accommodate our privacy here in the kitchen if she was aware of the need."

"I don't care to share the need, if you don't mind."

Obed stood. "Then we'll walk."

Henrietta couldn't stop the tears. Not since Herman died had she shed tears so freely and for so long. She was no match for Evangeline Moore, that was obvious. She could only imagine her now, sitting in the parlor with Obed, sipping tea and looking beautiful. No doubt she'd even offer to sing for him. She moved her chair closer to the window and let the breeze dry her wet cheeks.

Maybe she should consider Oscar's offer. She ticked off his attributes on her fingers. If she could get all fingers full, she'd have to do some serious thinking. He was a bit rough, but he was a well respected man—one finger. He owned a large ranch—two. Had plenty of money, according to rumors—three. And, she could well remember, when he still had teeth he was rather handsome—four. He was God fearing—five. That was one hand. Could she fill the other?

Had a nice home, though she could imagine it sorely needed a woman's touch—six. And... And... And he liked peaches—seven. She buried her face in her hands. It was the peaches that convinced him she was his intended bride, and it was Obed who didn't tell him the peaches were from him in the first place. And the peaches were the last thing she could count off on her fingers. Not enough. But maybe if she were to write them down it would help her think. After all, Herman's credits hadn't filled all ten fingers either. Not at first. But oh, how full he'd made her life.

She reached for paper and pencil from the drawer in the table beside her chair. Yes, she'd make a list. While she was at it, maybe she'd make a list of reasons why Evangeline Moore was not suited for the likes of Reverend Obed Mason.

She was busy writing when Tillie came into the room.

"What are you doing, Henrietta? Whatever it is, stop. Obed is here and wants to talk to you."

"I'm making a list of reasons why I should consider marriage to Oscar Wylie."

"You're what?" Tillie grabbed the paper. "This is ridiculous, even for you, Henrietta Harvey."

She plucked the paper from Tillie's hand. "Is it? You know, Tillie, I took your advice. I got ready, and was about to make my entrance, as you suggested, when I overheard Evangeline and Obed. Apparently you made muffins so they could have a little tête-à-tête in the parlor."

"I did nothing of the sort. I knew Obed was here and wanted to talk to you, but I had no idea Evangeline would waylay him right outside your door. I can't believe you would think that of me, and neither can I believe you'd actually consider marriage with Oscar Wylie."

"Well, believe it." She laid the paper in her lap. "Did you say Obed is here?"

"In the kitchen. He does very much want to talk to you. And you must let him. Remember the Proverb you read to me? He deserves a chance to be heard."

The curtain billowed with a puff of breeze, and at the same time revealed Obed and Evangeline, arm in arm, as they stopped right outside her window. Her heartbeat pounded in her ears and her chest tightened so much it hurt.

THIRTEEN

Obed allowed Evangeline to link her arm in his. After all, they were walking on uneven ground and it wouldn't be gentlemanly at all if he allowed her to stumble. "All right, Evangeline. What necessitates this talk?"

"Mr. Willie was right. He does know me."

"From Kansas City?" If that's where he'd gotten the bottle of whatever it was he splashed on his face, Obed understood why it smelled like the real stuff. It'd had plenty of time to age.

"Yes."

"And you didn't recognize him?" How could one forget the likes of Oscar?

She shook her head. "I would never have recognized him. Believe me, Obed, when I met him all those years ago, he was a very handsome man. He was also a very rich man. Both very strong attractions, I might add."

"And you were doing what in Kansas City? Performing on the stage, perhaps?"

She licked her lips. "The only stage I ever performed on was the top of a bar in a sleazy saloon. I was one of *those* ladies."

Obed swallowed. Did he want to know this story? "And that's where you met Oscar Wylie? I've never known the man to take a drink stronger than coffee. Of course, I've not been here long. And

I'm more than surprised that he would…would—"

"It's not what you're thinking. Mr. Willie came to Kansas City to sell cattle…and convert sinners like me. He wasn't in the saloon to drink or purchase favors. He came in with his gun and his Bible. I met him long before I met Thornton. I suppose you could say Oswald Willie prepared the way."

"Then you never—"

"I really don't care to divulge all the details of that time of my life. But I can tell you this, Oswald was always a true gentleman."

Her statement brought a measure of relief. "After you left, with your headache, he told me that you often had them, especially if he talked about taking you home with him."

She leaned her head back and laughed. "The only home he ever talked about was his heavenly home. He wanted to make sure I would be there with him one day. It made me quite uncomfortable. The only nice way I could think of not having to listen was to feign a headache."

"But you said your late husband took my church in Missouri. So, were you married to a preacher or not?"

"Very married. I met Thornton in a little church he had in an old store a few doors down from the saloon. Walked past one night and heard the singing, and I couldn't resist going in. Thornton knew from the start what kind of woman I was, but he loved me anyway. We married, and he got a church in Saint Louis to keep me from the prying eyes of old acquaintances. Those people never had a clue what kind of preacher's wife they had."

"But you didn't like the hills or the people in them, did you? I never knew an unkind soul in those hills."

"I hated every minute I was there. I grew up in hills like that. We were so poor we ate lard sandwiches, scraped ice off our water bucket every winter morning, and slept six to a bed crosswise so we could keep warm. I never knew an unkind soul in Missouri, either, but their kindness didn't feed us or keep us warm. They were all just as poor as we were. I vowed one day I would leave them and never look back. Going back to Missouri, seeing those poor women in their humble homes, being proud of what they had and never expecting anything better, brought more guilt than I could handle."

"And when you left those hills, you went to Kansas City? How could your life there been better than what you left?" They'd reached the back corner of the house and Obed indicated they keep going around. If they were going to stop, he preferred it be in full view of anyone passing to thwart any appearance of wrong doing.

"Kansas City was very kind to me...at first. I learned how to sew when I was old enough to hold a needle. I found a job as a seamstress, taught myself how to make hats, and I eventually opened my own shop, The Virtuous Woman." She scoffed. "A complete misnomer."

Obed shook his head. "What changed, Evangeline? How did you end up in a sleazy bar?"

She peered into the distance. "I got greedy. I discovered I could make more money making costumes for the madams. I could double that money by working for them. I was very young and didn't consider what would happen as I grew older. Too old, you see, to work in the finer places."

"Did Thornton know how you felt about moving from Saint Louis?"

She rolled her eyes. "Oh, he knew. I made sure he knew every minute of the day. I made life miserable for him. Something I'm not at all proud of now. At the time, it was my way of survival. But Thornton insisted he'd been *called*. I suppose one of my biggest questions will always be why God didn't see fit to call me while He was at it."

"He calls through His Word, Evangeline."

She stomped her foot. "You think I haven't heard that? But no one can show me where— Oh, never mind. I was wrong to oppose him so. In the end, those hills killed him. At least that's what I keep telling myself. It's easier, I suppose, if I can blame something instead of myself."

"You want to tell me what happened?"

"Jake Riley happened."

He frowned. "Jake Riley? I never knew a Jake Riley."

"No, you wouldn't have known him. He was an old client from Kansas City. He threatened to find me when I left, but we'd been gone so many years I'd forgotten all about him. Then one day he showed up in that little church in the timber. Walked in, called me out, and announced my sordid past."

"And the people turned on you?"

"I turned on myself. I couldn't bear to look at Thornton. Jake promised to not cause a problem if I'd go with him. He rode out, and I rode with him. It was the only way I knew to get him away from everything good that had ever happened to me. I…I didn't think Thornton would follow us."

"But he did?"

"Thornton always carried a rifle with him when he went into the timber. He hated snakes, probably the only thing he didn't like about those hills."

Obed's hands tingled. This was not at all what he expected to hear when Evangeline suggested they talk. "He shot this Riley fella?"

"He didn't shoot first. Jake did. By the time it was all over, they were both dead."

"What did you do?"

"I buried my husband with the help of those good people and left in the night so no one would find me. I caused his death, you know. I didn't pull the trigger, but I might as well have. You know, I really thought that once I gave my life to the Lord, everything bad would be over. My sins were forgiven—that's what Thornton told me, over and over again."

"And they are, Evangeline."

"Maybe. But the consequence of sin follows. The Bible says that we reap what we sow. I'm convinced we reap more than we sow. And we definitely reap in a different season."

"What you told us in Emma's Mercantile, about getting off the train and going to go look for a place to live. Was that the truth?"

"Partly. What I didn't include is the fact I got off the train and prayed I'd find a husband. I hate being alone. It frightens me. But I had no idea you were here, and that is the whole truth. The sad part, I'm ashamed to tell you, is once I met you I was determined to gain your attention—one way or another."

"Well, you did get my attention."

They rounded the corner to the front of the house, and while there was no wrong doing, Obed was relieved the street was empty.

She sighed. "Not your whole attention. I knew from the minute Harrietta walked into the little store that you were off limits. But I've never backed down from a challenge. Then again, I've never been up against the likes of Mrs. Harvey. I know when I'm beat, and I also know when it's time to move on."

"Why not stay here in Cedar Bluff? You can start all over again. What happened in the past is only between you and the Lord."

"And Oswald Willie." She smiled.

"I have a feeing Oscar will handle this revelation quite well. I think he'll be very pleased to know that you will now *go home* with him."

"I wanted you to know the truth. I'm tired of running."

He patted her hand. "You needn't run, Evangeline. You have your millinery and dress-making business. None of this story will ever leave my lips. If you want it told, you'll be the one to tell it."

"I want Harrietta to know this story."

"Do you want me to tell her?"

"No. I'll tell her my story. But you need to tell her you love her."

Obed bit his lip and scuffed forward another dozen strides, thinking. Evangeline was right. Oscar hadn't wasted any time telling Henrietta how he felt, and now it was Obed's turn. "I agree, Henrietta needs to know, and it needs to come from me."

No sooner had those words left his mouth than the window they stood beside slammed shut. Through the lace of the curtain he recognized Henrietta.

Henrietta turned to Tillie. "You were right, Tillie. Obed deserved to be heard. Well, now he's been heard, loud and clear. Please tell him I'm unavailable to speak with him today, or any other day. And never chide me again for making a list of Oscar's attributes. Please go."

Tillie planted her fists on her hips. "I heard him, too, Henrietta. But I'm telling you, we didn't hear the entire conversation. I'll tell him you don't care to speak with him. But if he wants to come in, I'll give him the key."

Henrietta gawked at her friend. "You wouldn't."

"I would. And I will. This is ridiculous. You love him, Henrietta. Anything you love is worth fighting for. Wash your face, put away Oscar's list, and be ready to receive company."

"I'm telling you—"

"Henrietta Harvey, you've lived your entire life telling others what to do, when to do it, and how. Now, it's my turn." Tillie slammed the door behind her.

Henrietta rubbed her arms. Tillie was right. She had told Obed what to read, and no doubt he fully understood her intent. Well, so be it. She stomped to her clothespress. If, by chance, Obed still wanted to talk to her, she'd be ready for him. But not in a green skirt and striped blouse. She had far more interesting items to choose from. For instance, one rust colored gown she'd ordered on a whim from Emma months ago. If brown caused her red hair to look red and her ample body to appear thinner, what might rust do?

FOURTEEN

Obed didn't need to look up to know it was Tillie charging his direction. Neither would he need an explanation.

Evangeline slipped her arm from his. "I think I best make myself scarce, Obed, but thank you for listening to me." She stepped past Tillie. "It's not what you think, Mrs. Rogers. I hope you allow him to explain."

Tillie threw her arms wide. "I just had this very same conversation with Henrietta. What were you thinking, Obed? Stopping right outside her window like that?"

Obed shrugged. "This may come as a surprise, Tillie, but I honestly didn't know it was Henrietta's window. It's not as if I visit her room often, you know. How much did she hear?"

"The same as what I heard. You agreed Henrietta needed to know something and you should be the one to tell her. Can you imagine what she thinks that might be? Evangeline hasn't exactly been subtle about her feelings for you."

"If Henrietta hears what I have to say, it will change things. And at some point, Evangeline will explain her side of it, too."

Tillie slapped both palms against her forehead. "Her side? So now there's a his side and a her side and somewhere in the middle is Henrietta?"

Obed grabbed Tillie's wrist. "She is not in the middle. Henrietta should be hearing this first, but you've forced me to tell you. I love Henrietta Harvey and intend to ask her to marry me. That's what I meant when I said Henrietta needed to know and that she needed to hear it from me."

"Then I suggest you tell her. I'll go warn her that you're coming." She moved away from him.

He grabbed her arm in passing. "Warn her? I'm not something or someone to be feared. No, you go see to Oscar. As I remember, you sent him to the parlor to wait for his coffee. I'll go to Henrietta on my own."

Tillie trotted after him. "Oh, my lands, I completely forgot about poor Oscar. Yes, you go. And keep Henrietta in her room so Oscar can't find her."

Obed laughed. "I found her first, remember? And the spoils belong to the victor."

They rounded the corner to the porch and found Oscar Wylie waiting in its shade. "Ya don't need to be worrisome about me, Preacher. I done heard how it is 'tween you and Henrietta. Guess I done shot outta the chute before they opened the head gate, didn't I?"

Obed's neck prickled with heat. This man could sneak up without a sound. Everything was out in the open now. He hadn't planned to talk to Oscar before he had a chance to explain things to Henrietta, but now it seemed the more necessary thing to accomplish.

He gestured to the house. "Oscar, let's go into the parlor, what do you say?"

"I reckon that'd be a good idea. You look like ya got somethin' a gnawin' at ya, an' I figger ya need to spit it out, man-to-man."

Tillie's face brightened. "I'll bring the two of you fresh coffee. How's that?"

Oscar smiled and snapped his fingers. "I done et all the muffins. Maybe ya got some spares?"

She laughed. "I have spares, Oscar, and I'll bring them."

In the parlor, Oscar settled onto the settee. "Ya know, I been a-thinkin' I might just up an' buy me one of these here big chairs. I got me an old hound dog what likes to be with me, but doggone if he ain't gettin' too big to crawl up on my lap." He patted the cushion beside him. "He'd fit right proper on somethin' like this."

Obed lowered himself to the chair opposite Oscar. How to start this conversation? He'd never talked man-to-man about his love for a woman, and for certain never about their love for the same woman.

Oscar crossed his legs. "This here talk is gonna be 'bout as toe curlin' as gettin' switched by a schoolmarm, ain't it?"

Obed nodded. "It is, my friend. I should have spoken up long ago, Monday night, to be exact. I should have told you right away I was the one who had the idea of bringing you the peaches. And I did it in the first place to keep Abe Mercer from asking too many questions." He leaned forward and rested his forearms on his thighs. "You mind listening to a long story?"

"Tillie ain't brung the muffins yet. Reckon I'll stay as long as got me somethin' to chaw on. Story-tell away. But ya better be saying 'the end' when you're finished, so's I know you're done."

Obed spilled the whole story, starting with his reading of the twenty-second verse in Proverbs eighteen, and ending with their sitting in the parlor now, trying to figure out what to do next.

Oscar chuckled. "It downright tickled my innards to think ya'all had a worrisome over me. Like I done said, I jumped outta the chute too fast. But I got me a good house, a good horse, and a good hound dog. That's more good stuff than a whole lotta folks. 'Course, a good woman woulda sweetened the cup a bunch." He scratched the side of his face. "Reckon ya can tell the news to Henrietta? I don't wanna be the one what breaks her heart." He slapped his thigh. "That's me spoutin' a funny, Preacher-man. Ya can go ahead and laugh."

Obed did laugh. "Then there's no hard feelings?"

Oscar shook his finger. "Never had me time to go heftin' a grudge on these boney shoulders. B'sides, as sweet as she be, Henrietta Harvey ain't the only lump of sugar in the bowl."

Well, my friend. You look into your own bowl, because she sure is the only sweetening in mine.

"Here you are, gentlemen, muffins and a fresh pot of coffee." Tillie entered the parlor and sat the coffee and plate of muffins on the table beside the settee. "Obed, could I speak with you? In private?" She smiled at Oscar. "I don't want to be rude, Oscar. It's just that—"

Oscar broke a muffin in two. "You go have your words. Ain't rude a'tall. Stuffin' this whole muffin in my mouth at one time, now that'd be rude."

Obed stood. "Is this something about Henrietta, Tillie? If it is, I don't mind if Oscar hears."

She shrugged one shoulder. "I just saw Evangeline heading for Henrietta's room."

Obed plopped back in the chair.

Oscar handed him a muffin. "I'm a thinkin' you might wanna gnaw one of these, Preacher-man."

"I think you're right, Oscar. And, Tillie, I hope the coffee is strong."

The knock on her door set Henrietta's heart racing. She took one last look in the mirror, then seated herself in the chair by the window and smoothed her skirt. Her mind raced with questions. What would she say to him? What would he say to her? Should she keep peering out the window or turn his direction? No. She'd not turn. It would be too much like she expected him. She'd peer through the window until he spoke her name. Decision made, she called in a quavering voice, "Come in."

The whiff of lemon verbena drifting through the room spoke volumes. Henrietta whipped her head around so fast her neck popped. "Evangeline Moore?"

The woman wrung her hands. "Could...could we talk?"

Henrietta's heart plunged to the tip of her toes. The last person she wanted to talk to was Evangeline Moore. But what could she say that wouldn't sound rude?

"Harrietta?"

Henrietta gave a little shake of her head to clear her thoughts. "Of course, Evangeline. Do come in." She would likely rue the invitation, but according to Proverbs eighteen, verse three, it would be wrong for her not to listen to what Evangeline had to say.

Evangeline perched on the edge of the bed. "I need to explain what you think you heard through that open window."

"I know what I heard. It was very clear."

Evangeline's shoulders heaved. "The words were clear, but the message behind them was left to your own interpretation. Hear me out. Then you may order me to leave, and I promise I'll not bother you ever again."

"I'll listen." Henrietta folded her hands in her lap in an attempt to hide their trembling.

"Thank you. You have no idea how difficult this is for me, but you deserve to know." Evangeline sat on the end of the bed and shared her story, and by the time she was finished they were both in tears.

Henrietta closed her eyes against the pain she observed on Evangeline's face. To think she almost refused her explanation. She reached across the arm of the chair and gripped Evangeline's hands. "I'm so sorry my behavior has caused you to reveal this part of your life that I'm sure you never wanted to revisit. Emma once told me I was jealous, and I was. But I was so wrong. I would very much like to be your friend. I do hope you will stay in Cedar Bluff."

Evangeline stood, crossed to the window, and peered out. "How would the fine people in this town welcome me if they knew the real me?"

"The real you is the person standing in front of me now, and that's all anyone else ever has to know. You would be an asset to our little town. You're a woman of many talents, you know."

"I doubt dancing on top of a bar would qualify."

"No, but you can design and sew hats. And you play the piano and sing. I've thought for a long time what we needed in the church was a choir. I'm sure Obed would welcome your contribution."

Evangeline knelt by Henrietta's side. "How can I ever thank you?"

Henrietta tilted her head. "You really want to know?"

She nodded.

"Inform Obed that I want to talk to him." She stood and smoothed her skirt. "Tell me, Evangeline, do I appear thinner in this color?"

FIFTEEN

Obed stood outside Henrietta's door, sent there by a grinning Evangeline Moore, and leaned his head against the wall. His heart raced and his palms were sweaty. He hadn't been this nervous when he was a youngster asking Clara's pa for her hand.

Maybe it was because he was older now and understood more clearly the depth of the commitment. He loved Henrietta. He was sure of it, though they'd never courted. He believed Henrietta returned his devotion. But what if all the doings of these past few days changed her mind? As nervous as he was to propose, to think of her rejecting him made his stomach hurt.

Maybe he should wait. After all, he hadn't discussed this with Albert, her only son. Was that proper? What would his church people say? What would he do if Albert objected to the marriage? Where would they live? It made sense to live in the parsonage, close to the church, but what if Henrietta didn't want to give up the boardinghouse?

The door latch clicked, and he straightened with a snap.

Henrietta stood framed in the doorway with a saucy grin on her face and one fist balled on her hip. "Obed Mason, are you going to stand out here all day? I would appreciate you hurrying up and asking me to marry you."

His heart melted, and he took her in his arms. One thing for certain, with this woman around he'd never again have to wonder what to do. She'd tell him!

"How do I look? And if you say ample, I'll cry." Henrietta primped in front of the mirror, adjusting the lace collar of her pale blue taffeta dress.

Emma tugged her hands away from the lace. "You're beautiful, my friend. But if you don't stop yanking at that collar, it's going to be limp."

Henrietta examined herself from neckline to hem. It had taken Evangeline a full three weeks to finished the dress, but it was worth the wait. She tried to smile, but her lips wobbled. "Do you think Obed will think me beautiful? Blue is his favorite color, you know."

Emma hugged her. "Yes, Obed will think you very beautiful. I doubt he even will see the color of your dress. He's marrying *you*, Henrietta. He'd marry you no matter what you wore."

"I think I'm going to cry. I shouldn't cry, should I? I should be happy."

Emma touched Henrietta's cheek. "Go right ahead and cry. Most likely everyone in church will shed tears right along with you. But they're happy tears. Now come, or you're going to be late for your own wedding."

When Henrietta and Emma arrived at the church, they found the yard full of buggies and farm wagons. Lone horses were tied to anything that would hold a rein, and people were lined up outside waiting to get in.

Henrietta grabbed Emma's arm, staring. "Is the entire county here? Oh, Emma, are all these people here just for us?"

"You are both very loved, Henrietta. And it's not often we are privileged to witness a union between two people your... Well, of two mature lovers."

Henrietta slapped Emma's hand. "Lovers? Oh, goodness, that sounds—"

Emma giggled. "Just like it should, my friend." She leaned close and kissed Henrietta on the cheek. "Now, as soon as the last people get seated, we'll go in. I believe you have one very anxious groom waiting for you."

Hours seemed to pass while Henrietta waited with Emma for the yard to clear. Finally they climbed the steps and crossed the threshold to the sanctuary. A hush greeted her when she entered the church. In that moment of quiet her gaze rested on Obed's face, and a cloak of peace surrounded her. How different from the excitement she felt with Herman. But a good kind of different. A right kind of different. Their future didn't hold the same questions she'd had as a young bride. Nor, perhaps, the same passion. Theirs was a quieter love. There was a calm certainty with Obed. She had no idea how many years lay ahead for their love to deepen, but she did know it would be exactly as long as God decreed. She intended to live every moment in that comfort.

Evangeline struck the first chords on the organ and the congregation stood. They began to sing, "'Praise God from whom all blessings flow. Praise Him all creatures here below...'"

Henrietta's heart quickened. Whose idea was this? Not hers. By the stunned look on Obed's face, it was a surprise to him, too. She turned to Emma. "Did you plan this?"

"It was Evangeline's idea. It's a choir. Isn't it beautiful?"

She waited until the song ended, and then tears flowed as Henrietta moved up the aisle. They flowed even harder when Obed came to meet her halfway to the front. He folded her hands in his and tipped his forehead against hers. "I love you, Henrietta."

She smiled. "I know. I love you, too. I set out a week ago to tell you, but got interrupted."

"I hope you never stop telling me, dear one."

She giggled. "You think you'll need to be reminded?" She rose on tiptoes and kissed his cheek.

Ty Morgan, serving as the preacher for their ceremony, cleared his throat. "I think they've forgotten we still have a ceremony to perform."

Obed winked. "We haven't forgotten, Ty. You're just slow."

Laughter swept through the room, Henrietta and Obed joining in.

Obed took her hand, and together they walked to the front of the church.

Henrietta squeezed his hand. Oh, how she loved this man, and he loved her. The ceremony proceeded without a hitch, and immediately after Ty announced them husband and wife, the congregation stood in one accord.

"'Praise Him above, ye heav'nly host. Praise Father, Son, and Holy Ghost.'"

Henrietta sang, "Amen!"

The end. For now.

In Sickness
and In Stealth

*"And as ye would that men should do to you,
do ye also to them likewise."*

Luke 6:31 KJV

To the *doctors and nurses* at
Newton Medical Center in Newton, Kansas:
From March of 1976 until New Year's Eve of 1994,
you gave to our family more than medical care.
You put literal arms around us, prayed with and for us,
cried with us, and rejoiced at every tiny ray of hope in some very
hopeless circumstances.
Thank you, thank you, thank you.
Our hearts will never forget.

ONE

October 1879
Cedar Bluff, Kansas

Tillie Rogers sat straight up in bed and pulled the covers to her chin. She was not the least bit bothered by dark and stormy nights. But the unmistakable squawk of the hinges on the cellar door and the subsequent screech as the door scraped across the kitchen floor set her heartbeat thrumming like snare drums in a fourth of July parade. If her business partner, Henrietta, was home, she'd just cover her head and go back to sleep. Henrietta would brook no intruders and by now would have investigated the noise, armed with a rolling pin and a broom. But Henrietta was on her honeymoon, and Tillie doubted rolling pins and brooms were anywhere close to what her business partner had on her mind on such a night as this.

She scooted her back against the headboard and hooked her arms around her bent knees. Maybe it was her imagination. There was a near steady flash of lightning—as if it somehow needed to show the wind which direction to blow—and thunder rattled the window panes. But no matter how hard she tried, she couldn't reconcile the noise of the autumn thunder storm with what she knew to be the opening of the stubborn cellar door.

Well, she couldn't wait for Henrietta to come to her rescue.

Few people in Cedar Bluff knew the *real* Tillie Rogers. Most people considered her the old maid... something—a more precise moniker had never been given to the title—who giggled too much but knew too little. And after such a long time, she had nearly convinced herself they were right. It was easier to let them think what they wanted than to reveal her past.

She sighed, threw the covers to one side and rotated her shoulders. Enough of that. The years behind her were just that—behind her. She stood and slipped her arms into her wrapper, then tiptoed to the wardrobe and dug into a small bag that hung on a hook behind her dresses. She didn't need light to retrieve the muff pistol she had stowed away. Henrietta would suffer an apoplexy if she knew Tillie owned such a firearm, let alone could shoot as well as many men. She put her hand over her mouth to stifle a giggle. Why did the urge to laugh always occur at the most inappropriate and inopportune times? But knowing that aiming the gun in any direction with both hands, while deliberately shaking as though petrified, was enough to make most grown men duck for cover did tickle her and gave her courage to face whatever—or whoever—had opened the cellar door.

She managed to open her bedroom door without a telltale click of the knob, and shouldered her way along the wall until she came to the kitchen. With lightning the only light she dare allow, it took awhile before she was ready to edge through the doorway.

"Who's there? I have to tell you I have a gun and I know how to use it. Come out, whoever you are."

Only the patter of rain against the window and the tick of the kitchen clock broke the silence. Unless the intruder could hear the tom-tom of her heartbeat.

Another streak of lightning lit the room long enough for her to see the door to the cellar stood wide open, and her heart thumped even faster. With her gun still drawn, she lit the lamp with one hand—no easy undertaking when her hand shook like the last leaf on the tree on a windy day. She couldn't just tromp down to the cellar without some plan of action. It was folly to try to get to the sheriff's office in the storm. Besides, Daniel Walker was no doubt home with his family. The most unruly citizen of Cedar Bluff was Emma Ledbetter's old mule, Dolly, who was known to have a penchant for garden vegetables and marigolds.

During the war, she'd faced illness and injuries of every degree and never backed away from what had to be done. More than once she'd stood in the doorway of the home she shared with her niece, Katie Rose, in Texas, waving her pistol in the air, just daring a drunken rowdy to take one more step. She'd never lost one minute of sleep over the ordeal.

So why is your heart racing and your palms sweating now, Tillie?

My gracious, I don't know. Maybe because I'm more afraid of the real Tillie Rogers being revealed then I am of the present dilemma.

She took a big suck of air, then edged to the cellar. With one shoulder against the rock wall for balance, she descended with her gun in one hand and the lamp in the other. Step. Listen. Step. Listen. Step—

"Don't shoot."

It was more a groan than a command, and it came from her right. She aimed the lamp that direction, and gasped as a man stepped out of the shadows.

"Are you Matilda Rogers, ma'am?"

She held the lamp higher to get a better look at the emaciated, disheveled person standing before her. How could this be? Her legs shook and she slumped to the steps. "Leon? Leon Rogers? But—but that's impossible."

"Careful, there." The man took the lamp from her hand. "Now, why don't you tell me why it's impossible for me to be Leon?"

Tillie's heart pounded. "Because—because he's—he's—"

"Dead? Is that what you're trying to spit out?" He lowered himself to the step below her and set the lamp between them. "Well, you see there's a small problem. That letter you sent Ma and Pa said Private Leon Rogers had died peacefully somewhere in Missouri. Course, it was quite a shock to Ma to learn Leon had him a wife. See, truth is, ma'am, *I'm* Leon Rogers, and I ain't quite dead…yet."

"Yet? Then who—"

"Who did you wed?" He swiped his hand down his face. "My twin, Lawrence."

Tillie gripped the gun with both hands as tight as she could to quell their trembling. "Mr. Rogers, it's been fifteen years. Why are you just now confronting me with this information? And how did you know where to find me?" It wasn't as if she had deliberately hidden away. It had never been her intention to deceive. The fact no one in Cedar Bluff knew of her past was simply because it was no one's business. And rankly, no one had ever asked.

The man crossed his arms across his stomach and rocked back and forth. Even in the dim light of the lamp Tillie could see beads of perspiration glisten on his forehead. "What? Sir, are you in pain?"

There was a barely perceptible nod of his head.

"Are you…are you ill?"

A crooked smile accompanied another nod of his head. "You might say that. Thus the reason I stated I was not dead…yet."

"And you took time to hunt me up to tell me this?"

"You're a nurse, aren't you?" He crossed his arms on the step above them, and rested his forehead on them.

"No, I'm not a nurse. What is wrong with you? Why are you here?"

"I understand you married me, or rather my brother, to fulfill his dying wish. You were a nurse then, and all I'm asking is that you do the same for me." His voice muffled against his arms.

"Marry you? Surely you don't expect that of me. It was war time, sir. I gave your brother the comfort of not dying alone. That's all he asked. And that's all there was to it. We never— He didn't live long enough to—"

"No need to marry, my dear." He sat up and withdrew a yellowed piece of paper from the pocket of his jacket. "According to this paper, Matilda, and because I can prove I'm one Leon Rogers, we already are married."

TWO

*B*e sure your sin will find you out. Tillie shivered. How many times had grandmother Landers shook her finger and repeated this dire warning? Now, sure enough, here in the cellar of Henrietta's boarding house, in the company of a strange man claiming to be her husband—and waving a piece of paper he said would prove his claim—it had come to pass.

Tillie yanked the paper from his hand then lowered herself to the step to take advantage of the light from the lamp. *This is to certify that I, Vincent Bohannon, M.D., did, on the thirteenth day of October, year of our Lord eighteen hundred and sixty four, join in Holy Matrimony, Private Leon Albert Rogers and nurse Matilda Ruth Landers.*

Her mouth was so dry she could hardly speak. "I've never seen this. Where did you get it?" Why had she never seen this certificate of marriage? It did have Doctor Bohannon's name on it, but could this man have forged the name?

"All I'm asking is that you stay by me until such time death do us part— Well, that and *one* more request."

She closed her eyes, as though that would ease the angst of hearing what more he had to say.

"You mustn't let anyone know I'm here. No one."

"What?" She pointed the gun his direction. "You broke into my house, told me we're married and that you're a dying man, and now you want me to hide you away until such time as you die? And then what? Suddenly produce a dead man and ask for help to bury him? No. I can't do that. I won't do that. I have a very good friend who is a doctor. If what you tell me is true, you need his help. And if you're in some kind of trouble, the sheriff in this town is a very nice young man. Oh, and Henrietta—she's the owner of this boarding house and I am just her partner—well, she just married the preacher and I'm sure—" Even to her own ears, it sounded like babbling—a desperate move that deep down she knew wasn't going to work.

"And you've managed to fool all these good people, haven't you? How do you think they'd take the news that the Matilda Rogers they know worked as an *unmarried* nurse during the war, married a young soldier, and is still a married woman?"

"You're threatening me? What kind of man are you?"

"A desperate man. A wanted man."

"You're a criminal? Why? What did you do?" She tightened the grip on her pistol. Could this get any worse, or any more complicated?

"I suppose you could call me a criminal."

"But what—what did you do?" *Oh, please, Lord…don't let him say he killed a man.*

His gaze narrowed. "I killed a man."

"You…you killed a man?" Would he kill her if she didn't let him stay?

He let out a huff. "I didn't pull the trigger, if that's what you're thinking. But I killed him nonetheless. The reason it was my twin you married is that I never took to killing of any kind, let alone another man. Lawrence thought the war would be short-lived, he'd go have his fun and be home again in no time. Well, it didn't happen that way, now did it?"

She relaxed her grip on the gun long enough to tuck a twist of hair behind her ears. "I'm sorry about your brother. But why did he use your name?"

"It was his way of protecting me. I was always the scrawny one, but Lawrence, he could fight like two fellas his size. When Lincoln called for seventy-five thousand volunteers, Lawrence announced he was going. He said he'd use my name and do battle for the both of us, didn't matter to him what they called him."

"What would your brother have done if falsely accused of a crime? If you didn't kill the man, why are you running from the law?"

"You wouldn't understand. Besides, I'm done running, Matilda, that's why I'm here."

"I could turn you in, you know."

He nodded. "Yes, you could. But I don't think you will—for the very reasons we've already discussed."

Tillie shook her head. "You haven't left me much choice, have you? So, what do you want me to do? You have to realize I can't bed you down in this boarding house."

He wiped perspiration from his brow. "Bring blankets, food, water…everything down here. There's a tunnel that I'm told was used during the war to help move slaves to safety. I'll take up residence in it, and if you're careful, no one need ever know I'm there."

"You know about the tunnel? How? Is that how you got in here?"

He stopped rocking and doubled over his bent arms that were still crossed around his stomach. "How I got in is irrelevant right now. You can be sure of one thing, Matilda. I mean no harm to you and only ask that you allow me to live out what remaining days I have per my request. Please. But for now, I need something for pain…whiskey, morphine—whatever you've got."

"You honestly believe I have morphine or whiskey at my disposal?"

"You said you had a doctor friend. Surely you could find a way to obtain one or both of them."

She waved the gun in his face. "This would work faster."

He stopped rocking. "And there may come a time I will beg you to do just that. But for now, that pretty little muff pistol is neither cocked nor loaded. Of course, you could holler *bang*, and I'll roll over and play dead if that would persuade you to help me."

Bolstered with determination, she stood and pocketed the gun. "I do not find that in the least amusing, Mr. Rogers."

He looked up at her, his eyes pleading. "Neither do I, Matilda. But the Bible says 'a merry heart doeth good like a medicine.' You do believe the Bible, don't you?"

"Of course I believe the Bible. I also believe one can make the Bible say most anything. Can you tell me where it says one person has the right to break into another person's home and compel them to do something as foolish as what you're asking?"

His shoulders heaved with a deep breath, and a groan escaped as he exhaled. "'And whosoever shall compel thee to go a mile, go with him twain.' I believe you can find that in Matthew, chapter five and verse forty-one. Please. I'm asking you to go that second mile with me." He moaned and gripped his stomach again. "I can almost guarantee there'll not be a third mile on this journey."

While common sense shouted in her head to run for help, compassion whispered to her heart to be the help. She'd heard that same whisper over the boisterous objections of family and friends when she left home to offer comfort and care during the war. It was considered morally wrong for a single woman to be subjected to all that was necessary to give aid to wounded men. More than one young woman was jilted by a suitor when her service was revealed. What this so-called journey would involve could very well put her in the same predicament. Abe Mercer had no problem with Emma tagging along with him on house calls of any kind. But would he be so tolerant of her? As far as he knew she was a single lady. Except for one incriminatory piece of paper that she hadn't even known existed, it was an accurate description.

She leaned against the wall. To maintain her own reputation would require stealth. Henrietta would notice food missing, and Abe would surely notice the disappearance of medications. She wasn't even sure she could manage such a deception. But what choice did she have? Clearly this man was not going away—at least, not until he left this earth. While the idea of turning away a dying man was loathsome, the idea of deceiving her friends was even more undesirable.

Tillie swiped her hand down her wrapper. "I'll do what I can. Doc

Mercer is out of town at the present time, but I have a key to his place. I can get medications for now, but I can't take enough at one time to last for any extended period. Doc will be home in a couple of days. Plus, once Henrietta and the preacher return from their honeymoon, they will take up residence here. It could very well be Reverend Mason will want to use this cellar for storage. Then what? I can't promise what we're doing won't be discovered."

He leaned against the opposite wall and gave her a wan smile. "I know, and I thank you. At such time I'm discovered, I'll attest to the fact that I compelled you to such deception."

She lifted the lamp from the steps. "Just so you know, I'm only doing this for the man I thought was Leon—not for you." At least Doc was out of town. If she was careful, and if she hurried, she could get in and out of his office without being detected.

Abe Mercer perched on the side of the bed in his hotel room. His trip to Topeka had been fruitful, and now he was most anxious to return to Cedar Bluff and to the company of Tillie Rogers a day ahead of time. It bothered him that she was alone in that big boarding house while Henrietta and Obed were away on their honeymoon. While Henrietta managed to take charge of most any circumstance that arose, Tillie seemed too flighty to even realize a bad situation should it occur.

He felt a bit guilty about not telling her the reason for his trip. It hadn't been as spontaneous as he allowed her to believe. In fact, he'd given it much thought and had decided at last that he would follow his heart and ask her to become his wife. He reached into his coat pocket and retrieved the box that held the ruby and pearl ring he hoped she would accept as his token of love and commitment. Thank goodness, Henrietta and Obed were still on their honeymoon. He didn't relish an audience to declare his intentions.

He and Tillie were no longer young, but they had as long as God ordained, and he aimed to make the years left to them the best ever.

One thing sure, Tillie was everything he'd ever hoped for in a wife, more than he ever dreamed he'd find. She was perhaps a bit more innocent and naïve than he imagined his wife would be, but she was God-fearing, hardworking, compassionate, and so honest she'd never be able to keep a secret without giggling if questioned. She wasn't a nurse, but then he had Emma to help him when needed, and Tillie would always be waiting for his return.

THREE

Tillie hung her basket over her arm and paused at the door of Emma's Mercantile. People for miles around declared Emma Ledbetter to be the *knowingest* person in Cedar Bluff. Some thought she had some kind of magic, but Emma always greeted that notion with a *pfft*. She claimed she just listened and watched, something anyone could do if they'd take the time. Until now, Tillie hadn't given it all that much thought. But what if somehow Emma could detect she was hiding something—or worse yet, someone?

Few were her choices, however, and short was the time she had to complete her mission. She'd managed to sneak into Doc's office and lift a bottle of laudanum from his supply cabinet. She could only pray that he wouldn't miss it right away. In the meantime, after a second trip to the cellar with blankets, water, and food, it was apparent Leon Rogers needed clean clothes. If he wasn't discovered by sight, his odor was sure to give him away. Her only recourse was to procure the needed articles and bury the old ones before Henrietta and Obed returned. Could she dare let Emma in on—

The clang of the bell above the mercantile door jolted Tillie from her hesitation. "Tillie? What in the world are you doing standing out here? I've watched you from inside for the last five minutes." Emma grabbed her hand and pulled her into the store.

"Oh, my gracious, Emma. I was just lost in thought." *That's no lie,*

Tillie. You're doing good so far.

"Well, you can think in here as well as you can standing outside with one hand on the doorknob." Emma smiled at her. "Let me fix you a cup of tea. You can sit here and sip and ponder while I make a quick trip to the post office. That way if anyone comes in there will be someone here to let them know I'll return shortly."

"Tea would be nice." While she would enjoy the hot drink, the fact she'd be alone for a time could well benefit her.

Emma disappeared behind the curtain that separated her living quarters from the mercantile, and Tillie took the opportunity to peruse her surroundings. She'd have to work fast to gather what she needed and figure out a way to conceal them. While she wasn't a stranger to the mercantile, neither had she spent much time looking for men's clothing. How did one determine the size?

"Here you go, my friend." Emma returned and handed Tillie a cup and saucer, then pointed to a chair by the counter. "You sit right here. That way you can see if someone comes in, and they can see you." She patted Tillie's shoulders as she gave her a gentle push onto the chair. "I'll hurry."

As soon as Emma was out of sight, Tillie set her teacup and saucer on the counter and rushed to the rack of men's shirts and the stack of folded britches on the counter next to them. She grabbed a pair of britches, held them up to her, and was satisfied that the width and length would at least cover the man's body. While holding them against her, the answer to her dilemma came.

Please, Lord. I have no right to ask You to help me, what with me sneaking around like this, but could You just keep people away for awhile?

She stuck the britches under one arm, yanked a shirt from a hanger, and made a beeline for the curtain behind the counter. Once hidden from view of anyone who might enter, she pulled up her skirt and petticoats and inserted one leg, shoe and all, into a leg of the very stiff piece of clothing. *My gracious, how do men manage this every morning?* She held her petticoats up with her elbows and shuffled to the wall. If she leaned against it, perhaps she could pull the other leg on without falling. A final yank, and she managed to be fully ensconced, but it was obvious the legs were longer than anticipated. Her skirts wouldn't fully conceal them.

With her rear end against the wall for support, she bent over and gave the hems a hurried roll, then grabbed the shirt and tied the sleeves around her waist. There wasn't time to look for a belt, but if she tied the sleeves tight enough, pinched her elbows against her sides as she walked, and prayed every step of the way, perhaps she could get home without her ploy being discovered. It was a good thing she was a bit on the *fluffy* side to begin with. With luck, Emma wouldn't question the extra bulk.

She finished in time to be in the chair, teacup in hand, when Emma returned.

"I'm sorry it took so long, dear. It seems I always find someone to visit with and time gets away from me. Thank you for being so patient." Emma laid the stack of mail on the counter. "Now, how can I help you this morning? I see you brought a basket so you must have some purchases in mind."

Oh, Tillie, you better come up with something fast because, unless I'm mistaken, your britches are falling. And on top of that—you're stealing.

Tillie stood so fast her lukewarm tea splashed over the side of her cup. "Well—uh—" She searched the shelves for something light. She couldn't possibly hitch up a pair of men's pants, carry a basketful of heavy items, and walk without waddling, all at the same time.

"Yarn. I—I need yarn." Good gracious, couldn't she come up with something better than that?

"Yarn?" Emma cocked her head. "You want a basketful of yarn, Tillie? My lands, my friend, you must have a large project in mind."

Tillie gulped. She was wading in deep water and her toes were barely touching bottom. "Yes. Yes. I'm making shawls...for the needy." She couldn't meet Emma's gaze.

"Shawls? For the needy? Hmm. The needy here in Cedar Bluff?"

"Well, you never know, Emma. There could be needy souls in Cedar Bluff. I—well, winter is coming and then Christmas will be here, and I just thought—"

No, Tillie. You didn't think…but you should have.

Emma flicked her wrist in Tillie's direction. "Don't mind me. I think it's a very fine gesture. I have several lovely colors to choose from. Come. We can look at them together." Emma motioned toward the back of the store.

Tillie bit the tip of her tongue. Why hadn't she asked to borrow a book instead of yarn? How would she manage to toddle to the back of the store while keeping a pair of men's trousers from falling around her ankles? And the worst part…it was all one big, terrible lie.

With Emma's back to her, Tillie set her teacup on the counter, pressed her elbows against her waist, and followed. When she passed the cheval glass that stood by the rack of dresses, she caught a glimpse of something amiss. She stopped, took a step backward and looked again. One pant leg had chosen to unroll itself and now hung like a lolling tongue below her skirt.

Oh, double gracious. She couldn't bend over in the aisle and roll it back in place. A small, squat-like maneuver lowered her skirts a bit. If she took a more skate-like stride, perhaps she could keep anything more from jarring loose enough to be observed.

Gliding across the wooden floor proved much more difficult than on ice on John Wenghold's frozen pond. She didn't dare look at Emma, but if she was going to maintain any resemblance of control over this situation, she must make every effort to appear nonchalant and interested only in the color of yarn available.

"I'm thinking perhaps gray would be best, or maybe brown?" Emma held the two skeins of yarn toward Tillie. "Or you thinking of something more cheery, like yellow or blue?"

"Yes." Tillie reached behind her to give what she prayed would be an unseen yank on the wad of men's clothing that had taken on a life of its own under her skirts.

Emma's forehead crinkled. "Yes? Yes, which one? Tillie, is something wrong?"

Wrong? Of course something was wrong. She had a strange man

in her cellar and men's clothing under her skirt that would most certainly fall around her ankles if she loosened her grip.

Tillie shrugged. "I'm fine, Emma. Why do you ask?" She rolled her lips to quell a very inappropriate giggle.

"Well, it looked as though you were having a difficult time lifting your feet high enough to take a step—more like you were skating. And now, you're clutching your back."

If only she'd have taken the risk of washing the stranger's clothing. "Just a little crick in my back is all. Must have slept on it wrong. Nothing to worry about." She shuffled closer to the yarn. "I believe I'll take some of each, Emma." She fingered a skein of soft, blue yarn.

"Each? You mean each of the colors I mentioned?" Emma lifted skeins of gray and brown from the display hooks. "How many of each?"

"Oh, my. Let's see, perhaps... Oh, just fill the basket. And you choose the colors, but I do favor the blue a bit." Maybe by purchasing so much unwanted yarn, she could make up for stealing the clothing. Shame flooded her. She knew better than to rationalize sin.

Be sure—

Tillie cringed. As plain as day, she could hear Grandmother Landers' warning. An image of the ruffles on her grandmother's white day cap bobbing in rhythm with the shaming finger clouded her eyes. She'd cry—oh, it would be so very easy to blubber right here in Emma's Mercantile—but what good would that do?

"There you go, my friend." Emma piled the last skein of yarn into the basket. "Enough yarn to knit shawls for all of Cedar Bluff if you so desire. I'll just put this on a ticket, and you can pay me later. I can tell by your face that you're hurting, so I'll not ask you to walk back to the counter. Should I go get Dan Walker and see if he would drive you home in my buggy? Dolly would welcome the exercise."

"My gracious, no." Just what she didn't need—climbing into a buggy with the sheriff. "I'll be fine. Walking might even be good for my back—loosen it up, you know."

Emma leaned and kissed Tillie's cheek. "Go then, my dear. Put your feet up, and I'll bring you some soup after I close for the day."

Another giggle threatened to erupt, but from experience Tillie knew if it made it past the lump in her throat, it would be followed by uncontrollable sobbing. She smiled, nodded, and prayed Emma wasn't in one of her better *knowing days*.

Thank goodness Abe wouldn't return home until tomorrow. She was in no condition or mood to see him any sooner. Not that she lacked the desire to see him. No. Not at all. Rather, it was fear. Face flushing, heart pounding, palms sweating fear. And it saddened her heart.

FOUR

"Cedar Bluff, next stop." The conductor stopped by Abe's seat and patted him on the shoulder. "I believe this is where you get off, Doc. Always good to have you ride with us, though."

Abe extended his hand to the man. "Thank you, Arnold. Enjoyed the trip, as usual, but all too glad to be home again."

"You still go home to an empty house? You know, my wife has a cousin who—"

"No, no." He raised his hands to stop the man. He'd been introduced to far too many cousins to even think about another. Besides, he had other plans. "Won't be empty for long." He pulled the box from his pocket and opened it to reveal the prized ring inside. "Can you keep a secret?"

The man chuckled. "Better than you, I expect. You haven't even asked the lucky lady yet, have you?" He shook his head. "Never would have pegged you as a gambling man."

Abe's smile slid off his face. "You think it's a gamble?" Maybe it was. Though he had made up his mind, he'd never talked with Tillie about the possibility of marriage. Just figured she got the hint.

Arnold shrugged. "I wouldn't even venture a guess. Who knows what goes on in a woman's mind? That is a purty ring, though. Hard for a woman to turn down something like that, even if it is a pudgy, middle-aged man asking for her favor."

Doc patted the conductor's belly with the back of his hand. "You're one to talk about pudgy, Arnold. And look at you, you're all married up, aren't you?"

He laughed. "Married good and tight, I am. But did my asking when I was still thin as a rail. Guess you could say we did our *growing* together." He clapped Doc on the shoulder. "Good luck, my friend." He whistled his way down the aisle.

Abe examined the ring box in his hand. Had he gotten ahead of himself? He'd never courted before meeting Tillie. Maybe this wasn't how it was supposed to work. Should he have asked her and then purchased the ring?

One last lurch as the train came to a halt interrupted Abe's questions. One thing sure, he'd better get some advice before he did something foolish.

The late afternoon sun felt good on Abe's back as he stepped from the train. He rotated his shoulders, then pulled his watch from his pocket. He'd intended to go straight to Tillie's. With Henrietta and Obed still on their honeymoon, he and Tillie could have time alone, but the conversation with Arnold had changed his mind. He'd go to Emma's first. She'd know how to advise him. At least maybe she'd have an idea how Tillie would respond to his proposal.

Emma was standing by the rack of men's shirts, head cocked to one side and hands on hips, when Abe entered the mercantile. If she heard the bell above the door, she gave no indication.

"Emma?"

She jumped. "My lands, Abe. How long have you been standing there?"

"Haven't been standing. Just walked in. Something wrong?"

She cupped one elbow in her hand and pointed to the shirts. "I'm not sure. I think I'm getting old. I thought sure I had a brown plaid shirt in stock. The hanger is here, but the shirt is gone, and for the life of me I can't remember selling it." She shrugged. "But enough of that. I'll think of it sooner or later. Now, how can I help you today?"

She turned to leave the rack of shirts, then stopped. "Wait. You're home early aren't you? Now I have to ask the question—is something wrong?"

Abe leaned against the counter near the folded britches and pulled the ring box from his coat pocket. "I don't think there's anything wrong. Just not sure of the timing. Hoping you can help me."

Emma took the box from him and opened it. "Oh, my, Abe. This is beautiful." She placed the box back in his hand. "But you know, I can't accept it." Her mouth pulled down at the corners.

"Well I— No, you— Emma, don't do that." He wiped his forehead, but the heat was still there.

She laughed until the tears rolled. "You should see your face, my friend. It's as red as the ruby in that ring."

"*Hmmph.* You sure do know how to make a fella uncomfortable. You know I think very highly of you and—"

She gripped his forearms. "You better stop before you dig a deeper hole. Now, you're fixing to ask Tillie to be your wife, aren't you? You do know this won't come as a surprise to anyone, except maybe Tillie herself?"

So Tillie would be surprised? "You don't think she suspects anything?"

"Should she? Have you given her any reason to believe this would be a possibility?" She moved around him. "You go on back to my kitchen and I'll lock up for the evening. We can talk better over a cup of coffee."

The beefy aroma of simmering soup made Abe's stomach rumble as he entered the kitchen. Come to think of it, he hadn't eaten since breakfast. Maybe Emma would share a bowl of the soup, as well as a cup of coffee. How nice it would be to one day soon walk into his own kitchen and have food waiting that he hadn't prepared himself.

Emma tapped him on the shoulder as she swept past him on her way to the cupboard. "You can start talking. I can listen while I pour the coffee." She sat two cups and the sugar bowl on the table.

"You asked if Tillie would have reason to suspect my trip to Topeka was to purchase a ring."

"That's not exactly how I stated it, but go on." Emma poured the coffee then sat down across from him. "My point was whether or not you'd declared your love and devotion."

"Well..." He spooned sugar into his coffee and tapped the spoon on the rim of the cup. Anything to buy a little time.

"Oh, for pity sakes, Abe, you're blushing again. You came to me for help, remember?"

He spooned another lump of sugar into his cup. "Guess I wasn't expecting you to ask questions. But since you did, the answer is no. I've never declared my love in so many words."

"So many words?" Emma clasped her hands together and leaned across the table. "Three words, Abe. I. Love. You." She ticked them off on her fingers.

He ran his hands over his face. "I tried...once. But she giggled."

"I can imagine." Emma nodded. "Tillie giggles at most everything, even if it's not appropriate. It's a nervous habit, like you spooning sugar into your coffee until it turns to syrup." She moved the sugar bowl from his reach.

"Do you think Tillie has— Well, do you think she has feelings for me, too?"

"I'll not even attempt to answer that, Abe. It's not my place. Besides, I think you already have a good idea what she'll say, you're just stalling." She stood and stepped to the stove. "I told her I'd bring her some soup for her supper. I think you should be the one that takes it to her—would give you a good reason to call on her. Sharing a table always seems to ease tensions."

"Why were you taking her soup? Is she ill?"

Emma stood, ladle poised above the pot of soup. "I don't know how to answer that. She was in earlier today and was definitely not herself."

"In what way?"

"Well, she held her one arm close to her side as though she didn't want to move it, and she clutched her back with her free hand. And she walked funny, squatted down a bit, and had more of a skating motion than a step."

"You think she hurt her back?" What had she tried to do without help?

She shook her head. "I questioned her, but she said she thought she'd just slept on it wrong."

"I imagine that could happen. If she was still walking, I'd not worry too much."

"But she wasn't her normal self. In fact, come to think of it, I don't remember that she giggled one time. Oh, and she purchased enough yarn to fill a rather large market basket. Said she was going to knit shawls for the needy in Cedar Bluff."

"The needy? In Cedar Bluff?" This concerned him. Not that Tillie was knitting the shawls, but had he missed seeing need? He was out in the community much more than Tillie. How could she be aware of such privation and he completely miss it? "Can you think of anyone in such hardship, Emma?"

She rubbed her forehead. "I've been thinking ever since she mentioned it. The only family that came to mind were the Tolivers out south of town. But I can't imagine big, burly Harold Toliver wearing a shawl anywhere in public."

Doc stood and poured himself another cup of coffee. "I know the Tolivers quite well. They don't have a lot of money, but they're proud people. They work hard, and even with their passel of kids, Ruby Toliver keeps a clean house and sets a good table. Kids wear patched clothes, but they're clean."

"Here, I'd take some more of that, too." She held her cup for Abe to fill it. "I can tell you this, Abe Mercer. If Tillie agrees to marry you, if and when you decide to ask her, you'll be a fortunate man. You won't find anyone more kindhearted. I don't expect she'd turn away the devil himself if he showed up bleeding at her doorstep."

"Where'd you put that sugar bowl?"

She laughed. "It's still on the table. Go ahead, sweeten 'til your heart's content."

He sat back at the table. "I'll deliver the soup, Emma, but I'll not ask her to marry me yet. You're right. I expect there's some words that need said before I do anything else. It'll give me a chance to see how she's feeling."

Emma pulled back the curtain under her sink and retrieved two jars. She ladled soup into the jars and set them in a basket, along with a loaf of bread. "There, that will be easier to carry than a hot kettle. Tell Tillie I want the basket again when she thinks of it."

He stood and lifted the basket. "Thank you, Emma. And—well, you won't tell anyone of our conversation, will you?"

She flicked her wrists. "What conversation? Now, go. She'll be surprised to see you."

Dusk was already blushing the sky when he stepped out of the mercantile. The streets were quiet, except for a dog barking in the distance and a few robins still chirping their good night songs. Would this be the night he would actually say the words Emma scolded him for not uttering?

He gripped the basket in one hand and stuffed his free hand in his pocket. He'd never uttered endearing words to a woman. How did one go about it? *You know how much I care for you, Tillie.* Well, that wouldn't work. How was she supposed to know when he'd never told her?

A buggy rattling down the street stopped him at the corner, and he welcomed the delay. While one part of him wanted to hurry to her, another part told him he'd better figure out what he was going to say first. *You know, Tillie. I've been thinking perhaps we should...* Should what? Get married? Go courting? The ring would say marriage, or at least a promise. But shouldn't courting come first?

How did other men go about such a thing? Should he get down on one knee? But then what? *Is there any chance you have feelings for me, Tillie?* Shouldn't he know that before putting himself in such a position? And what if he couldn't get to his feet again?

He reached the boardinghouse porch, but no lamplight in the window greeted him. Apprehension tightened his chest as he climbed the steps. Maybe Tillie was worse off than Emma realized. Had she fallen? Maybe she couldn't walk. He juggled the basket on one arm and turned the doorknob, relieved that it wasn't locked, and stepped into the hallway. "Tillie? Tillie are you here? It's me...Abe. I brought soup from Emma's."

No giggle, no footsteps. Only silence greeted him.

FIVE

Tillie froze on the cellar step, supper tray for Leon in her hands. Her heart skipped a beat. That was Abe's voice. But how could it be? He wasn't due back until tomorrow.

"Sounds like you have company, Matilda? A suitor, perhaps?" Leon's exaggerated whisper drifted to the top of the stairs.

"Shh!"

"Were you expecting someone? You didn't go to the sheriff, did you?" Leon scrunched to a sitting position and leaned against the rock wall. "You gave me your word."

"I did no such thing. I said I'd help you because you left me no other choice. And why didn't you stay in the tunnel like you said you would?" At least she'd shut the door behind her, hopefully before Abe was in the house. She sidestepped down the stairs and set the tray on the floor. If Abe opened that door looking for her, she'd not be able to explain a tray of food.

"I'm sorry. I should have stayed put, but if I don't move around a bit I'll get so weak you won't be able to help me. You better answer him. What if he comes looking for you?"

"You can't get much weaker than dead, you know. Isn't that the plan? And you want me to answer him? You think he wouldn't come down here if I yelled, 'Here I am'?"

Abe's footsteps thumped above her head. "Tillie? Answer me,

please. Where are you?"

She held her breath. *Please go away, Abe.*

Leon pushed himself to a wobbly upright position. "If you help me, I can go back to my hideaway."

"Stop talking. You got out here just fine, you can get yourself back. And blow out that lamp."

"Please."

"Please what?"

"Blow out the lamp, please."

She reached into the pocket of her apron and withdrew her gun. "You know, I still know how to use this."

"Sure you do. You think a shot from that gun will make less noise than our whispering?"

The creaking footsteps seemed to stop by the cellar door, then they receded, as though someone was in a hurry. Would Abe go home, or would he go for help? If he was going for help, then others might look for her down here. One thing sure, she couldn't be found in this cellar.

"I think whoever it was is gone, Matilda. If you go now, you'll be safe."

"How do you know?" She hissed at him, though she felt like screaming. "This door squawks when it's opened, and if he's still in the house, he'll hear me."

"Only if you want to be heard. Lift up on it just a bit and it will clear the floor enough that it won't squawk. And the hinges won't squeak, either."

"And how do you know this?" She wasn't at all sure she wanted to find out. How long had this man been in the boardinghouse before he was found?

"Well, for one thing, I'm a man, and that door isn't the first one I had to go through without making a sound. And secondly, you wouldn't know I was here if I hadn't wanted you to hear me. My only fear was that the storm would drown out the noise and I'd go another day without food."

"Then—"

"Look, Matilda, every minute you stand here fussing at me is one less minute you have to get out of here and redeem yourself. Leave the tray and dishes here, but take the lamp. Open the door like I told you. Go! I'll find my way back to the tunnel. Just don't forget I'm here. Oh, and thank you for the new clothing. It's been awhile since I've had anything clean to wear."

Like she would forget he was there or hadn't noticed how bad he smelled. But there was no time to argue. She did as he suggested, and she managed to open the door without a sound. Though Abe was nowhere in sight, a basket holding jars of soup and a loaf of bread sat on the kitchen table. He'd come home earlier than she expected, and he'd stopped at Emma's. What might Emma have told him? She had seemed a bit perplexed about the large purchase of yarn.

Well, there wasn't time to worry about it now. She'd hurry to light the lamps. With luck, she wouldn't appear frazzled when Abe returned. Because she was most certain he'd return.

Gasping for air, Abe stumbled into the sheriff's office just as Dan was leaving. "Wait... Need...help." He was so out of breath he could hardly get the words past his lips. Besides that, he'd tripped on a rock, landed in a puddle, and he was wet, muddy, and cold.

"Doc? What's wrong?" Dan stepped closer. "And what in the world happened to you?"

Abe bent and put his hands on his knees to catch his breath. "Tillie's...gone."

"What?" Dan ran his hands through his hair. "Gone? You don't mean she's—"

Abe straightened. "No, not...not dead." He took a deep breath. "I...she's not home."

Dan gripped Abe's arm. "She's not home? Doc, start from the beginning. I don't understand why you're so upset. Was she expecting you?"

By the time he caught his breath enough to explain why he was so upset, he could see concern in Dan's eyes as well.

"I saw her earlier, Doc. She walked past here and I assumed she was going home." He scratched his head. "Come to think of it, she did walk a bit strange. Did you check her bedroom? Maybe she decided to lie down. That would explain why there were no lamps burning. Could also be the reason she didn't answer you when you called her name. She might have been sound asleep."

Doc hung his head. "I didn't even think to look there."

Dan stepped from the porch. "Let's you and me go back to the boardinghouse and take another look. If we still can't find her, I'll get a search party together." He gripped Doc's shoulder. "Don't worry, my friend. I'm sure there's a reasonable explanation. My horse is right outside. We can ride double...save you a trip on foot and perhaps keep you out of the mud."

When they rounded the corner to the boardinghouse, Daniel reined his horse to a stop. "You say the house was dark when you were here earlier?"

Doc peered around Daniel's shoulder. Even from a distance, welcome circles of light emanated from the parlor windows. He breathed a sigh of relief. "You were right, Dan. She must have been napping."

"Well, let's go check and make sure she's all right."

"I feel a bit foolish, you know. I left before I thoroughly looked through every room. When she didn't answer, I—"

Dan chuckled. "I would do the same thing, although the chance of being greeted by silence is zero in our household."

"You're a fortunate man, Daniel Walker. I'm sorry I've kept you from your family. I expect Rachel is wondering where you are."

"Rachel has adjusted to this new responsibility of mine quite well. She knows the risks but is willing to take them because she knows how important this line of work is to me. You're right, Doc. I'm a very, very fortunate man. Now, let's get you to Tillie. Something tells me your own good fortune is in that boardinghouse."

"Could be, Daniel." He gave the horse a nudge with his heels. "Never can tell, but sure could be."

Tillie rearranged her skirt on the settee for the third time. She thought sure Abe would return to look for her, but it was taking longer than she expected. Maybe she was wrong. Perhaps he only came to deliver the soup Emma was going to deliver. Oh, what had she done? And the bigger question...what was she doing?

She lifted her Bible from the table beside the settee and turned to Matthew twenty-five. She read verses thirty-five and thirty-six. *"For I was an hungered, and ye gave me meat: I was thirsty, and ye gave me drink: I was a stranger, and ye took me in: Naked, and ye clothed me: I was sick, and ye visited me: I was in prison, and ye came unto me."*

Well, Leon Rogers wasn't naked or in prison, but he was a hungry, thirsty stranger. Although who would believe he was a stranger to her when he had a wedding certificate in his possession? She knew the passage well enough to know it said what she needed to hear. Was she using God's Word to excuse her behavior?

Footsteps on the porch caused her heart to race. She stood, and before she could take a step, Abe burst through the door and enveloped her in his arms. "Tillie Rogers, where have you been? You scared me to death." He held her at arm's length. "I thought... I was so afraid you..." He pulled her to him. "Oh, am I ever glad to see you." He pushed her away again. "Didn't you hear me call your name?" He pulled her to him and cradled her head against his chest.

She wiggled her head from his embrace. "Abe Mercer, if you don't stop pulling and pushing me, I'm going to be so dizzy I can't stand."

A subtle throat clearing intruded. They both turned to the sheriff. "I hate to break this up, but will you need a ride to your house, Doc? Looks like things are good here, and I'm getting hungry."

Tillie cocked her head to one side. "Emma brought soup." Guilt stabbed. She knew full well Emma hadn't brought it. "Do you want to eat here, Abe?"

Abe released his hold on her and held his hand to Daniel. "Thank you, friend. Sorry I panicked."

Daniel shook his hand. "Nothing to be sorry about. I'd have done the same thing in your situation."

Abe closed the door behind Dan, then turned to Tillie. "You say Emma brought you the soup? How do you know? Did you see her?"

Tillie prayed he'd not be able to see the heat rise to her face. "No, I...I think I must have been napping. Or something." Definitely something. "I assumed Emma brought it because she told me she would come later with soup."

He took her hands in his and rubbed his thumbs across her knuckles. "Well, I brought the soup. I stopped at Emma's when I got back to town, and she told me she was concerned about you. Since I planned to surprise you with my early return, she gave me the task of bringing the soup she promised."

"Was it a task, Abe?" She smiled up at him. "It is a surprise. I didn't expect you until tomorrow."

"I know. What say we have some of that soup? We can talk while we eat."

Tillie's mind raced. It would be logical to eat in the kitchen, but that was too close to the cellar door, and she wasn't sure Leon had returned to the tunnel like he promised. What if he stumbled or coughed or any made any number of possible noises that would alert Abe to someone's presence?

"How about we celebrate you coming home early? Let's eat in the dining room. I'll set the coffee on the burner and bring the soup and bread." She pulled her hands from his. "And you...you can set the table. We'll use the good bowls. You'll find them in the china cupboard in the dining room."

Oh, gracious. Had Emma told Abe about Tillie's back? Now she'd be forced to skate again. Was there no end to this deception?

SIX

A light mist was falling as Abe tied his horse and buggy to the hitching rail in front of Emma's Mercantile. Though not his normal routine, he'd felt compelled to visit outlying ranches today—namely that of Harold and Ruby Toliver. It concerned him that Tillie had discerned needs in the community while he had been oblivious. Why had he not noticed? It did warm his heart that Tillie, *his* Tillie, cared enough to not only see a problem, but took it upon herself to do something about it. She would have made a good nurse. She'd make an even better wife. If only he had the nerve to propose. But Emma was right, he'd never uttered the words he supposed every woman needed to hear at least once before accepting a proposal.

Emma and Daniel Walker were deep in conversation when Abe entered the mercantile. "You two look as though you were assigned to solve the problems of the world." He leaned his hip against the counter. "Trouble in Cedar Bluff?"

Dan turned and folded his arms across his chest. "Emma asked if I knew of any needy families around town."

"Tillie's got us thinking, doesn't she?" Abe reached for the jar of gumdrops but Emma slapped his hand away. "I'll pay, Emma, just need a little sustenance after a long day out and around."

"No one fed you?" Emma removed the lid and scooted the jar his direction. "So did your visits today confirm Tillie's observations?"

He grabbed a handful of the sugar coated candies then shoved the jar to Dan. "Every home I visited fed me." He glanced at his handful of gumdrops and smiled. "I'm not hungry, but you know I can't resist these things." He sorted through the candies until he found a red one then slipped it into his mouth. "In fact, I found nothing that would indicate lack of food or warm clothing. Nothing, Emma. And believe me, I tried. Even made a special effort to check out things at the Tolivers. Harold wasn't home. Ruby said he took the older boys to cut wood. But there were four loaves of fresh bread on the cupboard and a big pot of chicken and dumplings simmering on the stove. You're sure Tillie said she was knitting shawls for the needy?"

"I'm sure. Why else would she buy so much yarn? But there is something bothering me."

"About Tillie?" Abe popped the last gumdrop into his mouth and brushed sugar from his hands.

Emma shrugged. "No, not Tillie. But remember when I was trying to remember who bought the brown plaid shirt?"

"You remembered?"

"No, I didn't remember who, because no one bought it. It just disappeared. I went back over all my tickets from that day, and there wasn't one shirt purchased by anyone. And that's not all. In my fussing about the shirt, I took inventory, and a pair of men's britches is also missing."

"You're not thinking Tillie has something to—"

The mercantile door banged open. "Doc! Doc Mercer! It's Pa. He nigh cut his leg off." Lonnie Toliver hollered from the doorway.

Doc and Daniel moved in concert toward the young man. "Where is he?"

"In our wagon. He's bleedin' somethin' awful."

Abe followed Lonnie out of the mercantile, and his heart sank when he saw the wounded man. The boy hadn't lied. Blood flowed from a gash that laid open the man's shin. Harold's head rested in the lap of another son, Duane.

"Take him to my office. Wait, let me get in with you." Abe crawled up into wagon.

"Is he gonna bleed to death?" Duane's face was void of color.

"Not if I can help it. You boys did good, bringing him here like you did." He patted the boy's knee.

"You need my help, Doc?" Emma peered over the side of the wagon.

"I'll bring her, you go on." Dan motioned for the boy to leave.

The wagon lurched, and Harold moaned. Doc put his hand on the man's shoulder. "Hang on, Harold. We'll have you fixed up in no time. What happened anyway?"

Doc witnessed a wan smile crinkle one side of the man's mouth. "Reckon I gave a chop to the wrong stump. Blamed ax handle was wet, and it slipped out of my hands."

Abe gritted his teeth. With Harold's size and his probable hefty swing, the ax blade had likely gone clear to the bone. Bleeding was only a part of the problem. Had the bone been splintered? Even without bone injury, they'd have to worry about infection. Without a doubt, Harold would be laid up for quite a spell. However, the Tolivers' needs wouldn't be met by a knitted shawl.

Dan helped the Toliver brothers get their pa into Doc's surgery while Doc and Emma readied the supplies for the job ahead.

Emma positioned herself at Harold's head. "You want him to have something for pain before you start to work, Doc?"

"A shot of whiskey would be good," Harold volunteered.

"I send you home full of whiskey and Ruby will have both our hides." Doc patted Harold's shoulder. "I'm going to let you sleep through this, Harold. Can't take a chance of you moving around on me while I try to see what kind of damage you've done to yourself."

"Don't take much to that kind of talk, Doc. Just as soon be awake so you don't up and cut off my leg without me knowin'."

"You about took care of that yourself. Trust me, I'm going to do everything possible to make sure you leave here with both limbs intact." He handed Emma the chloroform and a towel. "You want me to send someone to talk with Ruby so your boys won't have to do it?"

"That'd be good. But make sure she knows there ain't no need of her bundlin' up the young'uns to come here."

"I'll go, Doc." Dan spoke from the doorway. "Unless you need more help here."

"Go, and take the boys with you. I'm going to keep Harold here at least overnight anyway. No need for them to stick around."

The day had lowered night shades by the time Doc was satisfied he'd done all he could for Harold Toliver. He'd stopped the bleeding, and to his relief no major arteries had been severed. Nevertheless, the man would be weak from the loss of blood and had a long recovery time ahead of him.

Dan returned with Harold's wife, and he helped move Harold to a bed in Doc's clinic.

Abe gave Ruby's shoulders a squeeze. "You didn't need to come, Ruby. He's in good hands."

"Never doubted that for a minute, Doc." She leaned to kiss Harold's forehead. "But we never spent a night apart since we said our I do's. Just don't want a slippery ax handle to come between us tonight. The big boys can take care of things at the ranch." She took one of Harold's big hands in hers. "You figure he'll wake up soon?"

"I'm hoping he'll sleep awhile. One thing sure, he's gonna be hurting like crazy when he does open his eyes again. He'll likely not want you to see him like that."

"Oh, *pfft*. Ain't no bigger baby around even when he's got nothin' but a snotty nose."

Abe chuckled. "Well then, I'll be in the next room if you need anything." He led Dan and Emma out of the room, closed the door, and turned to Emma. "Sure do thank you for your help. One of these days I'm gonna have to hire you as my nurse."

"You can't afford me, Abe Mercer." She gave him a playful nudge as they ambled up the hallway.

"Dan, you mind seeing Emma gets home? Is it still spittin' rain out there?"

"No rain, but the wind turned to the north. I'll see to it Emma gets home just fine. I already put your horse and buggy in your barn and fed the horse."

Emma hesitated at the front door. "Was Tillie expecting you tonight? Maybe I should let her know what's happened."

Abe ran his hand over his head. "She didn't stop in at all today?"

"You forgetting I've been right here beside you most of the day?

"Well, I don't know what to say. I thought she'd invite me back after last night, but she didn't mention it. She seemed real nervous all evening, but I'm still thinking her back is bothering her and she doesn't want to admit it. No. I'll check with her tomorrow. You go on home."

After Dan and Emma left, Abe checked on Harold one more time. Other than being pale, he didn't have any visible signs of stress. He'd opted not to close the wound but had put a loose bandage over it so he could check for infection sooner.

He looked at Ruby, who sat in a chair she'd pulled close to the bed. "Sure hate to see you spend the night in a chair, Ruby. Are you sure you don't want to stretch out somewhere? I have two more rooms that are empty, and I'd be glad to sit here with him."

"Couldn't sleep anyhow, Doc. Just tell me what to do if he wakes up caterwaulin'. No need to keep you awake."

He stepped to his supply cabinet and lifted a partial bottle of laudanum. There should have been another full bottle right behind it, but it was missing. How could that be? He never let himself run low on pain medications. Maybe he put it in the wrong place. He rummaged through the other bottles on the shelves. Had he put it in his bag? He checked, but it wasn't there.

Abe handed her the bottle of brown liquid. "Don't give him very much of this at first. He's a big man, so he might be able to have more than usual, but I don't want him to have too much until we see how he handles it. In fact, you come get me before you give him anything."

Ruby shrugged. "Whatever you say. I sure do thank ya. Had no idea when you stopped by today that we'd be seein' one another so soon-like."

"We never know what a day will bring, do we? Just thankful I was in town when your boys brought him in. They're fine boys, Ruby. Did just what they should have. You can be proud of them."

"I reckon those words is about the nicest thing a ma could ever hear." She ducked her head. "They got a good pa. He's taught 'em."

No matter how hard he tried, Doc couldn't get to sleep. He didn't know when his spirit had been so troubled. It was more than Harold Toliver's injury. Much more.

The missing bottle of laudanum puzzled him.. Could he be getting forgetful? He'd not ever given much thought as to what he would do should the time come when he could no longer practice medicine. Misplacing a bottle of pain medication—if he indeed had misplaced it—was reason enough for concern, but what if he should forget something vital in the treatment of any of the good folk in and around Cedar Bluff? He prided himself on remembering such mundane things as the names of each babe he'd delivered the past thirty-odd years, and he hoped that small bit of memory meant something to each of them. But what if he forgot a step in a surgery, or misdiagnosed an ailment? What if he forgot the directions to the home of a patient who needed him?

Tillie added another layer to his worry. She'd seemed more nervous than happy to see him last night. What if there was something terribly wrong with her? Why hadn't she invited him back? With Henrietta and Obed still gone, it would have been the perfect time for them to be alone. But what if she...what if she didn't share his feelings?

How would he know, without asking? And what right did he have to ask, when he'd never told her how he felt?

SEVEN

Tillie checked the clock one last time before heading to the cellar with Leon's supper. If only she'd thought to invite Abe to visit again this evening—at least then she'd know what time he might arrive. The last thing she wanted was to be found in the cellar should he come calling. His early arrival yesterday had unnerved her, however, and it had been all she could do to get through the evening without allowing him to ask questions. She'd even refused his normal help with the dishes and didn't miss the look of disappointment when she stated she was too tired and would leave them until morning. He mistook her meaning and left early, saying he was concerned about her back and if she didn't feel better in a couple of days, he wanted her to be checked. Somehow, before the next time she saw him, she had to have a miraculous recovery.

She set the lamp on the tray and maneuvered the door open without spilling anything. Now to get to the bottom of the stairs without stumbling. This morning Leon had seemed more lethargic, and when she took him his dinner, she discovered he'd eaten very little of his breakfast. While she hated him being here, she dreaded the day she'd find him…not here.

"That you, Matilda?"

Tillie's light caught the silhouette of Leon leaning against the stack of shelves that normally hid the opening to the tunnel. "Of course it's me. Were you expecting company? What are you doing out of the tunnel?"

"I need more pain medication. And socks. My feet are freezing, and you buried the only pair I had."

"Socks? And just how do you think I'm going to manage that?"

He shrugged. "I don't know. How did you manage the other stuff?"

She had no intention of telling him anything. "Never mind how."

He shouldered away from the shelves. "Wait! You didn't manage anything, did you? You stole those clothes." He leaned his head back and laughed. "Oh, my—that's the first I've laughed in so long I can't even remember the last time. And to think my wife is a thief."

"Stop calling me that."

"Calling you what? Wife, or thief?"

"Both."

"Fine. I'll stop the name-calling. I'll even forego the socks. But I do need something for pain."

"How could you have possibly used that entire bottle of laudanum already? Leon, it lasted less than—"

"I know. I know. But…but it won't be much longer, Matilda. Trust me."

"I can't just go to Doc's house and swipe you another bottle of…of anything." She set the tray of food on the floor in front of him. "You have no idea what this is doing to me. And you don't care, do you?"

"I do care, believe it or not. This is no picnic for me, either."

"Then let me tell Doc Mercer. He has rooms at his clinic. You could stay warm, and at least he could keep you comfortable. And I wouldn't have to lie or steal to keep you that way." She handed him a bowl of mashed potatoes. "Eat. You haven't eaten much all day by the looks of things."

He spooned a small amount of potatoes into his mouth. "They need salt." He set the bowl back on the tray and wrapped his arms around his belly. "Please, Matilda. I need something for this pain."

"Go back to your pallet in the tunnel. There's no way I can get you anything tonight, but I'll try—all I can do is try—to get you something tomorrow. That's the best I can do."

His shoulders sagged. "I don't have a choice, do I?"

She raised her arms in exasperation. "Yes, you do have a choice, but you don't want to take it. You'd rather die here, alone, in a cold cellar than tell the truth and face the consequences."

His mouth twisted into a sneer. "And you, my dear, as much as you argue otherwise, don't want me to take it, either—and for the same reasons. I reveal who I am and it will force you to reveal who you are. Now, who doesn't want to tell the truth and face the consequences?"

Tillie pondered Leon's accusation the rest of the evening. She should never have agreed to this absurd arrangement in the first place. But she had—and had subsequently stolen from two of her very best friends. Now she was being forced to repeat the action.

Or was she being forced? The man was dying. So what if someone recognized him? They wouldn't haul him to prison in his condition. And then she—

She buried her face in her hands. She couldn't take such a big risk. Even if her friends should overlook the fact that she had worked as a nurse for the confederate army, there was the little matter of the wedding. She did, after all, still carry the name of Rogers.

Relief swallowed disappointment when the evening melded into nighttime and it became more and more obvious that Abe was not going to pay her a visit. Henrietta and Obed would arrive home before the week was over. And then what? Even if she were able, by some miracle, to keep the whereabouts of a living Leon Rogers hidden—how in the world would she ever be able to explain a dead man in the cellar?

Harold Toliver was awake when Abe checked in on him the next morning. "Did you get any sleep, Ruby?" He patted her shoulder. "Or did you have to listen to this fella whine all night?"

"I don't never sleep well away from home, but it weren't as bad as

I expected." She stood and moved away from the bed. "I reckon you want to take a look at that leg."

Abe smiled at her. "I do for sure. You can stay if you promise not to faint on me, otherwise I could use a good strong cup of coffee. The makings are in the kitchen."

"I'll make coffee. I wouldn't faint on you, Doc, but I could use a cup myself."

Harold used his elbows to push himself higher on his pillow. "Can she bring me one?"

"Don't see why not. How much laudanum did you poke down him last night, Ruby?"

"None. I reminded him I had eight of his young'uns and never once had to take nothin' from a bottle to get me through." She blushed. "That stopped his moanin'. Can I fetch him home after you take at look at that leg?" Ruby leaned against the wall. "I can do at home what I done here last night."

Doc lifted the bandage from the wound. "You're going to have an ugly scar, Harold, but you're lucky you have a leg. I'd like you to stay another day, though."

"It ain't putrifyin', is it, Doc?" Ruby looked over his shoulder "I kept sniffin' it last night, and it didn't show no signs."

Abe straightened. "How did you know what to check for, Ruby?"

"Pfft. Any southern gal worth her salt knows how to check for putrifyin' flesh. Besides that, I was a nurse during the war. That's how I met Harold and come to Kansas. Never in my borned days did I ever figger on leavin' the hills of Tennessee, but here I am."

"I never knew that. I figured you were from around here." He put a clean bandage on Harold's wound.

"Does that make a difference? Me being from the south, I mean. It never meant no never mind to me what they brung us to care for, blue or gray. They all bled red. And once them uniforms came off there was no sign a-hangin' anywhere what said who they fought for."

"Well, I doubt there'd be a soul around Cedar Bluff who'd take offense at what side a person took during that awful time. It was a shame, that's for sure—making brother go against brother like it did. I can tell you one thing, I'm sure any doctor you worked alongside was more than happy to have you. And Harold is lucky he got you to come to Kansas."

"Luck didn't figger in on it, Doc. Love is a choice. We're as different as night and day, but differences fade like blue britches in the bright sun. We still don't agree on everything, but even after these eighteen years and eight young'uns, we still take a-likin' to the makin' up part."

"You're quite a woman, Ruby Toliver." He turned to Harold. "Guess I don't have to tell you that, do I, Harold?"

"Not tellin' me somethin' I don't know, but a man likes to hear his woman is thought of in a respectful sort of way, that's for sure."

Abe nodded. "If you two think you can manage here for awhile, I'm going to mosey over to Emma's. Can I bring you anything?"

Ruby met his gaze. "Didn't come prepared to do no buyin'. Don't know how we're gonna pay up for what we owe you now. But we won't be beholdin' to nobody."

"I tell you what." Abe put his arm around Ruby's shoulders. "You fry me a chicken and bake me one of your apple pies, and that's all the pay I need."

"That there is a done deal." Ruby grabbed his hand in both of hers and gave it a shake. "And we'd be mighty honored if you'd sit at our table to partake with us. My ma always said more harmony comes from the sharin' of vittles than you'll ever hear from a church choir."

"Your ma was a wise woman." Abe pointed to the door. "You know where the kitchen is, Ruby. Make yourself at home. I'll go by Tillie's before I go to Emma's. She and Henrietta usually fix dinner and supper for any patient who has to stay here long enough to get hungry. Don't worry about paying—it's a service I provide."

"You don't say." Ruby tilted her head. "Lands sake, you hear that, Harold?" She wiggled his arm. "I kinda like this. I just might have to send you out to cut wood in the rain more often." She leaned down and kissed his forehead. "I'll bring you a cup of coffee."

A red morning sky and a cold north wind greeted Abe when he

stepped out of the clinic. He pulled the collar of his coat higher around his neck and stuffed his hands into his pockets. It wasn't that far to the boardinghouse, and he was as certain as he could be that Tillie would have the kitchen warm and a fresh pot of coffee hot and ready. But would she be glad to see him this early in the day? He didn't know a lot about a lady's morning habits. Truth was, he didn't know much about women, no matter the time of day.

There was still lamplight in the front window when he reached the boardinghouse, but the door was locked. He gave the brass door knocker three short raps, hesitated, then three more—the signal he and Tillie had devised would be his alone. In the past it was answered with hurried footsteps and a giggle that would transmit even through the closed door. Today both were notably absent, and his heart plunged.

Tillie's heartbeat doubled its tempo. There was no mistaking the knock at the door—the signal was loud and clear. While it always had a heart-skipping effect on her, this was not the flutter of anticipation she normally experienced. How long could she stall the inevitable?

She set the tray of food she'd prepared for Leon on the table and took off her apron. A quick glance in the mirror by the door that led to the parlor revealed the frustration warring within. Dark circles under her eyes spoke of her sleeplessness, and she was as pale as an unfrosted sugar cookie. A quick pinch of her cheeks would take care of her color, but there wasn't much she could do about the dark circles.

She made a deliberate effort to slow her steps to the door, and once there moved her head from side to side to loosen the kinks. A deep breath raised her shoulders and stilled her anxiety only somewhat. Now there was only one thing left to do.

Please, Lord, don't let him ask questions.

EIGHT

Tillie's hands shook as she opened the door for Abe. "You're out bright and early this morning." She stepped back so he could enter. "Is something wrong?"

Abe removed his hat. "Better this morning. Harold and Ruby Toliver spent the night at the clinic. I—"

"Are they ill? Did someone get hurt?" Maybe she could keep the conversation away from anything that would incriminate her.

"I'll explain everything over a cup of coffee." He nodded toward the kitchen. "And I bet it's warmer in there, isn't it?" He scooted around her.

She grabbed his arm. "Wait. Don't—"

He turned, his gaze full of questions. "Don't what? Tillie, is something bothering you?"

If only she could tell him. She shrugged. "No. No. I just...well, I just thought maybe you could start a fire in the fireplace in the parlor and we could have our coffee there. That's where we usually serve our guests."

He took her hands. "Am I a guest? Nonsense, Tillie. I'm as at home at your kitchen table as I am anywhere in Cedar Bluff. You know that, don't you?" He ran his thumb along her cheek. "Now, how about that cup of coffee?" He gripped her hand and pulled her with him into the kitchen.

He came to such a sudden stop that she stumbled against him. "You were expecting someone?" Abe ran his fingers along the rim of the tray of obvious breakfast makings.

Heat flooded her face. "You. I was expecting you." She couldn't look at him.

He took her chin in his hand and tipped her head back. "Tillie, you weren't expecting me. What is going on?"

She twisted away from him. "Nothing is going on. You didn't come to visit last night, so I...I hoped you would come this morning, and I wanted to be ready."

"And yet you seemed surprised to see me out...as you stated...so bright and early." His shoulders drooped. "I don't know what's going on, but you haven't been yourself since I returned from Topeka. I can only assume it's something that I've done, or haven't done. I came by this morning to tell you Harold and Ruby will be at the clinic for another day. I'd appreciate it if you would see that they had food." He turned on his heels and strode to the door.

She hurried after him. "Don't go, Abe. You haven't had that cup of coffee, yet."

He stopped at the door but didn't turn to her. "Perhaps another time, Tillie." When he opened the door, a blast of frigid air wrapped around Tillie's shoulders. But more than just the autumn wind chilled her, and she rubbed her arms against the shivers. Was there anything as cold as the back of a loved one as he walked away?

Abe kicked at a rock in the street. He couldn't remember the last time he felt so...so downhearted. Yes, that was the word...downhearted. In fact, he didn't think his heart could plunge much deeper if someone kicked it down Tillie's cellar steps—a fitting, cold, dank place for shattered hope.

He slammed through the door of Emma's mercantile, sending the bell above it jangling as though Cedar Bluff was on fire.

"I take it you're a bit upset about something?" Emma pointed her feather duster at Abe. "I bet your mama wouldn't have allowed such behavior."

His chin hit his chest. "You're right about that. Tell me, Emma, what goes on inside a woman's head?"

Emma leaned her elbows on the counter. "You talking about all women, or Tillie Rogers?"

He puffed his cheeks and exhaled. "Tillie."

"You had coffee yet this morning?"

He shook his head.

"Well, I'll bring you a cup, and if you talk fast maybe you can tell me what's bothering you before the ladies of Cedar Bluff stop by after their trip to the post office."

The bell above the door clanged again before Emma returned with his coffee. Dan Walker strode in.

Abe nodded to the man. "Sheriff."

"Doc." Dan leaned against the counter and crossed his arms. "How's Harold Toliver this morning?"

"Better. His wound doesn't show signs of infection, at least not yet. Ruby will take good care of him."

Dan frowned "Something else bothering you, Doc?"

Abe tilted his head. "Why do you ask?"

"Oh, I don't know." Dan chuckled. "Maybe it's the frown plowed all the way across your forehead, or maybe the way your mouth turns down at the corners. But mostly because your jaw ripples like water on a windy day." He clapped him on the shoulder. "Want to talk about it? Where's Emma, by the way?"

"I'm here, Dan." Emma stepped from behind the curtain. "I heard your voice so went back to pour you a cup of coffee, too." She set two cups on the counter. "Doc has woman problems, in case he hasn't already told you."

Dan gave Abe's shoulder a shove. "Woman problems? Don't tell me...it's Tillie Rogers."

Abe nodded. "Maybe it's my imagination, but I think she's hiding something."

"Tillie?" Emma shook her head. "I don't think Tillie could hide anything no matter how hard she tried."

"I used to believe that, too, but let me tell you why I'm worried about her." Abe recounted his visits with her—how she insisted they eat in the dining room, how she wouldn't allow him to help with dishes, the tray of food he found on the kitchen table after she insisted they have coffee in the parlor. He pointed at Emma. "And she didn't giggle once. Not once. Besides that, remember how she claimed her back hurt?"

Emma nodded.

"Well, sometime in the past two days she's recovered completely."

Dan shrugged. "Is that so unusual? I mean, if she just slept wrong or turned funny, would it be so strange for her to be over it by now?"

"I suppose. But—" If he uttered his suspicions, what would they think? And what if he was wrong?

"Finish it, Doc." Emma shoved the jar of gumdrops his direction. "Maybe sugar will help."

Abe took a handful of gumdrops. It wouldn't help, but it would allow him a bit more time to think. He popped a green one into his mouth and sucked on the sugary sweet until only a gummy lump was left.

"I think you're stalling, Doc." Dan plucked a black gumdrop from Abe's hand. "Share, please."

Abe took a deep breath. He was stalling, but it couldn't last forever. He might as well spit it out. "Emma, you know how you said you had a shirt and a pair of men's britches missing?"

She nodded. "Just in case you're wondering, I wasn't accusing Tillie."

"I know. But, well—last night I discovered I was short a bottle of laudanum."

Dan brushed sugar from his hands. "Laudanum? Are you sure? Who would steal pain medication? Wasn't your office locked while you were in Topeka?"

Abe nodded. "I lock it every time I leave, even if I'm only going for the mail."

"Was there any sign of a break-in?"

"Nothing that I detected at all." Abe rolled his lips. "But what I'm about to say could change a lot of things." His pulse swished in his ears, and he ran his tongue over his lips. How he hated to say the words—words could cause injuries that would never heal. "Tillie has a key."

Emma's eyes widened. "You don't mean to imply that—"

"I don't want to imply anything." His shoulders sagged. "Believe me, I've never wanted to be wrong so badly in all my life."

Emma slowly shook her head. "I can understand, a little, how she might have taken the laudanum if she was in pain. I'm sure she'd be able to explain if you would ask. But why in the world would she steal a man's shirt and britches?"

Abe shrugged. "I don't know. Only I'm sure that breakfast tray was meant for someone other than herself."

Dan ran his hand through his hair. "This is a very awkward time to bring this up, but I think you need to see this." He withdrew an envelope from his pocket and handed it to Abe. "Just came this morning."

Abe leaned his back against the counter and adjusted his glasses.

Dan. We have reason to believe that Leon Rogers is in the vicinity of Cedar Bluff, Kansas. Reliable sources say he is most likely to seek reunion with one Matilda Ruth Landers, a.k.a. Matilda Ruth Rogers, his wife. Since you're right there in Cedar Bluff and might possibly know this Mrs. Rogers, we're requesting you pursue the matter. Contact us if found. Don't let him run again.

—Maxwell & Layton

Abe's chest tightened, and he slapped the missive with the back of his hand. "Who are Maxwell and Layton?"

"My superiors in Chicago while I was still a marshal."

"Does this mean Tillie is somehow involved with this man?" It hurt to take a breath.

"It does."

Emma stepped between the two men. "Are you two listening to yourselves? Tillie Rogers is no more a thief than I am."

Dan hooked his thumbs in his pockets. "Look, Emma, don't forget I was an undercover lawman for a lot of years. I can't tell you how many times the most innocent appearing person in any given territory turned out to be guilty. I'm not saying Tillie is guilty, but the only way we're going to know if she's innocent is for me to investigate. Unless, of course, you choose to ask her outright, Doc."

Abe pressed his palms against his temples. "No matter what I do, it can't erase the fact that she's already a married woman. How could we all be so fooled? Emma, you know her better than anyone. Did you know she was married?"

"No, Doc, I didn't know. But there has to be some other explanation. Tillie is not a thief, nor a liar."

"No? Well, maybe you need to read this, too." Abe held the paper toward her.

"No, I don't even want to look at it." She pushed his hand away.

"Do you know what this fella looks like?" Abe reached for more gumdrops. "Are there wanted posters? Anything?"

"No wanted posters, but I'd recognize him. He's...well, he's well-known to lawmen."

"Then why can't you just go ask Tillie about this. Why so secretive?"

"Doc, there are times for the wellbeing of everyone involved that a secret is the best way to approach the problem." Dan folded the paper and put it back in the envelope.

Emma folded her arms across her middle. "I can't believe you, Dan. Or you, Abe Mercer. How can either of you believe Tillie has anything to do with this, no matter how incriminating it may seem?"

Abe gritted his teeth. "A rash can be covered up for a long time, but eventually it'll spread to places a person can't hide. More often than not, I don't see it until it can no longer be concealed...and believe me, by then it's mighty hard to treat." He pushed away from the counter and trudged to the door. He had no idea where he was going—home, or to pay Mrs. Matilda Rogers a visit. He just knew he had to have air so he could breathe again.

NINE

Dan caught hold of Abe's arm before Abe could turn the knob to exit the mercantile. "Wait, Doc. Don't do anything foolish. I'm sure when this is all figured out, there will be a reasonable explanation.

Abe shrugged loose. "What's reasonable about lying or stealing?"

Emma stomped toward him. "We don't know Tillie is involved in anything of the sort, Abe Mercer."

"Really? I tell you what, Emma, you go call on Tillie, and then let me know how it goes."

There was no further resistance of his leave-taking, and Abe stepped off the wooden walkway determined not to look back. He tucked his chin against his chest and turned his collar higher on his neck. Why did it feel like the whole town was looking at him? Laughter coming from the livery seemed to taunt, and even the distant bark of a dog was a jeer.

Like a horse that knew the way home without being driven, Abe turned the corner to his clinic without looking ahead. He knew by instinct that ten very long strides would get him to his porch, one more to the door, then it would be a matter of slipping inside without being heard. He regretted telling Harold and Ruby they had to stay another night. He wasn't ready to face anyone.

Ruby was in the kitchen when he entered the house. So much for not wanting to face anyone. "Harold still doing well?"

She smiled at him and poured a cup of coffee. "He's been sleepin' a lot, but that's good. When he's awake, he fidgets about what all needs to be done at the ranch."

"You think you could keep him in bed if I let you take him home?"

"No more'n I could catch a moonbeam in a jar, but I could keep him in the house, that's for sure." She handed him the cup of coffee. "Leastwise he could be a gruntin' out orders an' that would keep him happy. You thinkin' on changin' your mind about us goin' home?"

Was he? He'd already alerted Tillie to their presence and requested she provide food for them. If he sent Harold and Ruby home, it would necessitate another meeting with the one person he dreaded facing yet longed to see. He'd never put his personal life ahead of his commitment to the people in and around Cedar Bluff. Though he'd prefer to be alone, this was no time to shirk his first responsibility to provide continued care for Harold Toliver. Besides, keeping them here another night would also give Ruby a much needed break from her brood at home.

He shook his head. "Gave it some thought, Ruby. But think it's best you stay another—"

The unmistakable crash of breaking glass, followed by a loud thud and a moan interrupted their conversation. Coffee sloshed from Abe's cup as he slammed it onto the table and ran toward Harold's bedroom.

"That crazy man done tried to get up by hisself." Ruby panted close behind Abe.

The scene that greeted Abe confirmed Ruby's description of *that crazy man*. Harold lay unconscious in a mixture of shards of broken lamp, lamp oil, and blood. What had been the last of the laudanum trickled from the bottle on the floor. Not only was there fresh blood seeping through the bandage on his leg, but now a gash on his temple— probably sustained when he hit the side of the bedside table—sent a new flow of the life-giving fluid down the side of his face.

Ruby slammed her hands on her hips. "Well, now lookee what you done."

140

"We've got to get him back to bed. I'll need your help, Ruby."

She used her foot to clear away some of the glass, then knelt beside her husband. "Can't move him 'til we get this glass cleaned up or we'll be cuttin' him up somethin' awful." She pulled a handkerchief from her sleeve and pressed it against the slash on his temple.

Abe groaned. The square of cotton wasn't the cleanest thing to press on an open wound, but there wasn't time to be picky.

"Can I help?"

A voice from the doorway sent shivers through Abe's shoulders. "Tillie? Where did you come from? Why are you here?"

"I brought a meal for them, like you requested. I guess you didn't hear me come in."

"Did you knock?"

"Oh, pity sakes, Doc. Nobody knocks when they come here." Ruby looked over her shoulder. "Glad you're here, Tillie. Think you can find where Doc keeps his sewin'-up stuff?"

Tillie nodded.

"Good. You go get whatever you find. If we hurry we can stitch a real purty design on this crazy man of mine before he wakes up. Doc, you take care of his leg."

Abe opened his mouth, but couldn't spit out the words that seemed jammed in his throat. He wasn't used to taking orders from a woman, even one who'd been a nurse. But Ruby was used to shouting out commands and would probably brook no argument.

He lifted his gaze to Tillie. "Bring gauze and anything else you think we might need. We've got to get this blood staunched." Harold Toliver needed help, and he needed it fast.

Instinct overruled any reticence of Tillie's past being revealed. She'd not experienced so much blood since the war, but there was no time to dwell on such things. It didn't take her long to find what she knew from experience they would need. She put everything in a tin basin and hurried back to Harold's side.

"Have you ever had to sew up a wound?" She whispered to Ruby as she knelt beside her."

Abe reached for the basin. "Ruby was a nurse during the war. She knows what to do. Don't get in her way."

Tillie pinched her lips together. She hadn't meant for Abe to hear her question. But his retort caused her heart to skip. So Ruby was a nurse in the war? Where? Was it possible their paths had crossed but years had faded any recognition?

"You were a nurse in the war? What—"

"It doesn't matter what side, Tillie."

Ruby rolled her eyes. "Don't mind him." She leaned closer to Tillie's ear. "Confederate. Tennessee. You?"

"You two need to stop whispering like schoolgirls and help me here. Tillie, get a broom and sweep this glass away so we can lift Harold into bed."

"Wait!" Ruby's eyes darkened. "Let me get this gash knit back together, then we'll help you lift him. Be one less thing we have to worry about bleedin' all over the place."

"You forgetting I'm the doctor here?" Abe's face was red. "Did you talk to those army doctors the way you're talking to me?"

"Didn't have to. Why are you so all het up? I never said you weren't no doctor. And I ain't forgettin' who I am, or even who I was. But Harold here, he don't give no never-mind 'bout who's who. He just needs to stop bleedin' all over the place. I reckon I can do my part just fine and dandy, an' I reckon you can take care of the leg.

Tillie breathed a huge sigh of relief when Ruby and Abe stopped arguing and proceeded to care for Harold. Abe's crankiness had given Tillie a reprieve from answering Ruby's questions. Undoubtedly she'd have more once this crisis was over. Leon was in pain and needed medication. She'd already stalled him longer than she thought possible, but how was she going to leave this scene without making a bigger one? In her gathering the needed supplies, she'd found a bottle of opium and camphor tablets. Even if she took the entire supply, they wouldn't last long, but she couldn't risk being caught with the bottle in her hand. She'd slipped a handful of the tablets into her apron pocket. It would have to do for now. But this wasn't a good time to leave. She had to think of something...some way to dismiss herself without it being obvious she was in a hurry.

After what seemed an eternity, Doc sat back on his heels. "There. That will do for now. Tillie, fetch the broom and get the rest of this glass swept away before he wakes up and starts thrashing around. We need to put this big man back to bed. Too bad Dan isn't here to help like he was when he brought him in here."

That was her out. "I'll go get him." She stepped toward the door.

"Good idea, Tillie." Ruby stood. "I'll get the broom, and you run for the sheriff."

Abe heaved himself to his feet and grabbed Tillie's arm. "No! I'll... I'll go."

"And leave us women here alone to handle this grizzly bear should he up and decide to come out of hibernation? I don't think so." Ruby gave Tillie a gentle shove. "You go, Tillie. But hurry. I done saw Harold's eyelids flutter, and the only good that'll come from that is knowin' he's still alive."

"Doggone it, Ruby. You, too, Tillie Rogers." Abe put his hands on Tillie's shoulders and moved her away from the door. "I said I was going, and I'm going."

"And just want am I to do if he wakes up the dead a-hollerin' in pain? You got more laudanum?"

Heat rushed to Tillie's face.

Abe scowled. "No, and I'm still trying to figure out what happened. I was certain I had more, but I'm missing one full bottle." He tilted his head. "Tillie, did you happen to see anyone—"

"No. No one." Tillie's stomach tightened. "You don't think I—"

"I never said it was—"

Ruby stomped her foot. "Good lands. The way you two snarl at one another you'd think there was only one bone in the pile. Go fetch the sheriff, Doc. I'll look for somethin' for pain myself—can use a rolling pin if nothin' else. Surely ya got some morphine tablets, don't ya? Don't answer that. Just go." She reached behind him and opened the door. "Shoo!" She fluttered her hands.

As soon as he was gone, Ruby shut the door and leaned her back against it. "I think you an' me got us some talkin' to do." She moved to Tillie and put her arm around her shoulders. "I got me a feelin' it's words you ain't wantin' anyone to hear." She perched on the side of Harold's bed and patted the mattress beside her. "We might as well use us a soft place."

Tillie sat beside her and clasped her hands in her lap. "How did you know?"

"How did I know what? You was a nurse or you don't want to talk about it?"

She shrugged. "Both." She turned to the other woman. "Oh, Ruby, I'm in so much trouble and if anyone finds out they'll drum me out of town."

"*Pfft*. Ain't nobody gonna do no drummin' unless they be marchin' right along with you. Ever last one of us got some kind of parade we don't want no horns a-tootin' about. Now, while the good doctor is on his errand and my good man is still layin' there payin' for his own foolishness, why don't you tell me all about what's got you in such a dither."

Ruby's eyes held nothing but kindness, and the understanding chinked through the wall that Tillie had built over the years. And as words tumbled through the cracks in the mortar of guilt, the heaviness of the past crumbled and the terrible weight of pretense lifted.

But would Abe lay new bricks?

TEN

Tillie clutched at the lapels of her coat and prayed she could get back to the boardinghouse before running into Abe and whoever he found to help put Harold back to bed. What a relief to finally tell someone all that was weighing on her. Ruby had insisted that she leave before Abe returned, but it was only a matter of time before she'd be forced to confess to more than only Ruby Toliver.

Grateful she'd not encountered anyone before reaching home, she slipped around to the back and entered through the kitchen door, only to find Leon Rogers sitting at her kitchen table.

"What are you doing up here? What if someone sees you?"

One side of his mouth tipped up. "You worried about me being found, or what will happen to you if I am? Where have you been? Did you bring anything for pain?"

She took off her coat and hung it on a chair, then pulled the stolen pills from her apron pocket and plunked them on the table. "There. That's all I could find. I'd advise you to use them sparingly because I'm done stealing for you."

He propped one elbow on the table and cradled his head in his hand. "I don't suppose you could spare a glass of water so I could wash these pills down, could you?"

She got his water and handed it to him.

"Thank you. And by the way, I never asked you to steal anything.

145

That's your own doing." He popped the pills in his mouth and took a swig of water.

Tillie slammed the palms of her hands on the table and leaned until she was nearly nose to nose. "How else was I to get medicine, and clothes, and—"

"You could have washed my clothes. By the way, my feet are still cold."

She straightened and plopped her hands on her hips. "Washed your clothes? And left you naked in the cellar? I'm sorry your feet are cold, but I am not going to steal stockings for you. Answer my question. Why are you up here instead of in the tunnel where you promised you'd stay?"

"I need to give you this." He handed her a slip of paper.

She lowered herself to a chair and looked at the paper, but there were only two names, Luther Maxwell and Marvin Layton, and an address in Chicago. "What am I supposed to do with this?"

"See, I know you're worried about having to...well, having to get rid of me once I'm gone." He smiled. "That sounds strange, doesn't it? Once I'm gone you have to get rid of me."

"Two names and an address tells me how to go about getting rid of you once you're...once you...after you're no longer here?" Why did he look so strange? His head lolled and his eyes rolled back. Surely he wasn't going to die right here, right now. "Leon? Leon, are you—"

He frowned and rolled his head from side to side. "There'sh a... there'sh...tell Schigago I'm—" His head bobbed, and like a cooked noodle sliding down an old man's chin, he slithered from his chair and fell to the floor.

"No!" She jumped to her feet. The pills were gone, every one of them. Why hadn't she been more careful? Was he trying to kill himself? She bent over him. How in the world would she get him back on his feet? Or for that matter, how could she get him back to the cellar?

She straddled him and shoved her arms under his, but he was limp as a piece of string and she couldn't even budge his shoulders. There was no way he could help himself. She shuffled backwards and grabbed his ankles. Land sakes, his feet were cold. Maybe she could pull him. But to where? She couldn't pull him down the stairs without his head hitting every stone step. She couldn't pull him upstairs and hide him in one of the empty bedrooms. She couldn't pull him anywhere. Even as gaunt as he appeared, he was too long, too limp, and too heavy.

Tillie knelt beside him and held her finger under his nose. At least he was still breathing. A slap on the face did nothing to rouse him from his stupor. She stood and grabbed what was left of the glass of water and dumped it on him. Nothing. He didn't even blink.

She forced herself to think. A man—a very long, heavy, limp man— lay on her kitchen floor. She couldn't budge him, but she couldn't leave him there. She gasped. She could try rolling him.

Roll him where? She tapped her chin. How tempting to get him to the cellar door and give one big shove. But getting him there was already proving harder than she expected. She sank to her bottom and scooted so she could plant her feet somewhere in his middle. Then she leaned back on her arms and shoved for all she was worth. He might as well have been a boulder. She scooted a bit closer, and gave one more heave. Was that a moan? Maybe he was waking up.

"Leon? Leon Rogers! Please wake up." She flipped to her knees and leaned closer. She drew back in dismay. Snoring! The man was snoring. Each breath increased the volume.

Without warning a giggle erupted. She didn't feel the least like laughing, but she couldn't stop giggling until, at last, the tears came. Then she couldn't stop crying. What was she going to do? She couldn't push him, pull him, or roll him. Until he woke up from an apparent overdose of opium and camphor—*if* he woke up—he couldn't help himself.

She stood and wiped her eyes. Crying wasn't going to help in the least. At least he was in the kitchen and not the parlor. Abe was busy with Harold, and Ruby already knew her circumstances. Well, other than the fact this so-called husband could very well die right here under her kitchen—

That was it! She'd hide him under the table. She pulled back the chairs and maneuvered the table to fit over him. It took some doing— he hadn't fallen in a nice straight line so now the table was at a rather awkward angle, and it wasn't quite long enough to cover his feet. She got down on her hands and knees and pulled on his pant legs until she'd bent his knees enough to put his feet completely under the table. With a heave, she got to her feet and brushed at her skirts. She darted for the cupboard for one of the tablecloths they used for the big dining room table. It would be long enough to hide him, kind of like him being in a tent.

After she flipped the cloth into place, she discovered a problem. While the cloth did reach the floor on all sides, even puddled a bit, the chairs couldn't be scooted under the table as normal. She pushed them as close as possible and then hung her head.

Lord, I'm not sure You'll even hear this prayer, what with all my deception, but if You're listening, please don't let anyone come calling.

"For two cents, I'd tie you to the bedpost." Abe squeezed Harold's shoulder. "However, I think you've learned your lesson."

Harold gave a weak smile. "Hate like blazes to ask, since I brought this on myself, but I don't suppose you would have something for pain."

"I do, indeed." He nodded to Ruby. "You know where the supplies are. There's a bottle of opium and camphor pills. Bring those, but don't leave them where he can knock them off. We'd be on our hands and knees for hours trying to find them all should he give them a fling."

With the crisis over, Abe trudged to his parlor and sank into his favorite chair. He leaned his head against the chair's wing and propped his feet on the matching footstool. He was weary. So very, very tired that it was hard for him to concentrate on anything other than the emptiness in his heart. He'd chided himself for being so remiss in

Julane Hiebert

declaring his love and intentions to Tillie. But what good would it have done? Would she have admitted she had a husband? He shut his eyes against the pain. To realize Tillie—his Tillie—not only lied by omission but could possibly also be a thief was more than he wanted to bear at this time. What reasonable explanation could there be?

Two short raps on the door brought him back to the present. Ruby gestured toward the foyer. "Sheriff Walker is here, Doc. I told him he could come on in, but he said to tell you he'd meet you on the porch."

Abe sighed. "Thank you. I'll be right there."

Abe joined Dan on the porch. "Is it Tillie?"

"We'll talk on our way to the boardinghouse."

Abe's gut tightened. "You surely haven't found your man already."

"As crazy as it may sound, I think I have."

"Tillie's involved, isn't she?"

"I can't answer that until we hear her side of the story. I went there after helping you get Harold back into bed. But I went to the back—to the kitchen entrance."

"You were sneaking around her yard?"

"Not sneaking. That would imply that I was— Well, I suppose you could call it sneaking. Anyway, no blinds were pulled, and I could easily observe through the window. Tillie was there...with a man."

Abe longed to erase the picture that was forming in his mind. "And this—this man...could you hear them talking? What exactly were they doing?"

"I couldn't hear them. The man had his head cradled in his hand, like maybe he was sick or something. I wanted to get closer, but she turned toward the window and I was afraid of being seen, so I ducked down. That's when I decided to come get you."

"Isn't it possible it's just some weary traveler wanting to rent a room?"

"Of course. That's quite possible, but that's also what we need to ascertain."

"How do you plan to do that? Assuming you have a plan."

"I do, and that's where you come in." He looked at Abe.

Abe didn't want to hear it. Weren't they being as deceptive as they presumed Tillie was being? "I want to stay out of this."

"I know. But all I'm asking you to do is call on her. Keep her busy in the parlor, and I'll go in the kitchen door. If this man is Leon Rogers, then we'll have answers sooner rather than later." Dan grabbed Abe's arm. "Look, I know this is hard for you, Doc, but years of experience have taught me that everything will be done to protect and prove the innocence of all parties involved. Trust us."

Abe sighed. What choice did he have? He didn't want to believe Tillie had anything to do with this whole scenario. So why was he so reluctant to allow this investigation? Maybe because down deep he had doubts of her innocence. And perhaps that doubt was even more painful than truth.

ELEVEN

Three short raps of the door knocker...hesitation...then three more. Tillie's heart thumped. Abe. If she didn't get to the door fast enough, he'd let himself in. She ran her hands down her apron, gave a quick pinch to her cheeks, and prayed the anxiety in her heart would not show on her face.

"Good afternoon, *Miss* Rogers."

Tillie frowned. What was with the *Miss* Rogers?

Abe removed his hat. "I wonder if we might talk about...about the meals you normally provide for patients at my clinic." He rolled his lips.

"Of course, Abe. Won't you come in?" She swept her hand in the direction of the parlor. Something was amiss, but she couldn't put her finger on it. Abe wasn't himself. Not at all.

Once in the parlor, she perched on the edge of the settee. "Was there something wrong with the dinner I prepared?"

Abe shook his head. "No. No. It's just that—well, Ruby insists on cooking their meals herself, so your services are no longer needed. She doesn't like to just sit around, I guess."

Tillie studied her hands in her lap. Why was he acting so...so much like she did when she felt cornered and guilty? "I see. Is that all?"

"I thought—I thought you might offer me a cup of coffee."

She clutched at her throat. "Of course. I'll—I'll be right back." She stood.

"Wait. I'll come with you."

She raised her chin. "I can't let you do that, Abe. I'd be negligent if I didn't serve you."

"Why is it every time I suggest going to your kitchen, you refuse me? And the one time I did, there was an obvious tray of food fixed for someone. What's going on, Tillie? Who are you hiding?" He stepped around her and left the parlor before she could stop him. She lowered herself back onto the settee and waited for the inevitable.

It took longer than expected, but Dan entered the room and stood before her, not Abe. "I brought you coffee, Tillie." He set the cup on the table beside her.

"Is Abe still here?"

Dan shook his head. "No. He left a note for me to give to you." He handed her a piece of paper. The same paper that Leon Rogers had given to her. The paper that held only two names and an address. Scribbled on the bottom in Abe's handwriting was a note—*Mark 8:36.*

She didn't need to look it up. She'd memorized it many years ago. *"For what shall it profit a man, if he shall gain the whole world, and lose his own soul?"* Tears clouded her eyes. Had she lost her soul? She'd gained nothing…except guilt. But now it was too late for explanations. Who would listen anyway?

"That's not all." Dan opened his hand and revealed three opium and camphor tablets. "Doc found them on the floor. That's when he wrote the note."

"And did he—"

"Notice the snoring coming from beneath your table? Or the bare foot sticking from beneath the tablecloth on one end? Yes, I'm afraid he did."

She pressed her hands against her temples. "Oh, Dan! What have I done? What must Abe think of me? What am I to do?" Would Abe give her a chance to explain? If he did, what would she say? She was sorry—very sorry. But for what?

Dan took her hands in his. "First of all, dear lady, I'm going to move this man upstairs. You do have an empty room, don't you?"

"Yes, of course. But how will you get him up there yourself?"

"He's long, but from what I could see he's pretty emaciated. I won't have any trouble at all. You go on up and turn down a bed—preferably at the far end of the hall. Then... Well, then it will be time for a long talk, won't it?"

"Abe Mercer will never forgive me." She couldn't stop the tears.

Dan gave her a quick hug. "You don't know that for sure. Look, as soon as I get this man to bed, I'm going to fetch Emma. I have a feeling you will feel more comfortable with her present, and I know for a fact that she'll listen to whatever you have to say. You have friends here, Tillie. Don't assume the worst from any of them."

"But I stole—"

He put his finger over her lips. "Shh. You can tell your story later. Right now I have more pressing matters to tend to...like getting that man to bed before he wakes up again."

"*If* he wakes up. I have no idea how many pills he took, but enough to knock out several men his size, I'm thinking."

"He's addicted to pain medicines, Tillie. That's all I'm going to say for now, but he's abused them for so long I doubt this last little round will be the one that kills him."

Tillie pondered that statement after Dan left, but it did nothing to help remove the guilt that wrapped around her so tightly she could barely breathe. The man was addicted to pain medications? She, who had witnessed the likes during her stint as a nurse during the war, should have recognized the symptoms. Instead, she had fostered his habit, and committed a crime in the doing. Would she end up in jail?

Abe pulled the blind in his room, then slumped into the chair by the window. He'd been able to get back into the house without Ruby seeing him, and now he wanted to be left alone. His suspicions about Tillie were true—and this was one time having a correct diagnosis didn't give him any satisfaction at all. How could he have been so fooled? All this time he believed Tillie to be the one for him, the woman with whom he imagined he'd spend the rest of his life. The silly little giggle he once found so endearing now grated hollow and taunting in his mind. He braced his forearms on his thighs and clasped his hands together. He couldn't remember the last time he'd felt so defeated. Could he ever face her again? And what about his friends, Emma and Daniel and—

A knock on the door interrupted his pondering. If it weren't for the fact he had a patient in the house, he'd not even answer. "Who is it?"

"It's Ruby Toliver. What are you doing holed up in here like a rabbit hidin' from a hound? I hollered *supper time* three times. You gonna eat?"

"No, go on and eat without me."

She stormed into the room and stood in front of him, arms crossed. "Nonsense. Now, I don't know what happened since you left here earlier, but I have me a feelin' it has something to do with some woman. Your face couldn't be longer if you was Emma Ledbetter's old mule, Dolly. Now, you come eat. I don't take to fixin' food and havin' it get cold."

He shook his finger at her. "You know, if you were this bossy with the doctors you worked with, it's a wonder they didn't ship you to the North. I can't believe Harold has put up with your sass all these years. Besides, I'm not hungry."

She widened her stance. "Harold knows my sass has it's rewards. But that don't go for you. You got two choices—eat or talk. Come to think on it—you only got one choice—talk."

"And why should I talk to you about...about anything?"

"Because if you don't, whatever it is you got stuck in your gizzard is just gonna fester 'til you turn cranky and mean. I don't tolerate no cranky and mean comin' from one of my young'uns, and I don't intend to tolerate it from one growed-up man. I done told you, I think it's a woman what's eatin' at you, and I'd be wrong if I was to guess it was anybody b'sides Tillie Rogers." She sat on the side of the bed.

"You can start talkin' any time now, you know. I gave Harold a pain pill and he's sleepin', so there's nothin' stoppin' you 'cept your own stubbornness."

Ruby was right. He had to talk to someone.

TWELVE

Abe sat in the silence—silence that screamed louder than a banshee. He'd told Ruby everything. Everything from the first twinge of something more than friendship had turned his heart to Tillie clear up to leaving a note about the man under her kitchen table. Surely Ruby understood his pain and frustration. But the woman who heretofore had been more than ready to speak her mind, sat and eyed him like a hawk who'd just spied a mouse hiding in the grass.

He held his hands wide. "Aren't you going to say something?"

Ruby drummed her fingers on the bedside table. "So, you wrote her down a Bible verse. Now, ain't that real special. Just what is it you think she gained, Doc? And what has she done so bad she's gonna up and lose her soul?"

Abe slapped his knees. "Weren't you listening to a word I said? She's a married woman. But all these years she passed herself off as a...as a *not* married woman. Did you know she was married? I sure didn't. I was even gonna ask her to marry me, that's how dumb I am. And she...she stole clothes from Emma's and medicine from me. In anybody's book that makes her a liar and a thief. I said it over and over. Weren't you listening?"

"Did you ask her why she did them things? Or are you more worrisome about what people around here will think of you for havin' marryin' feelin's for her?"

"Ruby Toliver, if she were to go before a judge, she'd be found guilty. There's proof."

She shrugged. "Could be. But if she was gonna go before a judge, like you say, he'd give her a chance to tell her side of things. You're so big on Bible verses—well, let me give you one to look at. Proverbs chapter eighteen, verse thirteen says it's a plumb shame and foolishness to give an answer before you even hear the question. That ain't exactly how the words go, but you can look it up for yourself. This might come as a surprise to you, Doc, but you ain't God. You don't have no right to be passin' judgment without knowin' the whole story."

"Do you know something I don't, Ruby? I'd sure like to know what it is, if you do."

"I know what I know 'cause I asked questions. But I ain't about to give you answers to questions you ain't even trusted her enough to ask." She stomped to the door. "Now, I got me a man to feed and I ain't gonna say it more than once—if you're hungry you better come now cause there ain't no eatin' after I get the dishes washed up."

The door clicked shut behind her. Before he could push himself out of the chair, it opened again.

Ruby scowled at him from the doorway. "The sheriff is wantin' to talk with ya. I was tempted to tell him you were in here poutin', but I reckon he'll see for hisself." She didn't wait for a reply before shutting the door again.

He hated to face Dan, but there wasn't a choice. Ruby was right. He hadn't given Tillie a chance to explain anything. Now he felt like one of her young'uns, about to get a thrashing for being rude.

Dan met him in the hallway. "Emma's with Tillie, and you need to come listen to what Tillie has to say. You owe her that much, Doc."

"Owe her? She stole from me, Dan. I don't owe her anything."

Dan poked him in the chest. "For two cents I'd— Never mind. You just come with me and listen."

"You've talked with Tillie?" Abe grabbed his coat from the hall tree and flung it across his shoulders.

"Only a bit, but enough."

When Abe entered the boardinghouse parlor, he gave a jolt. Tillie sat beside Emma, but she didn't even look like the Tillie he knew so well. Her face was red and blotchy, perhaps from crying, and she wouldn't meet his gaze. Was she always so...so small and fragile appearing?

Dan motioned for Abe to sit. "I've asked Tillie to go first—to explain the events that have led to this meeting today. Then I will fill in what blanks are left." He nodded toward Abe. "Doc, I would appreciate it if you would let Tillie talk without interruption. You left a rather terse note, and we can surmise that you're angry. But if you will listen, perhaps some anger can be alleviated."

Abe leaned forward. "She lied to me." He swooped his hand. "She lied to all of us, and she stole from me and Emma."

Dan scowled at him. "I will say this and then I will thank you to keep your mouth shut. If you don't let this woman tell her side of this situation, you, Doc Mercer, will be the loser."

"Fine." He sat back in his chair and tented his fingers. Why was he suddenly the bad guy here?

"Start at the beginning, dear." Dan sat on the other side of Tillie and put his arm around her shoulders. Emma gripped her hands.

The beginning. That would be her stint as a nurse...and her subsequent in-name-only marriage to the man she'd thought was Leon Rogers. Tillie could barely form the words, let alone make them audible. If it was only anger, she could handle it. But there was pain etched in Abe's face, and she could hardly bear to look at him. Yet she wanted him to know that she hurt, too. She wanted him to understand. So she told her story. Every painful word of it.

An eerie silence greeted her when she finished—the kind of silence that preceded a storm, when it seemed even nature was holding its breath. Then Abe put both hands on the arm of his chair and leaned forward. Tillie braced herself for the fury that was sure to follow.

"So Milo Landers was her brother. Is that supposed to explain something?"

Dan stood and leaned one shoulder against a bookcase. "Milo Landers was perhaps one of the most well-known, well-loved, and well-respected United States marshals I've ever known. A legend, if you will, to us up-and-coming, still wet behind the ears undercover marshals who followed behind him. The highest compliment you could give a young lawman at that time was to call him a Landers man."

Abe scowled at Tillie. "But you went by Rogers—how was that supposed to protect Katie if she still carried the name of Landers?"

Heat rushed to her face. It was one thing for Abe to question her motives concerning her past, quite another to imply that she'd not protected Katie. "You didn't recognize the name, did you, Abe?" She pinned her gaze on him and dared him to look away.

"No."

"Well, neither did a lot of other people, and those who did soon realized that to get to Katie they would first have to get past me. One reason I kept the name of Rogers, even though the marriage was not a real marriage, was to protect Katie Rose. I won't apologize for it, and I'd do it again if need be. I could ride and shoot with the best of them, and today is the first day I've not had my gun with me since I found Leon Rogers in my cellar."

Emma gave her hands a squeeze. The comforting pressure gave Tillie courage to continue. "I know what I've done is wrong, but it's also right. It was wrong for me to never tell you...any of you...my past. I was afraid this very thing would happen. You're all sitting here with your own ideas. But never once have I asked any of you to reveal any of your lives other than what I've come to know since coming here.

"As far as stealing clothes and medicine, is it any different than what you or Emma did for the people you helped escape to freedom during the war? How many people in Cedar Bluff know there's a secret tunnel under this house? Or, for that matter, how many people know what roles you played in that secret hideaway? It might not have been stealing as such, but you knew what could happen if you were caught or if those poor people were found." She took a deep breath.

Dan widened his stance and crossed his arms. "Now will you please allow me to finish, Doc?"

"No, wait! I'm not through." Tillie stood. "What I did was right because the Bible says that when someone is sick or hungry or cold or thirsty, and I give them warm clothes and food and medicine, then I'm doing it for Jesus. I know, Abe—you'll argue that Jesus wouldn't want me to steal. But neither does He want you to sit here in judgment. That's what you've done."

She brushed a wisp of hair from her face. "Now, if you'll excuse me, there's a man upstairs who might very well be dying. Regardless of what you choose to think, the only thing binding us as husband and wife is a piece of paper that I didn't even know existed. But what does bind us together is his need for care right now—and my ability to give it."

THIRTEEN

Abe peered out Tillie's parlor window. Between Ruby Toliver's earlier scolding and Tillie's outburst, he felt like he'd been scrubbed and salted, and it was his own fault. He could feel the eyes of his friends on him, and knew they were waiting for him to give Dan the go-ahead to give his version of the events that had unfolded before them.

"You ready to listen, Abe?" Dan inquired.

"I'm listening."

"Would you care to join us? I don't really like talking to someone's back."

He sighed and returned to his chair. He didn't care to face them, either, but he'd do what was expected to get this over with.

Dan perched next to Emma on the settee. "First of all, Leon Rogers is not a criminal. He's actually a U.S. Marshal."

Abe's eyes widened. "Undercover?"

"Well, he was at one time. Obviously not now. I first knew him when I was working on the Queen ranch in Texas. In fact, if Sam Mason was here, he'd recognize him as one of the hands—they worked together. But that's another story. For now, you all need to know that I'm most likely the reason he came here. In our conversations during that time, he learned about my relationship to Milo Landers and began to put two and two together. He told me then he had a brother who'd married a nurse named Matilda Landers. He also told me how this brother had used his name. We had a good laugh about it then, but it's not so funny now."

Emma shifted sideways on the settee. "But why would he come here now? Did he think he could somehow make Tillie honor that piece of paper?"

Abe rubbed his forehead. "I guess I'm wondering the same thing."

Dan shook his head. "I don't think that was his plan at all. Leon feels he's to blame for his brother's death. I don't think he's ever forgiven himself. Over the years, he's recited the letter Tillie wrote telling of his brother's death so many times that he started believing he was the one responsible. Those of us who worked with him noticed a gradual change. First he drank, but he quit when he got shot one night because he was so drunk he couldn't even pull his gun. That gunshot wound resulted in him receiving pain medications—and that began a whole new chapter."

"So you think he found Tillie so she would help him get medications?" Abe crossed his legs. "He was taking a chance, wasn't he?"

"When a man is desperate, he'll take all kinds of chances, Doc. I don't think he knew Tillie would have access to medications. But I do think he sought her out knowing she'd been a nurse and hoping she could give him some measure of comfort."

Abe took off his glasses and wiped them with his handkerchief. "So if he isn't a criminal, why were your superiors looking for him?"

"To save him from himself. There's a kind of...I suppose you would call it a brotherhood...that develops among lawmen. My superiors in Chicago wanted to find him to help him find himself again. I think he came here believing he was dying, maybe even hoping he would."

Abe settled his glasses back on his face. "So is he dying?"

"If he wakes up from this last dose of medicine he put down his gullet, I think he might stand a chance of living. But, Doc, you know what happens to a man when he withdraws from that stuff. He's probably going to beg to die, and might even try hastening the event if left to himself."

"Then you're saying he needs to stay here until this is over, one way or another." Abe gritted his teeth and leaned forward to brace his elbows on his thighs. Did they think he would offer his clinic for this man's struggle to overcome the ravages of addiction? But how could he refuse? The man couldn't stay at the boardinghouse. "I can't be with him all the time."

Dan frowned. "No one person can stay with him the entire time. In fact, I'm pretty sure for the first few days it will take a man, maybe more than one, to contain him. That's where you and I will come in. If need be, we can call on Sam Mason. Mason is young and strong, and he knows this fella."

Abe pushed himself to his feet. "I have a patient at the clinic. I need to go see about him. Then I need to get a room ready for this Rogers person."

"No, you don't." Emma motioned for him to sit. "I'll go to Ruby, but you aren't going anywhere until you talk with Tillie. I can't tell you what to say, but I can tell you, you have to say something."

"I agree." Dan nodded.

"I have nothing to say." A lie. He had plenty he wanted to say.

Emma stood and stepped to his side. "Less than a week ago you were ready to ask Tillie to be your wife. Now you have nothing to say? I've told you before and I'll say it again, if you don't give her a second chance, then you're forgetting why Jesus died on the cross. You throw Bible verses around real free-like when you want to make a point. But maybe you should ask Him what to do instead of deciding you're so without fault you can pronounce another person guilty. Me and Ruby Toliver will get things ready at the clinic, Dan will see to getting Leon Rogers over there, and you, Abe Mercer, are going to stay here and make things right."

He fisted his hands at his sides. Why was it so hard to admit Emma was right? But what if Tillie refused to listen? What if he declared his love for her, in spite of all that happened? What if he told her that no matter what, they'd work through this... together? What if he admitted he was wrong not to give her the benefit of the doubt? What if he would ask...even beg for her forgiveness? Was he a big enough man to do all that? If he was, would she listen?

Tillie fingered the blue and white cloth on the kitchen table. She'd tried to answer all of Abe's questions, but she couldn't be sure he understood. There was so much left unsaid between them. She longed to tell him her biggest fear was losing his...what? If she were honest, he'd never declared love for her. He'd implied it but never said it. Oh, how foolish she'd been. How often did a woman her age find a life's companion? Henrietta was the exception. And maybe, maybe one day Emma. It must have been her own silly, wishful thinking that allowed her to even imagine Abe Mercer would love the likes of her. Now that dream seemed more a nightmare.

She clasped and unclasped her hands in her lap, and when she raised her eyes they locked on his. He opened his mouth, as though he were going to speak, but then closed it and looked away.

She sighed. "Was there something more you wanted to say, Abe?"

"I...I just wish I would have known all this before now." He glanced at her again. "I wish you would have trusted me."

"Tell me, Abe, were you born and raised here?"

"No."

"When you came to town, did you announce to everyone you met everything that had taken place in your life before Cedar Bluff?"

"Of course not. It was nobody's bu—" Light dawned on his face.

"Exactly. I don't need to know what skeletons might be lurking in your closet. Nor is it my business to ask. I didn't offer any information upon my arrival for this very reason. Even after you've known me these past years, rather than ask the reason for my unusual behavior, you became my doctor and diagnosed me on your own."

"But you could've asked for help, Tillie. You should have asked for help."

She tipped her chin to her chest. "I know that...now. But at the time, I...I thought...I hoped you had..." She waved her hand. "Oh, forget it. There isn't anything I can say that will change your mind about me at this point. You've heard my story. You've heard Dan's story. But I'm not sure you've listened to either. I think you've heard words, but you've been deaf to the heart behind them."

"That's not true."

She tilted her head toward him. "Really? Than tell, me, Abe, why are you here?"

"Why am I here? Because Emma said—"

"Point made. You didn't come to talk to me on your own. You came because Emma said you should. In fact, you didn't come to talk at all. Neither did you come to listen. You came with your head full of questions—questions I've already answered over and over again. Well, you can go now. I have no more answers."

She stood and swept her arm toward the door. "Goodbye, Abe."

Abe leaned against the wall outside the kitchen. What had he done? Tillie was right—he hadn't listened to her. And he had asked the same questions over and over. He'd gone in with such good intentions, such hope. He'd questioned her trust in him, and at the same time he'd not trusted her. How could any kind of relationship survive without that key element? But could he call what was between them, what he thought and hoped was between them, anything close to a relationship? So much taken for granted, so little admitted. So much implied but never spoken. Three words. Three small words that could build and mend and heal. Heal... Was it too late? He was a doctor, after all. Wasn't he supposed to be the healer?

No. Ruby Toliver had been right—he wasn't God. God alone was the Great Physician. Abe was but a tool or a vessel to be used. He could have been a vial of oil to be poured out, to soothe, to bring beauty. But he chose to be a hammer.

Abe pressed the palms of his hands against his eyes. A hammer. He'd pounded and pounded away at the same old doubts and questions, and instead of building anything he'd only driven a wedge deeper and deeper. At some point, a wedge driven deep enough, would split asunder that into which it was driven. Once split, whether it be a log or love, it separated, never to be joined.

"Tillie?" Abe stepped back into the kitchen. "Tillie, please, may I come in again? I promise to listen this time. I promise."

FOURTEEN

Christmas Eve 1879

The heady fragrance of fresh cut cedar filled the church. Wreathes of cedar surrounded candles that glowed in each window, and red bows marked the end of each pew. Tillie's hands shook as she gripped Daniel Walker's arm. "Thank you, Dan, for offering to give me away."

Dan smiled at her. "Not really giving you away, Tillie. I'm not sure whoever came up with that term. But whatever you want to call it, I'm proud and honored to be your escort."

"Look at all those people. Friends and neighbors, young and old. I think they're here for Abe. He's well loved, you know."

Dan took her shoulders and turned her to face him. "Tillie Rogers, don't you for one minute think these people are here only for Doc. Yes, he is loved. Lands sakes, he delivered a good share of the people here tonight. But you, my dear friend, are just as loved and respected. Oh, and I almost forgot." He pulled an envelope from the inside pocket of his jacket. "Leon Rogers asked that I give this to you on your wedding day."

She peeled back the flap, and her eyes puddled. Inside was the wedding certificate that declared her the wife of Leon Rogers—but it was torn into pieces. She fingered through the confetti-like remains of the secret she'd guarded for so long.

"He also sent his regards, and by now I imagine Leon has been reunited with his superiors in Chicago—a man free of the devastating addiction that plagued him for so many years. The best part is he's also relieved of the guilt." Dan leaned to her ear. "Are you ready? I think Henrietta is waiting for my signal."

Tillie nodded. She was ready, and as Henrietta hit the first notes of Mendelssohn's "Wedding March," she took her first step toward the future she never dreamed would happen after the events of the earlier months.

When she reached Abe's side, he didn't take her hand. Instead, he put his arm around her shoulders and pulled her close.

Obed Mason winked at them. "She's not going to run away, Doc," he whispered.

Abe pulled her even closer. "I'm not taking any chances. Could we please get started?"

"If you will both join hands and repeat after me, I think we can do just that, my friend."

Abe held her hands so tight it hurt, but the love glowing on his face gripped her heart even more.

"I, Abraham William Mercer, take you, Matilda Ruth Rogers, to be my..."

Could this be real? Tillie's knees shook. After all the events of the previous months, did he still love her enough to promise...

"...to have and to hold from this day forward..."

This day forward. No more worries about the past. Isn't that what Abe told her? They only had the future.

"...for richer, for poorer..."

No amount of money in the bank could make her richer than she was at this very moment. As a young girl she'd imagined this day, never once thinking she might be plump with sprinkles of gray among her once golden locks before she experienced the love of such a good man.

"...in sickness and in health—" Abe's eyes twinkled as he leaned closer. "That's *health* my dear, not *stealth*."

Oh, no! Tillie sucked in her lips, but it wasn't going to help. Why did this always happen at the most inappropriate times? First only a snicker escaped, but she couldn't pull her hands from Abe's in time to cover her mouth before a full head-thrown-back giggle erupted.

Reverend Mason chuckled. "I'm not sure what our good Doc Mercer just whispered to his bride, but it certainly has made her happy."

Abe put his arms around waist and drew her close. "Just pronounce us married, Obed. I'm not sure I can stop her now."

In the comfort of Abe's arms, all else faded. Not until his lips met hers did she realize the preacher had taken him seriously, and she was now Mrs. Abe Mercer.

She eased away from his embrace. "Abe, did I say 'I do'?"

He cocked one eyebrow. "You don't remember?'

She shook her head.

"Hmm. Now look who has secrets." He smiled at her, his eyes full of love. "But I won't tell, if you don't."

"But we're married. Right? I mean, well you know—"

"We're shout-it-from-the-rooftop married, my dear." He put his hands on her cheeks and kissed her again.

The preacher chuckled. "These two seem to have forgotten their manners, but since I am their pastor, and they've told me their plans, I'm inviting you all back to our boardinghouse for a reception. I think we might even be able to persuade Doc and the new Mrs. Mercer to join us." Reverend Mason tapped Abe on the shoulder. "You will be there, won't you?"

Abe nodded to Henrietta, who was still seated at the piano. "Play us the happiest song you know to get us back down this aisle and we'll beat you all there."

Henrietta swiveled on the piano stool, and Tillie giggled all the way down the aisle to the strains of "Joy to the World!"

Joy, indeed, beyond anything she could ever have imagined.

Much later that night, they cuddled in front of the fireplace in their room. Abe reached to the table beside the settee and retrieved a framed document. "This my dear, is proof that we are indeed married. You did question it, you know."

Tillie took the frame and held the signed marriage certificate. "When did you have this so beautifully preserved?"

"Henrietta did it as one of her gifts to us." He kissed her temple.

She pulled away from him and stood. "I have something to show you." She gave him the envelope containing the torn document that had held sway over her. "Leon Rogers left this. I guess you could say it was his gift to us."

Abe stood and walked to the fireplace. "I can't think of a better way to preserve his gift, can you?" He gave the envelope a toss.

Tilled giggled and rushed into his arms. "Do you think you might prove to me, once again, that we are truly married?"

The end.

'Til the Ranch Do Us Part

The heart of her husband doth safely trust in her...

Proverbs 31:11a KJV

To *all those who have found that true love* has no boundary of age,
and to *those who have found that age is no boundary* for true love.

ONE

New Year's Eve, 1879
Cedar Bluff, Kansas

John Wenghold peered into the mirror above his washstand and smoothed his mustache with two fingers, then straightened and plopped his Stetson on his head. "New Year's Eve soiree. That's 'bout the most flubber-busted idee I ever heard tell. Don't need no fortune teller to know whose silly notion it is neither. Henrietta Harvey Mason, that's who." He closed the door behind him and ducked his head against the bitter north wind. "Thought sure once she got hitched to the preacher he'd rein her in, but doggone if he ain't about as twittered as his missus." Jumpin' bullfrogs, it were enough to make a fella talk to hisself.

Thankful he'd hitched the buggy beforehand, he tucked the ends of a blanket under his legs and snapped the reins across the horse's back. "Hup, there, Charley. I'll give ya a nice handful of oats once we get to town." No doubt the poor critter would rather stay in the barn than tied in front of Henrietta's boardinghouse all evening on such a night. He flipped the collar of his jacket to cover his neck against the frigid wind.

"No need for another whoop-dee-do, that's what." Two weddings since the Fourth of July was more than plenty for most all of Cedar

175

Bluff to celebrate, and more than plenty for him. With luck, maybe nary anyone would venture out on such a cold night and Henrietta would have to admit her little party-givin' ways was over 'til come springtime.

The only good thing 'bout this shenanigan is Emma agreed to go with me. That thought warmed him enough that his toes tingled. Doggone if he didn't feel like a schoolboy, 'cept he didn't have no remembrance of any female making his toes buzz the way Emma could. He always did think she was right comely, but George, God rest his soul, was the one what seemed to tickle her the most. Leastways, he was the one what got to sit across the table from her for nigh onto twenty years. If it had been any other fella 'ceptin George, he might have been downright jealous. But George, he was just one of them fellers other people liked. He couldn't blame Emma for fallin' for him like she did.

He gave another slap of the reins. Funny how the soiree didn't seem so sorry now that he'd been givin' it a think or two. He leaned back and fished his watch from his pocket. He done told her he'd pick her up at six forty-five. One thing for sure, he didn't want to be late knockin' on Emma's door.

"Well, George, another year has come to a close and somehow I've managed to keep on living without you." Emma Ledbetter smoothed the frayed hank of yarn across the page that contained Elizabeth Barrett Browning's sonnet number forty three, and closed her copy of *Sonnets from the Portuguese.* Only on the last night of each year since her husband's passing did she allow herself to grieve his absence. It was a date made more poignant in that it was not only the date of his leaving, but also the anniversary of their wedding. Twenty years of marriage. Twenty years of hearing him recite his silly version of sonnet forty three—"How Do I Love Thee?"

She closed her eyes and savored the memory of his hand cupping her chin, his eyes searching the depth of her own, while declaring there weren't numbers high enough to count the ways he loved her. Then he'd kiss her forehead. Her hand involuntarily touched the spot that had so often received the tenderness of his lips. Had he somehow known on New Year's Eve eight years ago that it would be their last? Is that why he made her promise to never forget how much he loved her, or had he always asked for assurance?

The clock on the mantle above the fireplace struck six o'clock, and its rhythmic *bong, bong, bong* vibrated against the walnut case like her heart within her breast.

She chided herself for such silly thoughts. The last thing George would want for her was to feel sorry for herself on this night of all nights. How could she pity the years that had been so good? No, George would allow her the sweetness of memories, but would expect her to keep living. And tonight, for the first New Year's Eve in eight years, she would not sit at home alone in front of the fire.

Reverend and Mrs. Obed Mason request the honor of your presence at a New Year's Eve soiree to be held in their home, Henrietta's Boardinghouse, beginning at seven o'clock, December thirty-one, eighteen hundred and seventy-nine, the invitation read. Henrietta had distributed them with a flourish the evening of Doc and Tillie Mercer's wedding reception a mere week ago. John had accompanied her home that night, muttering the entire time about the nonsense of one more *whoop-dee-do,* as he called it. Yet, he'd asked her to attend the party with him and even squeezed her hand with the asking. While the invitation didn't specifically say, it implied that the guests were expected to stay to welcome the year 1880.

Emma laid the book of sonnets on the table by her chair and stood. She'd spent every evening of the past week in a flurry, sewing a new dress for the occasion. Would John even notice? She'd known the man forever, it seemed, and since George's death they'd become very good friends. But would it ever go beyond acknowledging the presence of one another, yet never conceding any emotion beyond friendship? If she were to confess, she'd have to admit to using this soiree as a way to manipulate Mr. Wenghold. The man seemed never at a loss of words, or an opinion, whether asked for or not. Now, if only she could manage to make him drop his jaw and leave him speechless, even for a few seconds, she would have accomplished what no other woman in or anywhere near Cedar Bluff, Kansas, had accomplished. And she'd not apologize if what it took was a few loose curls around her face and a burgundy colored taffeta dress to complete the mission.

At six-fifteen, Emma lifted the dress over her head and allowed it to fall to her shoulders without mussing the low chignon she'd so carefully arranged earlier in the evening. Satisfied the two wisps of hair on either side of her face didn't appear too indiscreet, she gave her cheeks a quick pinch and dabbed a bit of rosewater on her wrists. Then, for good measure, she patted a drop of the sweet fragrance behind each ear. Just in case—she told herself—Henrietta suggested a waltz, though the idea of John Wenghold doing anything but his usual pump and shuffle was a stretch of her imagination.

John slammed his hand against the side of the buggy. If this wasn't a cat's whisker in the cream jar. How could he have been so doggone careless? Never left home without checking every inch of the buggy. Until tonight. Now, here he was, still a good thirty minutes from town and the left wheel done rolled right off and lay at the side of the road, one spoke stickin' out like a tongue razzin' him for bein' so forgetful.

He fumbled under his coat and pulled his watch from the pocket of his britches, but even with squintin' he couldn't make out the time. The lamp had sputtered and died 'bout the same time the wheel went a *whooshin'* past like it wanted to race. One more thing he forgot to check—the oil in the lamp.

He leaned against the buggy and crossed his arms. It was a sure sign God agreed with him that this here party was a whole bunch of nonsense.

God didn't have no part of this, John Wenghold. You're gettin' old and forgetful, that's what.

Horse feathers. He weren't that old.

Must be. Old and stubborn. You do remember Emma's waitin' on you, don't you?

How could he forget? The only reason he gave even a granny's cat thought of goin' to such a doin's was because of Emma. He took a deep breath. Now she'd be a-frettin' 'cause he was late and there weren't no way of lettin' her know.

Only one thing a body could do at a time like this—unhitch the horse from the buggy and ride bareback to wherever he was goin' in the first place. Unhitchin' weren't the problem. He could do that easy enough, but gettin' seated on the animal did pose a bit of a stumble. It weren't like he could grab a hank of mane and swing hisself up, like he coulda done twenty years ago. This would take linin' the animal up just so, so he could clamor up the side and get his leg swung over before the old gelding decided it was time to go. Bouncin' on the bony spine of this old horse wasn't gonna be pleasant. For sure he couldn't ask Emma to hike herself up behind him, and it was too cold to expect her to walk to the boardinghouse. They'd have to hitch Emma's old mule, Dolly, to her buggy. For certain they'd be walkin' in late, and Henrietta would chatter like a squirrel that'd spotted granny's cat. This year weren't endin' real good.

At six-thirty, Emma took her black and burgundy plaid woolen cape from her wardrobe and laid it on the bed. She didn't want to appear too anxious, but she knew John well enough to know he'd huff and sputter if he had to wait too long.

By seven o'clock she became concerned, and when the clock chimed seven-fifteen, and John had not yet knocked on her door, she knew something was wrong. While he'd made it abundantly clear he thought Henrietta's party was a whole bunch of silly, it was not like him to ignore a commitment. He had asked her to attend with him, after all. The man could growl and fuss, but he was known to be a man of his word. He was also a stickler for good manners, and often muttered his disdain for people who arrived habitually late, stating— usually loud enough for others to hear—*it's plumb rude to waltz in like they's the only cracker in the barrel when it's soup for supper.*

Something must have happened. She hurried to the bedroom and slipped her cape around her shoulders. Everyone who might help look for him would be at Henrietta's. Her heart thumped as she pushed against the wind on her way to the boardinghouse.

Please, Lord. Keep him safe, wherever he is. I don't want to lose—

What was she thinking? Lose what? Lose who? It wasn't as though John was anyone she could lose, at least not in the sense that she'd lost George. He was a good friend. That was all. But she didn't want to lose a good...a *very* good...friend.

TWO

John hesitated outside the door of Henrietta's boardinghouse. Through the window he observed Emma in the middle of a circle of party-goers. Gathered around her fussin' about him not showin' up in time, no doubt. He sidled closer to the window to take advantage of the light and pulled the watch from his pocket. Seven-thirty. It weren't that late. Looked to him like she coulda waited a bit longer before gettin' all het up. She shoulda knowed he wouldn't just up and forget he asked to fetch her to the doin's.

He stepped away from the window and puffed a sigh of exasperation. He'd never been knowed—as far as he could remember—to break a promise. So's, the only choice left was to go in, say his sorries, and be ready for Emma to glare a furrow right through his middle. She'd not say a word. No need. That woman could say more by keepin' her mouth shut and pinnin' a look on ya, than them what yapped and yammered 'til they got little gobs of slobber at the corners of their mouths.

One step sideways would get him to—

"John Wenghold? Is that you? My goodness, I thought we would be the last ones here tonight." A woman stepped from the shadows of the walk, accompanied by a gentleman John didn't recognize.

John clutched the woman's hand in both of his. "Florence Blair. Well now, if this don't up and put a feather in granny's bonnet. I don't reckon I seed you since—"

She nodded. "Since that terrible Fourth of July so many years ago, when Robin was injured. Please don't remind me, dear friend. That's a night I'd rather not remember. However, I am anxious to see Ty and Robin. And I hear all the sisters are here in Cedar Bluff. How nice for you."

"Ahem." The stranger put his hands behind his back and rocked from his heels to his tiptoes, his head cocked toward Florence.

She pulled her hands from John's. "Oh, I'm sorry. I've been so remiss. John, I'd like you to meet Wynston Alexander."

John grasped the man's outstretched hand. "Please to meet ya." He glanced at the woman beside him. "You two—"

"Cousins, John. Just cousins. Wynston is an attorney in—"

"Philadelphia, I suppose?" Looked fancy enough anyway.

Florence shook her head. "No, New York City, actually. He's here to help me sell my holdings in Cedar Bluff."

"You're leaving us? For good?"

"Oh, I suppose I'll—"

"Excuse me." Alexander slipped his arm around Florence's shoulders. "Perhaps we could continue this conversation inside, out of the cold."

John chided himself. Why hadn't he thought of that? He must seem plumb unthinkin' to the likes of a fancy city fella. "Of course." John hurried to the door. "Here, let me get this for you. I gotta say, Florence, ya sure are a sight for sore eyes."

"Yes, well, that's one way to put it." Alexander smirked at John as he ushered Florence past him and into the house.

It didn't take long for the guests to spot Florence, and if anyone had been worried about John's absence, it seemed—to him, at least—that the appearance of this well-loved former resident of Cedar Bluff now had everyone's attention.

Except for Emma. Like a hawk what just spied a mouse cowering in the ditch, Emma strode toward him. "Where—"

John raised both hands, palms out. "Wait, wait, wait. Before ya scold me, give a listen to that there *where* question."

Emma's eyes puddled. "Why John Wenghold. I had no intention of scolding you. I was worried—worried sick that something had happened. I knew you wouldn't just—"

He narrowed the gap between them. "Ya suppose we could slip into the kitchen so's I could tell ya all about it?"

"I doubt anyone will miss us—they're all so busy with Florence and her man." She crooked her finger and motioned for him to follow her.

"He ain't what ya said."

Emma stopped so suddenly, John bumped into her. "He isn't what? What did I say?"

"Ya said Florence and her man. He ain't her man."

"And you know this because—"

He pointed to the kitchen door. "Could we maybe go in there to do our talkin'? Iffen somebody spies us in this hallway, they's likely to think we got somethin' goin' on between us."

Emma raised her chin.

He knew that there crank of her head, and it near always meant he done said somethin' wrong.

"Why of course, Mr. Wenghold. We certainly wouldn't want anyone to think there's *anything at all* between us, now would we? Of course, being found in the kitchen...just the two of us...while the other guests are all welcoming Florence Blair and —and whoever the man might be—would never arouse anyone's suspicions, would it?"

"Now, Emma-girl." He patted her arm.

She brushed his hand away. "I'm not your *girl*, John Wenghold. You've made that quite clear." She turned and her footsteps echoed in the tall-ceilinged hallway.

Did he think wrong, or did she stomp her way to the kitchen? He removed his hat and ran his hand through his hair. Tryin' to talk to this woman and not get in trouble was like walkin' across the corral and not gettin' muck on your boots. He squared his shoulders, puffed out a long breath, and followed her.

In the short time it took for him to get to the kitchen, Emma had cups of hot coffee sitting on the table and now sat all stiff-necked, with her hands folded in her lap. She didn't even give him a glance, but kept lookin' at the wall behind him. What he couldn't give for one of her icy-eyed glares.

He pulled a chair away from the table and straddled it backwards so he could lean his arms against the back. If he'd had any smarts, he'd a-kept talkin' in the hallway. His rear plumb hurt from bouncin' all the way to town without a saddle to cushion the jolt, and the wooden chair weren't any softer than the bony spine of his buggy horse.

Laying his hat on the table, he leaned forward. "Ya know I ain't good with sayin' the right words, but for certain I never meant to make ya mad."

Emma took her eyes off the spot on the wall she'd been staring at for so long, and met John's gaze. "Mad? I'm not angry, John. I was frightened…so very frightened. I worry about you every time you leave your ranch on nights like this. Even in good weather, if I know you're on your way to town, I pray you will make it here all in one piece. And I pray you home every time you leave. Do you have any idea what kind of terrible tragedy I can imagine?" She swiped her hand across her forehead. The last thing she wanted to do was cry, but the lump in her throat seemed to grow with each word.

"That ole buggy horse knows his way to town and back better'n me, Emma. Ain't no need for you to be so worrisome."

Well, that took care of the lump. Maybe she was angry after all. "Oh, really? Then tell me, John Wenghold, where were you at six forty-five tonight? How is it you arrived with Florence Blair and her— her whatever you want to call him?"

"It's her cousin, and I didn't arrive *with* them. And you ain't the onliest one who was worried. I done stopped to get ya, just like I said,

184

and doggone iffen the place were all dark. I pounded on the door and went around a-peekin' in winders 'til it was a wonder nobody called the sheriff. Then I figgered ya must've got tired o' waitin' and hoofed it on over here by your lonesome, so I did the same. Only I didn't hoof it. I climbed on the bony back of that ole buggy horse. I was a standin' out there on the porch tryin' to decide what to do. I could see you was a-talkin' to all them people in there and I figgered it were about me. If you'll just listen, I'll tell ya where I was at six forty-five."

He was worried about her? Why did that make a little tickle run down her spine? "I'm listening."

By the time John finished with his story, the lump had returned to Emma's throat. She'd acted like a fishwife, while he was doing all he could to reach her. Of course he had no way to get word to her. However, that was the point. With Ty and Robin on their own ranch, Sam and Wren in their cabin at Henry's Grove, and Albert and Lark living behind the post office, it left John at home alone. He could just as well have fallen in his kitchen, unable to get up, and he'd be helpless as a newborn.

"You ain't gonna say nothin'?" John turned his chair around and folded his hands on the table.

Emma scooted her chair closer to his and grasped his hands in hers. Oh, she had plenty she wanted to say, but how could she voice what was in her heart without putting him on the defensive? Only on occasion had he revealed any feelings toward her other than being a good friend. Would he chide her for her concern? She, Emma Ledbetter? The one others sought out for answers? The one who normally stayed calm when others around her jumped to the worst possible conclusions?

"That's the reason I worry, John. You're out there all alone. Anything could happen, and who would find you in time for help? I *knew* you weren't late on purpose, but when you still weren't there by seven-fifteen, all I could think of was to get help, a search party, anything to find you. I don't know what I'd do if anything were to happen to you." There, she said it. Would he discern what words weren't spoken?

He shrugged. "*Pfft*. Didn't look to me like nobody was breakin' down doors to come find me. They's all crowded around you like buzzards on a fresh kill."

She pulled her hands away from his, and jumped to her feet. "Excuse me?" A fresh kill? Why did her have to be so...so John? It was obvious he'd not heard a word she said. At least he'd not *understood* what she tried to say. "John Wenghold, you say it was seven-thirty when you checked your watch? Well, guess what? I hadn't been in this house a full ten minutes. I walked, you see, because the man who was to accompany me here was nowhere to be seen, and it took me awhile before I could catch my breath enough to talk. You—you—"

"Oh! There you are." Henrietta swirled into the room. "Why, Emma, you look downright pale. Are you ill? John, is she ill? And where were you, by the way? You had this poor woman scared out of—"

"I'm not ill, Henrietta. John had an incident with his buggy. That's why he arrived late. All is well." She couldn't look at John. Henrietta could smell a juicy bit of gossip a mile away, and if she—even for a second—sensed she'd walked in on an argument, the piece of news would be served to every guest as the main course.

"Well, that's a relief. Now you come on, you two. We're about to start the dance." She slipped her hand around Emma's elbow. "Oh, and you must meet Florence Blair's cousin. Wynston Alexander is his name, and he came here all the way from New York City. I never would have dreamed someone from such a fancy place would visit Cedar Bluff, Kansas. And here in my boarding house."

Harriet clutched her hands under her chin and quivered with excitement. "Oh, and did I mention he's an attorney? Can you imagine that? I didn't even know Florence had such a—such *distinguished* relative, did you? I don't suppose you did, either. But come along. He did say he was most anxious to meet you. I understand Florence has told him all about you, sang your praises from what he said. And can you believe such a fine specimen of a man has never been married? Never, Emma. Isn't that exciting? Wait! Oh, my goodness, Emma

Ledbetter. Now why didn't I notice this when you first arrived? You have a new dress. Why, it's downright stylish, too. My! My! And your hair! If I didn't know better, Emma, my dear, I'd say you had your cap set for someone tonight. Ooh! How exciting. How did you know Florence's cousin would accompany her?"

Henrietta twirled around and pointed her finger at John. "You arrived with Florence and her cousin. You must have known. Of course. You're the one who told Emma, aren't you? And now look at her—all prettied up in a new dress and hair style." She giggled and shook her finger at him. "Ooh, and here I thought you'd be the one to court this dear woman. But then, you've always been a sly one. Matchmaker. That's what you are."

Emma pulled on Henrietta's arm. "Stop. I told you John was late because he had a problem with his buggy. It's pure coincidence he arrived with Florence and her cousin. Please, Henrietta, don't make a fuss."

Henrietta fluttered her hand against her bosom. "Me? A fuss? Why in the world would you think I, of all people, would make a fuss? I just think it's quite nice that someone like the distinguished Wynston Alexander might be interested in someone from right here in Cedar Bluff, Kansas. After all, you can't wait on John Wenghold forever, you know." She tapped her fingers on John's shoulder. "And yes, I did intend for you to hear that."

Emma closed her eyes and counted to ten. For sure, as soon as she could manage it, without making a scene of her own, she would leave. Whatever made her think she could enjoy this night...of all nights?

Oh, George. How I miss you.

THREE

With Henrietta practically dragging her, Emma sucked in a deep breath and stepped into the parlor. Not the type of entrance she'd choose, had she had a choice.

"Oh, there you are, Emma." Florence Blair approached with her arms open wide. "I thought I saw you when I first came in, then you disappeared." She wrapped her arms around Emma.

Henrietta poked her head around Emma's shoulder. "Oh, I found her, Florence. In the kitchen...with John...alone."

Florence pushed away from the embrace and raised one eyebrow. "I see. That doesn't surprise me at all, but I do have someone I want you to meet."

"I told her about your cousin, Florence. And she's most anxious to meet him." Henrietta beamed with satisfaction.

"I—I didn't say..." Emma didn't want to sound rude, but neither did she want Henrietta giving anyone the wrong impression. Though, announcing she and John had been in the kitchen...alone...was more than impression enough.

"Wait here, dear." Florence patted Emma's hands. "My handsome cousin seems to attract a crowd no matter where he is. Just give me a minute to try to disengage him as gracefully as I'm able."

Henrietta sidled next to Emma. "I told you he wanted to meet you."

"And I asked you not to make a fuss, Henrietta. I'm afraid we've now become the center of attention."

"Oh, *pooh*. With your fashionable dress and new hair-do, it would have happened without my help. You surely didn't do all that for John's sake, did you?"

Emma shot her a glance she hoped would quiet any further discussion, but the chance of it working was like trying to preserve a pat of butter on a hot potato.

"There he is." Henrietta's breath puffed against Emma's ear. "Now don't act nervous. Just smile. He's no different than any man—except, oh my goodness, he is quite handsome isn't he?"

"You needn't point, Henrietta. I have eyes, and I saw him come in with Florence." She nodded toward a group of men gathered across the room. "Correct me if I'm wrong, but I do believe you have a brand new husband. I wonder what he would think of you calling another man *handsome?*"

"Well, you needn't be so saucy, Emma Ledbetter. I only said— You know I would never think any man more worthy than my Obed, don't you? I'm only trying to—"

"I know what you're trying to do, Henrietta. Please stop. I'm a grown woman and can very well make my own choices. And right now, I choose to go—"

"Here she is, Wynston." Florence planted herself in front of Emma. "This lovely lady is Emma Ledbetter. Emma, dear, this is my cousin, Wynston Alexander, and he's most anxious to make your acquaintance."

"Indeed I am."

"It's nice to meet you, Mr. Alexander." What else could she say, and still be considered polite?

"Please, let's get rid of the 'mister' moniker. My friends call me Wynston, and my very good friends address me as Wyn."

Emma didn't want to encourage his attention. After all, even with his tardiness, John was her escort for the evening. "I'll try to remember that should we meet again." She gave a quick glance

189

around the room. Where was the man anyway? She thought sure he'd follow her from the kitchen.

"Meet again, you say?" Wynston's eyes crinkled at the corners when he smiled. "The night is still young, my dear, and we've not yet said our farewells. Might I be so bold as to predict that by the time the new year rings in, you will address me by Wynston, and before my time in Cedar Bluff is done, Wyn will be the preferred title?"

"May I ask how long you plan to be in Cedar Bluff?" Emma bit the tip of her tongue. If only she'd thought that question through before asking. Now he might interpret her inquiry as a veiled hope he'd be around for quite some time.

He put his hands behind his back. "Well, I suppose that depends. There are several business transactions that must be completed for Florence. However, in the very short time I've been in your quaint little town, I've found I rather like the slower pace of living and the obvious neighborliness that I don't experience in New York. Who knows, with the right incentives, I might just decide to stay for... well, for much longer than I anticipated when I agreed to make this journey."

Henrietta's cheeks puffed like little pink pillows. "Oh, now, isn't that just the best news ever, Emma? Why, I'm going to get the musicians started, and the two of you can lead the first waltz." She bustled away clapping her hands. "Attention! Attention, everyone. If you will all choose a partner, we'll start the dance." She nodded to the knot of musicians. "Do play a waltz first. Emma Ledbetter and a guest, Florence Blair's cousin, Wynston Alexander, have agreed to lead with one turn around the floor—with me and Obed following, of course—then others may join."

Emma gasped. "We did no such thing, Henrietta. You are giving these good neighbors all kinds of ideas that simply are not—" She closed her eyes and prayed the music drowned out her protest.

"You can open your eyes. I'm quite sure no one heard that objection over the music." Wynston took her hand and led her onto the floor of the cleared-of-furniture parlor. "I'm sure neither you nor Cousin

Florence would ever be suspected of any wrong-doing." He placed his free hand on her waist and swept her into the *Blue Danube Waltz*.

"This is a small town, Mr. Alexander, and there's not a lot of newsworthy events. However, you are an unmarried man new to a locale which is home to many a single lady. Believe me when I say that every woman at this gathering will keep track of how many ladies you dance with, and how many times you stood up with the same woman." Goodness, she'd say one thing—he was no pump and shuffle dancer.

"And you?"

"Me, what?"

"Are you going to keep track of how many other women I dance with—and how many times?" He raised one eyebrow and smiled. "We could make it real easy, you know, if you'd agree to dance *every* dance with me."

Thankful other couples had joined them, and they were no longer the center of attention, she pulled her hand from his and stepped off the dance floor. His confidence and boldness made her most uncomfortable.

He followed her, his gaze questioning. "Did I do something to offend you?"

"No offense, exactly. While your suggestion to dance every dance with me is most flattering, Mr. Alexander, I'm afraid I must decline. I wouldn't want to deprive even one other woman of the pleasure of your company."

He shook his head. "Wynston."

"Excuse me?"

He leaned closer. "You used *mister* again. I'm reminding you my friends call me Wynston."

"I'm sorry. I'm not accustomed to being on a first name basis so soon after making the acquaintance of a gentleman. I meant no offense."

"Then the apology is mine, Mrs. Ledbetter." He tilted his head and gave a shrug. "The ladies I meet in my fair city seem to have no such inhibition. You must think me most conceited or self-assured."

"Perhaps a little." She smiled. "However, do you see the lady in the blue dress standing by the doorway?"

He turned to the door. "The blue dress with the white collar?"

"Yes. Every woman you see between her and the punch bowl is either a widow or a single lady, and they're all holding their breath in hopes you will invite them to dance with you."

"Really, now?" He ran his hands down the front of his jacket. "It does seem a bit like window shopping, though, doesn't it?"

Emma grimaced. "Oh, my! Please don't let anyone else hear you say that. Consider it an opportunity to become acquainted with more than one woman in our fair town. It's a far cry from the hustle and bustle of New York City, I'm sure. And I suppose our ways will seem very...old fashioned. Nevertheless, I think you will find the available female population of Cedar Bluff quite pleasant." She wanted to ignore the wrinkle that flitted across his forehead for just an instant. While the smile was still on his face, the twinkle in his eyes was dimmed. Had she been too dismissive?

"Then I shall take the *opportunity*, as you call it, and attempt to become more acquainted with the nice ladies of this fine town." He clasped her hand. "Thank you, Mrs. Emma Ledbetter. It's been a pleasure. I trust we shall meet again before Florence and I take leave of Kansas."

"Thank you. I'm sure we shall." Would he think that was an invitation for further social communication? Though he wasn't entirely unpleasant, he wasn't—

"Kinda cocky, ain't he?"

John. Obviously he was no longer in the kitchen.

"Did I miss somethin' important?" John hooked his thumbs over the pockets of his britches. "Guess you met that city fella, huh? I done met him when I was standin' on the porch."

She laid her hand on his arm. "Have you been in the kitchen this entire time?"

John shrugged. "Thought you'd be back once you met the man. Can't blame ya for keepin' me waitin', seein' as how I did the same to you."

"Henrietta insisted that Mr. Alexander and I lead on the first waltz."

He took his hands out of his pockets. "You mean you done danced with him? Did ever'body see ya a-twirlin' 'round the floor with him a-holdin' your hand?"

"You needn't make a scene. I didn't have a choice, John. And yes, there were people watching. Of course he held my hand. It was a waltz, for goodness sake."

His heart thumped. He weren't jealous, was he? He just didn't take to the notion of the pretty boy and Emma a-waltzin' when he was waitin' on her in the kitchen. Embarrassed is what he was...for Emma. Why, the man didn't have a mustache or beard or nothin'. Bet he couldn't grow enough hair on that pink face to cover his lip, let alone his chin. Emma surely noticed she was bein' whirled by a smooth-faced dandy, didn't she?

Emma shook his arm. "Were you listening to me? Why don't you say something?"

He took his forefingers and smoothed his mustache. That oughta make her notice. "Oh, I had me plenty words b'fore Henrietta came a-stompin' in, but don't reckon you wanna put your ear to any of 'em now. Not since you and that fancy New York fella traded words while ya was a-waltzin' right there where ever'body could watch ya...and him a-holdin' your hand and all."

"John Wenghold, when have I ever not listened to you?" She plopped her hands on her hips. "If I didn't know better, I'd say you were jealous. You're talking nonsense, and I've heard every word."

He put his hands on her shoulders. "Not ever' word, Emma-girl, 'cause I ain't said 'em all yet."

"Then you start talking, because I'm not going to stand here and fuss with you."

"Well, what them words was wantin' to say was…well, I was a-thinkin'—" He had no idee what he'd been thinkin', but one thing for certain, he'd better come up with somethin' real jackrabbit quick. "I was a wonderin'—"

"Oh, for mercy sakes. Spit it out. What is it you were wanting, or thinking, or wondering about?"

If only he could make those fiddlers stop their fiddlin'. They was so loud he couldn't think straight. He took a deep breath. He was a prayin' man, and he surely did hope when he opened his yapper, God would let some words come a-slidin' out 'cause he done got himself in a real pickle. "I was a-wonderin', Emma Ledbetter, if you'd—"

"You're going to have to speak up, John. I can't hear you."

He gripped her shoulders tighter. "Well, have ya ever thought— What I want to say is—"

She wiggled loose from his grip. "You aren't talking louder, you're just squeezing my shoulders until they hurt."

Doggone them fiddles. Louder is what she wanted? Louder is what she'd be gettin'. "WHAT DO YA THINK ABOUT YOU AND ME GETTIN' HITCHED?"

He groaned.

Well, now, God. Them ain't exactly the words I had me in mind.

FOUR

John never reckoned on the fiddlers to stop their fiddlin' right when he shouted them words. No, siree.

"It's about time, John."

"Way to go, Wenghold."

"Can't believe it, but congratulations."

While the men hooted, slapped John's back, and shook his hand until it was numb, the women gathered around Emma, gigglin', huggin' and wipin' tears.

What had he up and done? And how could he untwist it? It weren't like he didn't think real highly of Emma. Fact is, it weren't the worst thing he coulda hollered for all of Cedar Bluff to hear. No, it was the look on Emma's face what made his gut hurt. Even now, from what he could see, she had water a-runnin' down her cheeks, and her lips were a-turnin' t'ward the floor instead of up and smilin' all happy-like.

Henrietta kept flittin' around like a moth around a candle. "Oh, this is just the greatest news. Now, John, you go get your intended bride. You musicians, you strike up another waltz, and John and Emma will take a turn around the floor. Oh, goodness, take two turns. Go on, John, go get her."

The men around him had sense enough to give him room, but gettin' through the tangle of women was gonna be like swattin' at spider webs.

"Wait a minute, please." Wynston Alexander stepped from the sidelines. "I realize I'm new here and therefore not familiar with your customs. However, in New York City, where I make my home, it is customary for the bride to *accept* the proposal before taking the turn around the floor as intended husband and wife." He put his hands behind his back and rocked up on his toes. "Of course, there's been such a clamor of well-wishers, that perhaps I missed hearing Mrs. Ledbetter's reply."

Well, if that wouldn't curdle water. *It's a good thing the man is bald-faced, 'cause if he weren't I'd pluck ever' hair on those pink cheeks and pointy little chin with a pliers.*

One thing certain, them women scattered like shelled peas hittin' the floor and left Emma standin' where he could step right up to her. He weren't real fond of havin' to twirl around the floor—two times— whilst ever'body was watchin'.

"Take me home," Emma mouthed.

"Now?" Weren't she gonna say somethin'?

"Now. This very minute." She lifted her skirt with one hand and walked toward the door.

"Emma, wait." Doggone it was quiet.

He beckoned to Henrietta. "Could you please have them string-scratchers to start fiddlin' again? Ain't no need for ever'body to be listenin' to us." He catched up to Emma. "I can't take you home." So much for fiddlin'. Could'a heard a piece of straw fall from a loft.

Her skirts swished around her ankles when she turned to him. "And why not? You invited me here in the first place. Remember?"

He raised his hands, palms up. "Course *I* remember, but I had buggy problems. Do *you* remember? I rode here on Charley."

Florence Blair hooked arms with John. "Let us help. I know this is quite awkward, and I apologize. Wynston was out of line, but he did have a point. Emma needs time, you know. We can drive her home in our buggy, and perhaps you can visit with her tomorrow."

"Now wait just a granny's cat minute." John pulled away from Florence. "I ain't about to let that there cousin of your'n go traipsin' off with Emma all by their lonesomes."

"You misunderstood, John." Florence patted his arm. "I will go along, of course."

It was mighty hard to ignore Emma's gaze when her eyes were all puddled like they was about to run over. He nodded to Florence. "Sorry. Guess if you're gonna be there, I ain't got much choice"

"It isn't your choice, anyway, with or without Florence." Emma wiped at her eyes. "Thank you, Florence. I'm thankful for your offer."

Alexander approached, Emma's wrap in hand. "There's a blanket in the buggy so you won't get chilled." He laid her cape across her shoulders.

"Thank you..., Wynston. That's very considerate."

"Aha!" Alexander patted Emma's shoulder. "Didn't I predict you'd call me Wynston before the new year arrived?" The man smiled so big his teeth showed, all pearly and straight. It was enough to make a real man wanna make the smart aleck swaller one of 'em.

John fisted his hands at his side. Even with the fiddles fiddlin', to thump the guy a good one would more'n likely cause a big hoopla. *Wynston, before the new year.* Now weren't that real special? One thing for certain, Alexander might be takin' her home, but sure as fire was hot, he'd be followin' behind. He rubbed his chin, right proud it were scratchy. T'weren't any way he was gonna let that smooth-faced city slicker get the last word. He pulled his watch from his pocket. Twenty minutes. He'd give Alexander twenty minutes to walk back through Henrietta's door. After that time—back or not—he'd pay Emma a visit hisself.

John paced the hallway between the front door and the kitchen. Why did he give 'em twenty minutes? Fifteen were plenty long. He lifted his coat from the hall tree and flung it over his arm. Five more minutes and he'd be on his way.

"You aren't thinking of doing something stupid are you?" Obed Mason joined him and leaned against the doorway into the parlor.

John shrugged. "Not stupid, but I ain't goin' home 'til I have me a sit-down talk with Emma."

"You are going to wait until Florence and her cousin return, aren't you?"

"I gave 'em twenty minutes."

"Oh, I see. You gave them a time limit. Does Emma know this?"

"Ain't none of your business."

"But giving them a time limit was yours...is that what you're saying?"

"Twenty minutes is plenty time."

"John, are you aware of what happened here tonight?"

"I knowed what happened."

"You spoke before you thought, didn't you?"

"No... Maybe... I don't for sure know. Me and Emma hitchin' up ain't a bad idea, is it? I mean, look at you and Henrietta, and Doc and Tillie."

"No, my friend, marrying Emma is not a bad idea at all. It's the way you went about asking her that leaves something to be desired. Are you familiar with Proverbs chapter twenty-nine, verse eleven?"

John leaned against the opposite wall and sucked in a deep gulp of air. "I reckon I'm gonna get familiar with it."

Obed chuckled. "'A fool uttereth all his mind: but a wise man keepeth it in till afterwards.'"

"So, you're sayin' I'm a fool? Now you wait just one doggone minute."

"Those aren't my words, friend—they're God's. But tell me this, was it your plan to propose to Emma tonight?"

He swallowed. "No."

"Was it your plan to propose to Emma, say, in the next week?"

He ran his hand under his collar. Henrietta must've stoked the fire. "Hadn't gave it much thinkin'."

Obed squeezed John's shoulder. "That's what I mean. You didn't think. And your not thinking embarrassed the very person I'm sure you didn't mean to embarrass."

"Them fiddles stopped playin' too soon. First I couldn't hear nothin' but them a scratchin' away on them strings, then the next thing I knowed, I done yelled out a— Well, you heard what I hollered. But she never said nothin' about agreein' to do it, so I reckon it won't stick."

"Oh, it will stick, brother. She may never agree to be your wife, but how you went about proposing will stay in her mind like her ABC's. And believe me, she'll put that memory, along with anything else you've said or done all these years, into words, and those words will write a story you may never want to read. Unless, of course, you're somehow able to redeem yourself."

He pushed away from the wall. "So how do I do that there redeemin' thing?"

Obed shook his head. "You'll have to figure that out yourself, John, but don't do anything until you've taken the time to give it a whole lot of thought and done some serious praying."

"Then you don't reckon I oughta go see her b'fore I go home?" He didn't like the idea one bit that Wynston Alexander would tell her g'night.

"I can't tell you what to do, but I can warn you about what not to do. If you go, don't even mention Florence Blair's cousin. That's what started all this in the first place, isn't it? You were jealous."

"Weren't jealous. Didn't cater to the idee of them a-holdin' hands and twirlin' around the floor is all. Can't call that there bein' jealous."

Obed laughed until his face turned red. "What would you call it, John?"

"I don't reckon I got a word for it. Like I et a green apple. Belly all tied in a knot. Felt real bad for Emma."

"You felt bad for Emma? Why?"

John shifted his coat to his other arm. "Ya mean it slipped right by ya? That there city fella don't have nary a hair on his face." He poked Obed's chest with his forefinger. "No mustache, no beard, no whiskers. I'd bet my ranch he can't even—"

"I guarantee you, Mr. Wenger, I can."

When'd Alexander sneak up behind him? "Wenghold, sir. Wenghold."

"I prefer to stay clean-shaven. Much easier on a woman's tender face, you know." The feller smirked. "Oh, by the way. Did I return in the allotted time?"

"What?" John swiped his hand across his forehead. Was this man a wizard? Doggone, if that weren't another reason for him to stay away from Emma.

"You know, the time you allowed before you planned to come looking for us. I saw you pull your watch from your pocket as we were leaving. Tell me I'm wrong, and I'll apologize."

"Emma's my woman, ya know." It were a right good thing Obed was standin' there or he'd clobber the guy.

"Emma is her own woman. I'm surprised you don't know that." Alexander leaned one shoulder against the wall and gripped his lapels.

"Well, that might be, but I'm the one who done proposed to her."

"And I shall repeat my earlier statement—I didn't hear her accept. Did you?"

"Don't matter. Emma ain't a big talker, 'specially when so many ears are a- listenin'. She'll tell me when we're alone."

Wynston reached into the inside pocket of his coat. "I almost forgot. Emma asked me to give this to you." He handed John a folded piece of paper.

"What is it?"

"Well, I can't be certain, but I think, by the looks of it, that it could be a note of some kind."

A real smart aleck, this baby-face. "Ya think I'm stupid?"

"I don't know you well enough to tell you what I think. Perhaps by the time I leave Kansas, I'll be able to answer that question."

Obed motioned toward the parlor. "I tell you what, Wynston. Why don't you and me go back into the party and let John read his note by himself? I'm thinking this conversation needs a chance to cool down a bit."

"Whatever you say, Reverend." Wynston gave John a punch on the shoulder as he left.

John waited until both men were gone, then made his way to the kitchen. Somethin' gnawin' way down deep told him he oughta be sittin'. He lowered himself to a chair, but laid the note on the table. No matter what them words said, he had him a feelin' it weren't gonna be good news. He knowed she had some purty pink paper to write on, but she writ these words on plain paper. A shudder wiggled across his shoulders. Couldn't put it off no longer.

The paper crinkled as he unfolded it, and he moved the lamp on the table a bit closer. Them were little letters she put in them words, and there weren't very many of 'em.

John:
I need time.
Emma

Time? Time for what? It don't take a whole lot of time to say yes… and no was even shorter. Did time mean he should stay away tonight, or tomorrow, or the next day? He propped his elbows on the table and cradled his forehead in his hands. Doggone if he knowed what to do next.

Three words, and he might as well've been gut punched.

FIVE

Emma settled into her chair in front of the fire and opened her
Bible. The night had been long and sleepless. Today, with New
Year's day being an official holiday, there would not be the normal
routine of waiting on customers to keep her busy enough to not dwell
on last night's fiasco. She turned to Psalm sixty-two, her reading for
today, and her gaze drifted to verse five, which was already underlined.
My soul, wait thou only upon God; for my expectation is from him. When had
she underlined this verse? And why?

She rested her head on the back of her chair and closed her eyes.
To mark in a Bible was considered a sin, according to her papa. Yet,
she'd found it to be comforting, and most of the time knew where to
look for a special verse, even what side of the page. But this one—

A knock on the door broke her reverie. Callers before daylight
would mean one of two things. Trouble, or—

"Emma? You awake?"

Trouble, or John, and right now it was impossible to tell the two
apart.

She stood and went to the door, opening it only a crack. "I'm
awake. Didn't Wynston give you my note?"

"He did, but I got me some words I need to say. It won't take long."

She opened the door so he could enter, and he went straight to the
kitchen table and straddled a chair.

"It is too early for coffee?" He blew into his hands and rubbed them together. "Right cold out there this morning."

"Did you ride in from the Feather this morning?"

"No. I bedded down at Henrietta's boardinghouse last night. Doggone if I could sleep, though. I'm headin' home now. Just had me a few words I want to tell ya b'fore I take my leave."

Emma poked a couple of sticks of wood into the stove, and sat the coffee pot on the burner. "Shouldn't take long for it to heat. You shouldn't be here, you know. If anyone sees you here with me, alone, it will cause gossip." She sat down opposite of him. "Besides, I told you I needed time."

He rubbed his chin. "I knowed what ya said. Ya had all night, ain't that enough?"

"No, John. That isn't enough time."

"I guess I figgered all ya'd need to utter is yes or no."

"It's much more complicated than that. Did you even hear what you chose to yell at me last night, with nearly all of Cedar Bluff present?"

"Didn't rightly choose to holler, but I did have a right hard time a-hearin' myself think 'til them fiddles stopped, and them words done rolled past my lips so fast I couldn't stop 'em. I do recollect askin' ya to marry up with me."

Emma crossed her arms on the table and leaned across them. "No, John. You didn't ask me to marry you—you asked what I thought about you and me getting *hitched*."

"Don't them words say the same thing?"

She stood and made her way to the stove. "When you want to come to town in the buggy, what do you have to do?"

He frowned. "Is this here one of them trick questions where no matter how I answer I'm gonna be in trouble?"

"No, it's not a trick question." She took two cups from the shelf by the stove and set them on the table. "What do you do to get to town in the buggy?"

"I reckon ya already know the answer, but just so's we's clear, first thing I do is hitch up old Charley."

"Exactly." She lifted the coffee pot from the stove and filled their cups before sitting again.

"Whew! I said that one right? Thought sure as crankin' a man's nose will up and make his eyes cross, you was gonna try to make me say words what would prove somethin'."

Emma closed her eyes and shook her head. "Let's try it one more time. Where's Charley now?"

"Out front, unless he done took off."

"And what did you do to keep him from running away?"

He grinned and waggled his finger at her. "Ya done gave me another easy one, didn't ya? What I done was loop them reins two times 'round that there hitchin' rail. See—if I'd wound 'em three times, it'd be too tight, and iffen I'd a twirled it 'round one time that old geldin' would more'n likely toss his head and pull it right loose, then off he'd go like one of them horseflies lookin' for a horse's rump." He tilted his head. "Course, him already bein' a horse 'n all, I reckon that don't make much sense."

The man just didn't understand. The lump in Emma's throat threatened to block any words, but she swallowed. "I think you should leave now. It's getting light, and if anyone should see Charley *hitched* out front—with today a holiday—they might think it inappropriate."

"But we ain't talked, yet, and I still got coffee. You kickin' me out, Emma-girl?"

She stood and walked to the door. "Not kicking you out, John. I've already told you—I need time. Please, give me at least a week before you ask me again."

He hesitated just a bit at the open door. "I surely do wish I had me an idee what words it was ya was expectin' me to say." He brushed his knuckles across her cheek. "I'll give ya time."

With the click of the door as it closed, Emma allowed the tears to roll. While she'd tried to get him to understand how she felt about his word choice, he uttered one sentence that spoke louder than his so-called proposal. *I surely do wish I had me an idee what words it was ya was expectin' me to say.* Expected him to say. Last night was a fiasco because she'd *expected,* and she'd learned a long time ago that a disappointment was nothing more than a broken expectation. And for the most part, it was because she'd put an expectation on someone or something that had no idea or power to fulfill the hope it embodied. Only upon God—her expectation must come from Him alone.

From the time John invited her to go to Henrietta's party, until right now, she'd expected things from him that—had she been honest with herself—she knew he would never do. She'd been foolish to anticipate his reaction to her new dress or hair style. He could tell you at a glance if a horse was sound, or judge the weight of a steer on the way to market. He could look at the clouds and predict the weather, and knew every inch of his Feather ranch as well as a she knew every detail of her mercantile. But to expect him to notice her dress, or hairstyle, or even speak words she wanted to hear—well, she'd set herself up for that disappointment.

In the first place, by the time John got to the party, he had to be frustrated. To have buggy trouble so far from town, on such a cold night, certainly wasn't something he planned. And secondly, John Wenghold was never known for his eloquent speech.

She wiped her tears and poured herself a fresh cup of hot coffee. How she hated to admit there was a third factor. Wynston Alexander. She'd welcomed his flattery, even though his boldness made her uncomfortable. It had never been her intent to make John jealous, and she certainly hadn't expected his proposal, but she had to admit that down deep it pleased her that he'd noticed Wynston had singled her out for special attention.

She'd asked for a week, but for the life of her she didn't know why. If John hadn't had buggy trouble, he would have taken her home from the party, and if he'd proposed to her—using the very same words— as they sat snuggled against the cold, she would have said yes without hesitation.

Pride. It was nothing but pride. There was plenty of women around Cedar Bluff who would jump at the chance to take John Wenghold up on such an offer. No, he wasn't a smooth talker or a fancy dresser. In no way would he ever be content in a city. But he was kind and honest, and his integrity was unquestionable.

Fresh tears rolled down her cheeks. What if during the week of time she'd requested, he decided he no longer wanted to know what she thought about her and him "gettin' hitched"?

John slid off of Charley and inspected the buggy he'd left by the side of the road last night. For sure it weren't goin' nowhere 'til he got the wheel fixed, but first he'd need to come back with a wagon to carry it to town. No way he could hitch anything to it 'til—

He slammed the palm of his hand against his forehead. Hitched. It were the *gettin' hitched* what was the wrong words. He shoulda knowed what she was tryin' to tell him, askin' them dumb questions on things she already knowed. He paced the length of the buggy and back. He'd sit, but his rump were sore from bouncin' on the horse's backbone, and he were still a far piece from home.

One thing for certain, he'd not be utterin' them words again real soon. No, siree. *Marry me.* Them's the words she was a-wantin' to hear. He wiped his hand down his face. Could he say 'em? He reckoned he could utter 'em real fine, it were the meanin' part what stopped him. Those nieces of his was always yappin' about love, but how was it a man knowed when it were love? He'd never said nothin' of the sort to any woman b'fore, 'cept his ma, and she'd utter them words right back at him.

For sure he weren't about to ask Obed or Doc, 'specially since they was hitch—married up with Henrietta and Tillie. They'd spill to their women. Askin' Henrietta to keep a secret were like tellin' a tornado to stop twirlin', and Tillie would up and giggle ever' time him and Emma were in the same room, even if it were in church. No. He'd have to figger this out for hisself. He had time—Emma told him give her a week. Seemed to him that were plenty. Seven days was a long time to go without sleepin'.

He grabbed Charley's reins and led him to the buggy. He needed the extra height to be able to heft his leg over the old horse's back. Jumpin' bullfrogs, this gettin' up in years weren't no fun.

Emma carried the empty coffee cups to the sink, then went back to her small parlor and put another log on the fire. She'd had her cry, and enough was enough. With no customers today, she had the entire day to do whatever her heart pleased, and the headache that accompanied long spells of tears was not on her agenda.

After a restless night, she needed sleep, and reading was always a good sleep-maker. There was nothing new in her small library, but she'd close her eyes and choose. That would at least be a surprise. Standing in front of the shelves that housed her precious collection of books, she put one hand on her chair—for balance—and closed her eyes. She fingered along the spines.

"One…two…three…I choose thee."

She pulled a volume from the shelf, but a knock on her kitchen door prevented her from looking at it. Hadn't she just told John to give her a week? What was he doing back so soon? She laid the chosen book in her chair and with great reluctance went to answer the door. She rotated her shoulders and took a deep breath, then pulled the door open.

"Why are you here again, Joh—"

If only she'd not been so hasty.

SIX

"Flo–Florence. Wynston. My, I wasn't expecting visitors so early." Emma swallowed and willed her hands to stop shaking. She wasn't expecting them at all, and certainly not so soon after John left. "Won't you come in?" *Come in and leave soon, please.*

"Thank you, dear." Florence stepped past her. "I apologize for calling at such an hour without invitation. We were both concerned about you." She sat a basket on the table.

Did they plan a picnic? "I thank you for your concern, but I'm quite fine."

Wynston removed his hat and cocked his head toward Emma. "My cousin seems hesitant to tell you we were here earlier."

Emma swallowed. "Earlier?"

He laid his hat on the table and clasped his hands behind his back. "Yes, quite early as a matter of fact. However, it seemed you had company and we thought it best to wait."

Emma bristled. There was no need to deny his insinuation. She and John were adults, and though it might not have been the most proper thing to be alone, she was not going to succumb to Mr. Alexander's implication. "Yes, John came by on his way back to his ranch. We had some things to discuss that required—"

"Secrecy?" Wynston raised one eyebrow.

"Privacy, Mr. Alexander. John Wenghold and I have been friends, very good friends, for a very long time. You know that, Florence. I can assure you that nothing the least bit improper occurred."

"Of course I know that, Emma. I'm afraid my cousin is just a bit overprotective."

Emma forced herself to make eye contact with Wynston. "John Wenghold is the very last person from whom I need protection. He would never do anything to hurt me."

His eyes darkened. "It wasn't your physical safety that concerned me, Emma. Rather, your reputation."

Florence put one hand on her hip. "Wynston Alexander, I'm embarrassed and ashamed of you. To question the reputation of a woman like Emma Ledbetter is unacceptable, and I think you know it."

"You're right, dear cousin." His gaze hadn't wavered, but it had softened. "Please accept my most sincere apology, and I do ask for your forgiveness. As much as I hate to admit it, I was...well, I was jealous and completely out of line."

He was jealous? "Apology accepted, and I do forgive you." She prayed her face wasn't as red as it felt. She'd only seen him as rude, bold, and way too confident. To think he might be jealous was a whole new thought.

Florence rubbed her arm. "Well, now that's settled. We can get on with the real reason we came. We hoped to catch you before breakfast, thus our early visit." She lifted a platter from the basket and removed the towel she'd wrapped it in, revealing a heap of plump, brown, sugar-coated sweets of some sort.

Emma took one and studied it. "Would I be terribly rude if I were to ask what they are?"

Florence and Wynston looked at one another, then both laughed. "You have no idea how disappointed I'd be if you didn't ask," Florence replied. "These, my dear Emma Ledbetter—who is the best cook in all of Cedar Bluff—are called New Year's cookies. They're a fried sweet dough with raisins."

"I've never heard of them." She took a bite. "Oh, my! Those are delicious. How did you come to know about such a delicacy?"

Florence withdrew a piece of paper from the basket. "I have a sweet neighbor in Philadelphia—a German Mennonite lady—who introduced me to this wonderful pastry." She handed the paper to Emma. "This is the recipe. In English they are called New Year's cookies, but I've never been able to pronounce the German name for them, *neeosh coca,* or something like that. My attempt to say the words are usually meet with a smile and a shake of the head."

Emma took the paper and studied the words. *Niejoash Koaka.* "I think I'll stick with the English pronunciation." She waved the paper in the air. "May I keep this recipe?"

"Of course, my dear. I think my neighbor would be pleased to know I shared it with others."

"Was this delicious treat served only on New Year's day?"

Florence shrugged. "I think you could serve them any time, but it did seem to be a traditional New Year's treat."

"I have coffee if you would join me. I'll share these *neeush coca.*"

Florence smiled at Emma. "Yes, by all means stick to the English pronunciation."

It was almost ten o'clock before Florence and Wynston wished her a Happy New Year, and left to return to the Blair home. Emma stacked the dirty dishes and placed them in the sink along with the coffee cups she'd left before. She'd never been in the habit of leaving dirty dishes, but this was a holiday, and she intended to spend what time was left of it doing what she set out to do.

The fire had long gone out in the parlor, but she stirred the hot coals and added more wood, and it didn't take long for it to roar to life once again. *Ahh!* Now to put her feet up and read.

John sat on the floor and stretched his legs toward the fire as far as he could without catchin' his socks on fire. By the time he got home from Emma's and finished morning chores, his feet were numb from the cold. 'Course, he was plumb lucky they weren't frost bit. Charley were a good buggy horse, but he had one gait and one speed—well, one speed anyway. Slower than a fat lady in a sack race, that's what. As for his gait—well, doggone if it weren't like that same lady bumpin' and hoppin' ever' which way so's she can cross the finish line. Funny how he'd never took a notice 'til he had to straddle the animal's bony spine.

He needed to get the buggy wheel fixed. Trouble was, if he was to go back to town, say like tomorrow, he'd have a real hard time not goin' into Emma's. For sure, people would notice, and then he'd have to give 'em an answer, and he weren't about to say Emma told him to stay away. He scratched his head. Well, come to think of it, that ain't exactly what she said. What she said was to give her a week b'fore he asked her again. She never said to stay out of the store. He could do that, by gum. He could go in, like any other customer, but he wouldn't say nary a word about them gettin' hit—married.

He leaned back on his elbows. His feet tingled somethin' awful with the feelin' comin' back. It hurt like thunder, but it were better than havin' 'em froze. One thing for sure—that there fire felt gooder than a skinny-dip on a hot day. He lowered himself to a prone position, and put his hands behind his head. It'd feel real nice to get him some sleep, bein' how last night were nothin' but a toss and tumble. Yes, siree. It'd feel right good.

Morning dawned worse than the night before. A glaze of ice encased everything, making even the grass treacherous underfoot. Tree limbs creaked and popped with the weight of the frozen precipitation, and wind driven snow threatened to make things even more worrisome. There weren't gonna be any way he'd take a horse and wagon out in this just to get a buggy wheel fixed. He couldn't hurry. Be his luck to have one leg go north and the other one south. Doggone it. That'd split him clean up the middle. Sure hoped Emma would give him a "yes" so there'd be somebody here to know if he up and got himself in a pickle.

Emma rubbed a peep-hole through the frost that coated the inside of the big window of the mercantile. Though she didn't expect any customers on a day like this, it wouldn't surprise her to see John trudging down the street. She asked him to give her a week, but she also knew him well enough to know that he'd somehow rationalize his coming earlier. She lit the lamp in the window and unlocked the door—just in case—then hurried back to the warmth of her kitchen.

A bit later, with a hot cup of coffee in front of her, she nibbled on one of two New Year's cookies she'd saved from yesterday. John would like these. He liked anything coated with sugar. She could picture him now—napkin tucked under his chin, taking a bite and brushing the sugar off his hands before taking a sip of his coffee. His eyes would crinkle with satisfaction, and he'd bemoan the fact she'd only saved him one. An involuntary smile parted her lips. If they were to marry, she'd have to put the gumdrop jar under lock and key.

She finished her sweet treat and though tempted to take a bite from the one remaining, she put it back in the biscuit tin. She'd save it for John.

SEVEN

Five days later

John heaved the broken wheel into the back of his wagon then climbed onto the driver's bench and gave the reins a flip. "Hup, Charley, gotta get to town b'fore sunset."

Sunshine for two days, accompanied by a warmish south wind, had made short work of the ice and snow. Though muddy, the road was passable. Ever-changing fluffy white clouds freckled the blue sky, and an occasional meadowlark whistled from atop a stump.

If it weren't for Emma bein' in Cedar Bluff, he'd be content to never leave his ranch. He loved every inch of this prairie and the hills that cradled it. By the middle of spring it would be a sea of grasses, their fronds rollin' like waves as far as the eye could see. Red-winged blackbirds would sway on long stalks of big bluestem, or switch grass, while turkey buzzards circled high above the earth, their keen eyes keepin' watch for signs of food.

John took a long whiff. Oh, the aroma of the prairie. Even today, though the grasses were brown and damp, there was a distinct fragrance that was as sweet to a man who loved these hills as rosewater all packaged up in them blue bottles at the mercantile. Would Emma like it out here so far from everything familiar. Would she miss talking with her lady friends every day? At the end of a long day would she be ready to sit on the porch swing and listen to the night sounds—the howl of the coyotes, the distant bawl of a cow, or the late evening recital of a mocking bird's repertoire? Would she appreciate a stroll to the top of the hill to watch the sun set across his beloved Feather ranch?

How about the winters, during the occasional days on end when travel was impossible, yet chores were demanding? Or—no matter the season—the oft times of not seeing friends or neighbors except on Sunday? Could he ask her to give up the convenience of having all her supplies within a few steps? Of the ability to walk to church, or to visit neighbors without the need of horse and buggy?

One thing sure, stewin' about it weren't gonna fill his belly, and his was a-rumblin'. He climbed onto the wagon seat and gathered the reins. "Hup, Charley. Let's try this here goin' to town again."

Emma unlocked the door to the mercantile and turned to survey her store. George had always unlocked the door. Funny how one simple action triggered the sweetest memories, and how those same recollections unlocked a picture book of memoirs. George would unlock the door, then methodically make his way back to the front of the mercantile, touching each display table as though he were giving it his blessing. He loved this place and the people who entered through its door. She loved it, too.

Would John come to have the same affection for a place so different than his? He was a rancher—had been all his life. His roots joined those of several generations, long before Kansas had been declared a state, and his family tree was as sturdy as a mighty oak. Hard work seemed a tonic for him, the unpredictable Kansas weather nothing more than a challenge. He still sat a horse straight and tall, his body moving in smooth rhythm no matter the animal's gait, never a speck of sunlight between him and the saddle. Would he ever consider a move to town? Could he understand her reluctance to leave?

How could it be that she, Emma Ledbetter, supposedly the knowingest woman for miles around, had no clue as to how John might respond? Well, because he was John, that's why. And sometimes she didn't think John even knew what he planned to do next.

Her shoulders heaved with a sigh. This was no time to stand around. The storm had passed and there would be an influx of customers as people from outlying farms and ranches could once again make it through to purchase supplies. She made her way to the front, straightening anything she found out of place, and breathing in the fragrance of new leather, lamp oil, and candle wax. George would be pleased she'd kept the store.

The clang of the bell above the door announced her first customer of the day, and she turned to greet them—only to come face to face with John. He removed his hat, gave her a sly grin, and locked the door behind him.

"Mornin', Emma-girl." He narrowed the space between them.

Emma's chest tightened and a lump in her throat threatened to block her air supply. She opened her mouth to speak, but he took a step closer and laid his finger across her lips. It was a good thing. She couldn't have uttered a sensible word anyway.

"I know it ain't been a week, like ya told me, but I'd been here sooner iffen ole Charley could skate. I figgered out what it were what got ya so het up 'bout what I hollered at ya when we was at Henrietta's party, and I'm right sorry. I ain't ever gonna use that word again iffen I'm yappin' 'bout you and me." He bent to look her in the eyes. "Ain't ya got nothin' to say back at me?"

She rolled her eyes and pointed to her mouth. Only John, who could spot a snake in the grass at twenty yards, couldn't see that while he had a finger over her mouth, she was unable to speak.

He pulled his finger from her lips as though they were hot. She could only pray they weren't.

"Sorry. Didn't want ya yammerin' b'fore I had a chance to say me them words."

Is that all he had to say? Did he lock the door only because he wanted to tell her he figured out what he'd said that bothered her? Oh, how silly she'd been to get so upset over mere words. She doubted anyone in the room that night thought he was out of line. He was just...John. That fact alone had always been good enough for her. But to tell him now would be like asking him to propose again.

"I was kinda hopin' ya'd have me an answer, but I reckon you're waitin' to hear purtier words. I can say 'em, ya know." He leaned against a table display of pots and pans and crossed his arms. "Can't blame ya none for not talkin'. Don't s'pose you was expectin' me to holler out like that." He ran his hand around the collar of his shirt. "Truth is, it weren't somethin' I took a thought to b'fore I done it."

If only she'd answered him before he started to ramble. He hadn't planned to propose—if that's what she could call it? He could say *purtier* words if she wanted to hear them? She'd told God she would remove all expectations from this man, but perhaps she'd been a bit premature to make such a promise. So John hadn't meant to propose, but now he wanted an answer?

"Doggone it, Emma-girl, ain't ya gonna say nothin?" He pushed away from the counter. "They's customers a-gawkin' in at us. Reckon I'd better unlock the door. Sure wish you'da said somethin."

She grabbed his sleeve. "If you'd just stop talking long enough, I have plenty to say. With one breath you say you want an answer, and with the next you tell me you hadn't planned to propose to me, that it was a surprise to you, too." She glanced toward the front of the store, and sure enough, people were lined up, some with their foreheads pressed against the glass of the door and large front window, gawking. Well, let them look.

"Exactly what is it you want me to say, John? Would it make you happy if I agreed to be your wife? Or would you feel trapped? And what if I said no? Would you be relieved, or discouraged? All these years, and you've never mentioned marriage."

"Well, you was married to George."

"What? John Wenghold, George has been gone for eight years. Eight years! That hasn't been enough time for you to let me know you cared, even a little?"

216

One of his hands cupped her chin, his blue eyes meeting her gaze without a flinch. "Emma-girl, I done cared for you whilst ya still wore pigtails. Then ya up and married George, and I figgered he were too good a friend for me to make a fool of myself bein' all jealous actin' and such."

"But George is gone, John."

He nodded. " I know, but ya know I ain't good sayin' things the right way. It ain't like I never gave a thought to comin' home to ya ever' night and wakin' up beside ya. I had me lots of them kinds of things a-whirlin' around my mind."

"Would it help you to know I had those same thoughts?"

A smile pushed dimples into his cheeks. "Ya did? Iffen I was to say them words again would you—"

"I would."

He grabbed her hands. "Ya mean you'd hit—you'd marry up with me? For real?"

All she could was nod her head. His eyes held the love his lips found it hard to proclaim. But it was enough.

He gathered her in his arms, and the crowd outside erupted in whistles and cheers. "B'fore I unlock that there door... When?"

She could hardly breathe he held her so tight, but she wouldn't complain. "When what?"

"When shall we do it? I figger Obed'll be askin."

She put her hands on his chest and gave a gentle push so she could look at him. "I need a bit of time to think about it. Do you mind?"

He shook his head. "A week again?"

"A few days, at least."

"Five days then. 'Til Sunday. I wanna stand up in church on Sunday, all proud-like, and tell ever'body they's invited to the happiest weddin' day Cedar Bluff has ever had." He gathered her close again and kissed the top of her head. "Ya know that reddish dress ya was wearin' at Henrietta's party?"

So he had noticed! "It was new. I made it especially for you."

"I'd be right down pleased if ya was to wear it when we wed. When

I seed ya in it I knowed it was new, and you was the purtiest thing my eyes ever looked at." He ran his finger down her cheek. "There was little bits of hair a-floatin' on your cheeks, and I just up and wanted to plant me a kiss on 'em."

She chuckled. "On my hair? You wanted to kiss my hair?"

"No, woman—these. I wanted to kiss these." He took her face in his hands and kissed both cheeks. "Truth is, I wanted to do that many a time."

His mustache prickled against her face, but she relished the affection. Not at all what she'd expected—yet hoped for—from the John Wenghold she'd known for so long. A red wedding dress isn't what she ever envisioned, either, but she'd accomplished her goal of getting his attention. And if it pleased him, what did it matter? Maybe he had expectations, too.

EIGHT

Emma stood in front of her wardrobe and studied its contents. The ensuing days had passed in a blur, but now it was Sunday and John would soon arrive to pick her up for church. She'd made him promise to stay home—at least not to come to the mercantile—until today. First of all, she didn't want him traveling back and forth when it was so cold. And secondly, she needed the extra days to think about a date for the wedding, and how she might approach him with the idea of moving to town. The date she'd decided—the last Sunday in January. But convincing John to become a merchant would take some careful thought.

Getting married at the end of the month seemed hurried, in a way. On the other hand, she already had her dress, and it would give John time to adjust to his new surroundings before the spring rush. John was not one to hem-haw around, and if he said no to her first invitation to share the mercantile, it would also be her last. She would need patience to wait for the right time to engage him in a conversation about such a drastic change to his lifestyle.

After fingering through her dresses, she settled on a brown wool with peacock-blue piping around the collar and cuffs and a matching brown hat with the same blue ruching lining the brim. It was modest, yet fashionable, and she knew the blue complimented her silver-streaked hair. She slipped the dress over her head, careful not to dislodge the carefully placed wisps on her cheeks, then took a quick peek into the mirror. In reality, her hair wasn't silver-streaked at all. Gray would be a more accurate description. Still, blue did make it appear more silver. George loved her to wear blue, but would John even notice?

A knock on the door sent tingles down her spine. John was early. John was never late, but seldom early. Was he as anxious to see her as she was to see him again? And how should she receive him? As a friend? As her betrothed? Oh, this was silly. He was both her friend and her husband-to-be. How to greet him had never been an issue. Most days he'd enter, head straight for the jar of gumdrops, and she'd swat him with her feather duster. But the mercantile wasn't open today, and somehow his knocking on the kitchen door and her greeting him with a feather duster didn't seem appropriate this morning. But to fall in his arms was even more inappropriate. She'd never even fallen into George's arms. Oh, it had been so long since she'd been courted. Here she was, the one who always had advice to give, with no idea how to go about this change in her life.

Another knock, and she gave her shoulders a shake. How long had she been standing here, doing nothing to welcome this man? She took a quick peek into the mirror to insure the wispy curls she'd purposely let fall free around her face were still in place. One quick pat on each cheek—she didn't want to appear too pink—and she scurried to open the door.

"Good morning, Emma." Wynston Alexander removed his hat and gave a curt bow. "Your chariot awaits, m'lady. You are going to attend church services this morning, aren't you?"

Did he think she would be impressed? What was he doing here, and what made him think she would attend church with him? He'd not been in the mercantile since the morning he and Florence brought the sweet treats on New Year's day.

"Yes, I do plan to attend church. It's very thoughtful of you to offer, Mr. Alexander, but I have a ride, and he will arrive very soon."

"*He*, you say? Tell me, does this happen to be that Wenger character?"

"Wenghold. His name is John Wenghold, and yes, he's the one."

Disappointment crossed Wynston's face. "I see. Please tell me you won't find it necessary to climb into a buckboard. He does have a buggy, doesn't he?"

"He has a very fine buggy, but if he should choose to bring his buckboard I will be most happy to climb into it. You will see many more farm wagons than buggies in the churchyard today, given the weather and condition of the outlying roads. Safety and convenience are much more a necessity than prestige, here in Cedar Bluff."

Wynston's shoulders lost their proud carriage, and he licked his lips. "Well, then. Perhaps I shall get my bid in earlier next week. Would that be Cedar Bluff proper?"

What to do with the persistent man? She should invite him in, out of the cold, but she didn't want to encourage his company. Neither did she want John to find him in her kitchen, and he'd be arriving any time. "I'm sorry. Next week won't work, nor any time after that. You see, John has asked me to marry him."

"What? You mean that ridiculous display of unfettered restraint when he yelled about *gettin' hitched* at the New Year's eve soiree?"

"Well, there was that. However, we've talked since then, and he made a very proper proposal."

"And you accepted?"

She nodded. "I accepted."

"Do you love him?"

What kind of question was that? And why did he think it appropriate to ask her? She straightened her shoulders and looked him in the eye. "The fact that I accepted his proposal should be a sufficient answer."

His countenance darkened and a frown crept across his forehead. "I see. Forgive me for asking. I must say, however, how pleased I am to have met you after you were so highly touted by Cousin Florence. You're everything she said. I'm only sorry that I didn't meet you before John Wenghold."

Emma gave what she hoped he'd interpret as a friendly smile.

There was no need to beget rudeness with rudeness, but she did want him to understand that her relationship with John went far beyond a proposal of marriage. "I don't recall a time when I didn't know John Wenghold. It was nice meeting you, Wynston Alexander. I'm sure our paths will cross again before you leave Cedar Bluff, and I do hope this conversation will not prove awkward in that meeting."

"No. No. My business dealings with Florence will be wrapped up in another week or so—that is if I can get her back on a train to Philadelphia. She seems more reluctant to leave as each day passes. There must be something about small towns that I don't understand."

"We're very much like a family, you see. There are times when there are arguments and misunderstandings. There are times when we don't much like one another. Yet, at the end of the day, all that is put aside. If one family member is attacked, then all the others will defend. If one is ill, there will be help to fill the gap. It's because we know one another, Mr. Alexander. We don't just pass on the street with a nod."

He tilted his head. "And apparently you know one another so well that you overlook what an outsider might consider rude, uneducated, and simplistic."

Oh, the nerve of that man. "We're simple people. We're not uneducated, and only in a few instances might we be considered rude." *Like this very minute when I would very much like to slam the door in your face.* "Now, I really must close this door. We are both cold from standing like this, and I fear it will take all day for my humble dwelling to get warm again. I trust you and Florence will be in church?"

"Most certainly. Have a good day, Emma Ledbetter. John is a very lucky man, but I must warn you...I don't give up easily." He tipped his hat and walked away with a swagger.

Emma shut the door, then leaned against it. Her cheeks puffed with a long exhalation of air. What did he mean, he didn't give up easily? Didn't he say his business dealings would be finished in another week or so? Did he really think she could be swayed with so much ease? Bold and confident didn't even begin to describe his attitude. Proud and arrogant was a much more fitting description.

She moved from the door and pulled a chair away from the kitchen table so she could sit while she waited for John. Her heartbeat swished in her ears and her face felt flushed. Why were her knees shaking so? Mr. Alexander had done nothing to frighten her or endanger her in any way. However, his insinuations and questions left her troubled. Did his declaration that he didn't give up easily mean he would attempt to woo her? There was no doubt the man was used to getting his way. But why would he question her love for John? And why did it bother her now?

While they'd never declared such, John's love for her, and hers for him, was just…understood. George never said those three magic words, either—until their wedding night. But she knew, she always knew. John's affection for her was no different. Well, perhaps a bit different, but just as deep and steady. They were not young lovers. She'd known the love of a good man for twenty years of marriage. While John had never had a wife he, like a lot of ranchers in the area, would often claim his Feather ranch as his mistress. And in a way she supposed that was a fitting portrayal of his devotion to his patch of Kansas.

People in these parts always spoke of Kansas in the female gender, the prairie as her bosom and the tall grasses as her flowing hair. She was loved in spite of her haughty dry spells when she seemed unwilling to produce anything but wind and dust, or her long periods of tears that would flood the creeks and rivers that were as much a lifeline as blood in her veins. Such mood swings were tolerated because they knew—like a man knows the woman he loves—that after throwing a fit, soft breezes, like warm kisses, would be the reward of the day, with the promise of nights so fragrant and sweet they'd beg dawn to tarry so they could rest in her embrace a bit longer.

Emma rested her elbows on the table and clenched her hands. How could she ask John to give up the Feather? How did the wives of these men share their love for the land? Were they jealous? Did it mean giving up their own needs so that the needs of this so-called mistress might be met?

Yet, her love for the mercantile was just as deep and strong. A dichotomy of character, perhaps, with both its refusal to pander to or be known as either male or female, opting rather to satisfy the needs of both. That's what made the partnership with George so meaningful. They worked together, long and hard, to provide their customers with both the essentials as well as the frippery. As male and female, husband and wife, they understood the needs of their respective gender, while giving ear and respecting the oft times unspoken needs and wants of the opposite sex. It wasn't that she was more knowing than others, but rather that she'd learned to listen with her eyes and heart as well as her ears.

She stood and went to check her appearance again. With her hands on her hips, she leaned close to the mirror. If only the image reflected could tell her what to do.

...whither thou goest...

"That doesn't apply to this situation, Lord. Ruth was following her mother-in-law."

...where thou lodgest...

"Isn't Your word relevant to men as well as women? Couldn't You bring this to John's mind, as well as my own?"

The heart of her husband doth safely trust in her...

"You mean he can't trust me if he moves into town? You mean I—"

Emma stopped. She was arguing with God, of all things. And out loud at that.

Oh, John. Please hurry. We can be early to church for a change.

NINE

John slipped his arm around Emma's waist. It were a good thing Reverend Mason waited 'til after he uttered them last "and give you peace" words b'fore announcin' their planned nuptials. Ever' lady popped up from where they was a-sittin' like a firecracker done exploded under their pew, and now they was a-circlin' like they were comin' in for the kill. He leaned to Emma's ear. "Ain't heered so much cacklin' since there were a skunk in the henhouse, and doggone if I don't feel like the skunk the way them women are a-carryin' on."

She smiled up at him. "Not a skunk, dear John...a sly old fox."

Well, now, if that didn't slice him the biggest piece of pie. He'd been named a lot of things, but couldn't recollect *sly old fox* bein' one of 'em. 'Course he'da liked it better if that there *old* weren't connected.

"Old?" He winked at her and didn't much care whose tongue would wag about it. She was his intended, and by granny, he'd wink all he wanted. "Emma-girl, that'd make you my little vixen."

She jabbed her elbow in his ribs. "You behave yourself."

He'd never understand how she could say words without movin' her mouth, but it pleased him that she turned pink as a summer rose.

Henrietta Mason pumped her way through the crowd of women, and they parted like the Red Sea. She stopped square in front of him and Emma and took a deep breath. She were standin' so close, it was a wonder they didn't get sucked right in. 'Twas plumb scary to think that suck of air was just primin' the pump. Enough words were gonna come gushin' out it'd be like gettin' caught in a Kansas thunderstorm. She clapped her hands twice and ever' mouth that were open slammed shut like they was on a spring.

"Oh, I'm so happy for you both. I told Obed, when I heard John had been at your house so early on New Year's day, I said to him, 'Obed, dear, you mark my word. John Wenghold is asking Emma to marry him. You just wait and see.' Of course, Obed told me to not say a word, and I said to him, I said, 'Now, Obed dear, you know I don't gossip.'"

John slid a bit sideways. If he so much as took a deep breath, Emma would punch him a good one in the ribs again.

"Now, do tell us all, when is the wedding day? I'll play and sing, of course, and Tillie can bake the cake. And there are others who will be most happy to pitch in and help." She nodded to the crowd of women. "Wouldn't you ladies?" Heads bobbed like a woodpecker on a dead branch. "See, I told you. And you'll need help packing for your big move to John's ranch. Oh, my. Whatever will you do with your mercantile? I can't imagine—"

John raised his hand in hopes it would stop her yappin'. "They's things Emma and me ain't talked about. I reckon we need us a bit of time b'fore we start announcin' more than what you heard the good reverend say. All we got for ya today is we are gettin' married. 'less, of course, Emma wants to say more'n that."

Emma gripped his hand. Hard. "Like John said, we—we haven't had a chance to discuss everything. However, I did choose a date...if John approves, of course."

He shrugged. "Reckon you're the one what got the movin' to do, so it don't matter to me." He wrenched his hand away and put his arm around her shoulders to pull her close.

"Well, then, I've chosen the last Sunday of this month for the wedding."

All them heads stopped their bobbin', and now the mouths what slammed shut were open in big round Os. Doggone if they didn't look like a whole bunch of birdhouses...'til he realized his own chin was hangin' loose. No woman had lived at the Feather since Rachel and her young'uns moved out when she and Daniel got married. Emma were a right bit more persnickety than him 'bout things. He weren't sure he could get all them rooms ready for her in two weeks.

He patted Emma's shoulder. "That don't give ya much time to close up the mercantile, does it? I'll help, if it's worrisome for ya."

She rolled her lips and a frown wrinkled its way across her forehead. Had he up and used wrong words again?

"We'll talk about that later, John. Later, when we don't have an audience."

Them words didn't sound real friendly. Brought back memories of his pa announcin' he'd meet him behind the barn. For certain, that weren't never good.

Emma clasped her hands tight on the way back to her house after church. She expected the women of the community to be excited for her, and she should have known Henrietta would ask such pointed questions. This wasn't at all the way she'd hoped to discuss her desire to have John move to town and help her run the mercantile. What was he thinking? She didn't know if he was waiting on her to talk first or if all the commotion after the announcement of their engagement caused him to be so quiet. John knew everyone in the church, so it should be no surprise to him that there was so much excitement.

They reached the mercantile and John climbed from the wagon, tied Charley to the hitching post, and went around the side of the buggy to help Emma disembark. "You been awful quiet, Emma-girl. Did I say somethin' wrong?"

She gripped his arm with both hands. "You didn't say anything wrong, John. I was concerned that I was the reason you were so quiet. I'm sorry I didn't discuss the date of the wedding with you on the way to church this morning. I thought we would have time to talk after dinner. I should know better. I know she means well, but Henrietta has a way of—"

"That woman talks too much. You s'pose she yammers like that at home all the livelong day?"

"You two have managed to butt heads since the first day you set eyes on one another. I'm sure Obed sees something in her that you've refused to see all these years. Henrietta does talk a lot, but she's a dear friend."

They linked arms and walked to Emma's kitchen door on the side of the mercantile. He opened the door and motioned for her to enter ahead of him.

She slipped her cape from her shoulders and reached for his coat, then stepped into her bedroom and laid them on the bed. If only she knew how to approach him with the idea of living in town.

He lowered himself to a chair by the table and indicated for her to sit across from him when she returned to the kitchen.

"Are you upset I chose the date without talking to you?"

He reached across the table and folded his big hands around hers. "Emma-girl, I'd a-married ya today iffen I didn't think a real weddin' was important to ya. I got a heap more worry 'bout gettin' the Feather all purtied up b'fore you make it your home."

If she was going to say anything, it should be now, but those work-hardened hands held hers so gently, and his eyes said words she didn't suppose he could utter. How could she ask him to leave all that he loved so much? Yet, how could she leave what she and George had labored so long to build? "John? We need to talk."

His eyebrows arched. "Ain't that what we been a-doin'?"

"We have, but this is—" She swallowed and took a deep breath. It was now or never. "The truth is, John, I...I hoped you would agree to move to town. Here. With me." She wasn't prepared for the absolute silence that followed her statement. The clock above the mantle in her small parlor might as well have been a bass drum banging through the house. She leaned closer in an attempt to make him look at her. "Aren't you going to say anything?"

228

He studied their hands for a bit, then slowly released his and leaned back in his chair. "Is you sayin' you don't wanna move to the Feather? I never knowed ya didn't like it out there. All these years, and I never knowed it. Ain't there somethin' in the Bible 'bout you lodgin' where I lodge?"

"There is, but that's what Ruth told her mother-in-law when they left Moab. It wasn't between a man and a woman." How could she make him understand? "It's not that I don't like the Feather. I do. I've always loved it out there. It's just that me and George worked so hard for so long to get the mercantile where it is today. People for miles around depend on me, depend on it being open."

"And there ain't nobody around who could keep it goin'? Is you the onliest one what can order goods, put 'em on the shelves, and sell 'em?"

"It's more than that, John. When was the last time you took a good long look in a mirror?"

"This mornin' right b'fore I come to town." He grinned. "Wanted to make sure there weren't no stray hairs a-stickin' outta my mustache just in case I was to up and plant a kiss on ya."

She put her elbows on the table and rubbed her fingers across her forehead. "Be serious."

He turned sideways in his chair and leaned one elbow on the table. "I ain't never been more seriouser in my life. What is it you was a-wantin' me to see in that mirror?"

"The same thing I see when I look in mine. I see gray in my hair. Crinkles at the corner of my eyes. Smile lines etched around my mouth. Age, John, that's what I see. How much longer do you think you can keep the Feather running like it should? I worry about you. I worry about you being out the cold hunting for strays. I worry about you falling on the ice. I hate it that you have to chop wood all summer so you can keep warm all winter. What if the ax slips? You could bleed to death before anyone would even know you were injured."

His gaze bore into hers. "The onliest thing you said what would be different if I was to move to town, is I wouldn't be huntin' for strays in here." He shook his head. "Ice is ice, no matter where it is. You could take a tumble on it on it, too. And last I knowed, ya have to have somebody cut wood for you so you can keep all warmed up for the winter." He stood and reached for his hat. "I'd sooner up and die in my barn, than have to be cooped up here for the rest of my borned days. Don't never ask me to leave the Feather. I can't do it. I can't."

She looked up at him. "And I can't leave here. I'm sorry."

He plopped his hat on his head, then put his hands on either side of her face and kissed her forehead. "Emma-girl, I was hopin' you'd make the Feather your home, but I won't never ask you to move away from this, if this is what you want."

He opened the door and didn't even bother to close it behind him. Though his shoulders slumped, and his boots lumbered across the porch, he never looked back.

TEN

Emma ran her feather duster over the counter in front of her and prayed no customers would come in today, though there was not even the slightest chance the prayer would be granted. Henrietta, as well as most of the town women, were every day visitors, all with questions and big plans for the wedding. She'd not yet told them there might not be a wedding. John hadn't come back into the mercantile since he walked out on Sunday. If only she knew what to expect. There was that word again. She should have known better than to think, even for one minute, that John would agree to give up his ranch..

Sleep was no longer her friend, and today she wasn't at all sure she could endure Henrietta's shrill voice. She'd run out of believable answers long ago. Tomorrow was Sunday, and no doubt would reveal the truth. Last week she'd been surrounded by well-wishers, but if John didn't come to church tomorrow, how would she respond to the inevitable circle of long faces and questions?

She shuffled to the chair beside the wood stove in the middle of the store. Her head pounded with every step, her shoulders ached, and she could barely swallow against the ever present lump in her throat. Was it possible to be any more miserable?

"Emma? Emma? Oh, there you are."

Henrietta! Emma massaged her temples. Hadn't she just wondered if she could be any more miserable? Evidently the answer was in the affirmative. She stood and turned to greet her friend. "I'm right here, you needn't yell."

"Oh, yes, of course. There you are. Well, so what do you have to tell me today? I have news for you. Did you know Florence's cousin left on the train this morning? Florence didn't go with him, though. Do you think they had a disagreement? I don't know where he went. I asked Carl Rempel, over at the train depot, but he wouldn't—"

No, she didn't know Wynston Alexander had left, but neither did she care. She had much more important matters to think about. "Can we please sit, Henrietta?" Emma indicated another chair by the stove. "I have a feeling this is going to take awhile, and my head hurts too badly to stand."

Concern swept across Henrietta's face. "I'm so sorry, Emma. Here I come in, blustering like usual without giving one thought to how you must feel—what with all the gossip that's going around about you and John. Of course, I wouldn't repeat it, but they are saying that there isn't going to be a wedding after all. But what do they know? All those busybodies. I told them, I said 'if there wasn't going to be a wedding, I'd be the first to know.'" She patted Emma's clenched hands. "You do know John hasn't been to town all week, don't you?"

Emma's eyes misted. She hated to cry, especially in front of Henrietta, but tears flowed with free abandonment no matter how hard she tried to keep them inside. "I am more aware than anyone that he hasn't been to town. It's my fault, you know. I proposed that he move here to Cedar Bluff and help me run the mercantile. I should have known he couldn't leave the Feather." She pulled a handkerchief from her sleeve and wiped her eyes. "Now I don't know what to do."

Henrietta fanned herself with her hands and scooted her chair away from the stove. "You mean you don't want to move to the Feather? Oh, my. I suppose that—"

"You didn't move to Obed's house. Tillie didn't move to Abe's. Why should it be a surprise that I don't want to move to the Feather?"

"I would have moved, Emma, but Obed insisted we live at the

232

boardinghouse. He said Cedar Bluff needed such an establishment, and there was plenty of room there for him to still have an office to conduct church business."

"And Doc and Tillie?"

"Well, you've seen Doc's house. He only used one room and the kitchen for himself, the rest was clinic and patient rooms."

"Do you think I should give up the mercantile?" Did she just ask Henrietta's advice? Well, it was too late to retract it.

Henrietta stood and pulled Emma to her feet. "I think— Oh, stars and fudge, Emma, you're the one who always has the answers for everyone else. I can't believe you're asking me. But since you did, I— Well, I think everything has moved so fast, and John only has one speed. You've been married, but John hasn't. And until the party at my house on New Year's Eve, you both seemed content to continue as you've been since George died. As good friends." She put her arms around Emma. "Give him time."

Emma pulled away from Henrietta's embrace and plopped back down on her chair. "What if he changes his mind? What if the Feather is more important to him than I am?"

"And I imagine John Wenghold is thinking the same thing. Maybe, to him, this mercantile represents your life with George. You're his first love, but he isn't yours."

"Does it bother you that you're not Obed's first love?" She couldn't imagine Henrietta being intimidated by anything, but she had to ask.

Henrietta shook her skirts and moved her chair closer to Emma. "I never knew Obed's first wife, and he didn't ask me to live in the home they made together. But John and George were the best of friends. George's presence still fills the mercantile...and your mind, Emma. I'm sure John must feel it every time he steps in here. I know everyone else does."

Emma jumped to her feet and slammed her hands on her hips. "That's not true. I even changed the name of the store after he died. Remember? It's no longer Ledbetter's Mercantile—it's Emma's Mercantile."

"Oh, my dear friend. You can name it anything you want, but that doesn't change the inside one tiny bit." Henrietta covered her eyes with her hands. "First display table on the right when a customer enters this place—blankets. And to the left— galoshes in the winter, and shoes and boots for the entire family in the summer. Next, on the right—"

"And what do you think that proves?" Emma tried to swallow the lump that threatened to block her airway. Couldn't Henrietta see that there was a purpose for the arrangement?

Henrietta stood and gripped Emma's hands in her own. "It proves that anyone who is familiar with this mercantile can walk in blindfolded and still find exactly what they are looking for. It proves that nothing, absolutely nothing, has changed here on the inside of this place since George left us."

"That's because this arrangement is—is the most effective for purchases." Emma pulled her hands from Henrietta's. It was, wasn't it? George had a reason for everything, and it served them well over the years. He used to tell her, *If it doesn't squeak, there's no need to grease it.*

She folded her arms over her chest. "You don't understand marketing. There's a reason for repetition. A customer doesn't need to waste time looking for what they need when it's right where it was the last time they purchased it."

"Repetition also makes deep ruts—ruts deep enough for you to get stuck in, and thus your chance of ever seeing anything new diminishes. And marketing isn't the reason you've not changed anything. You're afraid that if you don't keep everything just as George left it, you will somehow be disloyal to him."

Emma didn't much like this side of Henrietta—a sensible side that was seldom revealed.

The clang of the bell announced another customer, and a welcome reprieve from Henrietta's newfound *knowing*. Why Henrietta, of all people?

"Go, Emma. I must get back to the boardinghouse." Henrietta gave her a peck on the cheek. "Try not to worry." She turned to leave, then twirled back around. "Florence is the customer. Be sure and ask her about her cousin." She turned again and nodded to the woman who'd entered. "I was just leaving, Florence. Now, if you have anything you want to tell Emma, you can do it in private."

Emma pressed her palms against her forehead. Just what she needed—Florence Blair with news, no doubt, about Wynston Alexander leaving Cedar Bluff. She met Florence in the aisle and attempted a smile. "I imagine you heard Henrietta's not-so-subtle remark."

Florence nodded. "Wynston's leaving is the very reason I'm here. I'm not surprised Henrietta is curious. All of Cedar Bluff seems to have their own opinions as to my dear cousin's departure."

"Please sit." She indicated a chair for her customer and sat back onto her own. "Now, what is it about Wynston's leaving that brought you here?" Anything to get her own mind off John.

"Thank you for asking, because I wasn't at all sure how to start this conversation." Florence seated herself next to Emma and straightened her skirt. "I'm sure Henrietta has apprised you of the town's predictions concerning you and John Wenghold."

Emma leaned her head back and stretched her neck from side to side. "Oh, Florence, you really don't think Henrietta would pass up such an opportunity, do you?"

Florence studied her hands. "No, I suppose not."

Emma fidgeted with the cuff of one sleeve. Over the years, she'd been the one to listen to other ladies' woes, but had never felt it necessary to share her own. Yet, she'd never known Florence Blair to be anything but honest and discreet. And now, more than ever before, she did need to talk with someone. Her shoulders heaved as she took a deep breath. "Well, the truth is, I have no idea what is happening. I asked something of John that I had no business asking. He left, Florence. He left without even so much as giving me one last look, and I've not heard from him or seen him since. If he doesn't come to town for church tomorrow, then I think I can assume the wedding is off."

"You would *assume* without talking with John? Oh, Emma, I don't think that's wise. Whatever you asked of him, whether you should have or not, can't be bad enough to call off your wedding. You don't know why he hasn't come to town. Perhaps he's ill. Or maybe he feels he needs to be at the ranch for some reason. It isn't like John to just walk away."

Worry struck hard. "Why, I didn't even think he might be ill or hurt. My request included those very reasons. Do you think I should check on him?" She stood, but Florence pulled her back onto her chair.

"I do, but wait. Let me tell you why I'm here before you go. You know that Wynston left, but you don't know the reason. He had business in Chicago and doesn't plan to return to Cedar Bluff."

Emma bit the tip of her tongue. He didn't plan to return to Cedar Bluff? What happened to his not giving up easily?

Florence tapped Emma's knee. "Are you listening, dear? You seem to have wandered away from the conversation."

"I'm sorry." Emma straightened her shoulders. "Please, continue."

The slightest frown creased Florence's forehead. "I'm wondering, depending on what you and John decide, of course, if you'd consider accompanying me back to Philadelphia. I could use the companionship, and if things don't work out for you and John, I'm guessing you could use a time away yourself. You don't have to give me an answer now, but please consider it."

Emma's mouth was so dry she wasn't even sure she could get words past her lips. "Philadelphia? And what would I do about the mercantile? I—I don't feel comfortable leaving it closed." Wasn't that the argument she'd used to try to persuade John to move to town? What would he think if she were to leave now?

"I thought of that, and don't have an answer. I'm sure, should you decide to travel with me, something can be worked out to your approval. I'm not asking for a commitment today, but please pray about it."

"Oh, Florence, I've prayed so hard this past week, but it seems the heavens are closed. I no longer even have the words and my mind wanders so much I feel guilty. I can't remember the last time I felt the Lord was so far away."

Florence leaned her head against Emma's. "God hasn't moved, Emma. You'd be the first one to tell anyone that very thing. We don't always need words, you know. He knows our hearts. Just rest in His presence." She stood and rubbed the small of her back. "Now, I must get on home, and I think you're wanting to get to John's. Tomorrow is the Lord's Day. Let's see what He has in it for us."

Emma followed her to the door, and locked it behind her. She had no idea how John would react to her visit, but she couldn't sit at home and wonder any longer.

ELEVEN

John poured two cups of coffee and sat one in front of Emma and one at his place at the table. "If I'da knowed ya was comin', I'da had somethin' besides coffee to offer ya."

"I didn't come to eat, John. I came because—"

"B'cause I acted like a spoiled boy? Can't say I blame ya none. My ma woulda switched me good for walkin' out like I done, Emma-girl. I ain't one bit proud."

Emma wound her fingers around his. "I came because I was worried about you—and to ask you to forgive me for trying to persuade you to do something so very much against who you are."

"Who am I? I been doin' a whole lot of thinkin', and doggone if I can figger out how a man like me—a crippled up ole piece of rawhide what knows more about cows and horses than about the ways of a woman—ever thought a lady like you could be happy livin' stuck out in these here hills like a rose in a potato patch."

"You're not—"

He put his finger over her lips. He weren't through talkin'. If she shut him up now, he might never get it all said. "I reckon I know plenty about what I'm not. I ain't fancy talkin' like some others ya know. Them words are right smooth soundin' in my head, but when I spit 'em out they's all tangled. I dance like I'm pumpin' water, and mama cows has kicked and wallered me so much I walk with a hitch."

He folded his hands on top of the table. "Mostly, Emma-girl, I ain't... and can't never be...George." There, he done said it. Been thinkin' on it all week, but never let the walls hear him utter the words.

"I know you're not George. I never wanted—"

He reached across the table and grasped her hands. "The two of ya was so close, it were hard to tell ya apart iffen ya wasn't standin' side by side. We was real good friends, me and George, but it's plumb foolish for me to think on takin' his place when ya ain't never really turned loose of him. I knowed it all along, but was hopin' again' it."

She pulled her hands from his and crossed her arms across her bosom. "It's been eight years, John. I've had plenty of time to 'turn him loose,' as you put it."

He nodded. "Plenty of time, but ya ain't done it. Ever'thing is the same as the day he done left us. I can't never move a candy jar without getting plunked by your feather duster."

"I *plunk* you with my duster because you steal gumdrops, not because you move a candy jar."

"Ya got three jars of sweets on the counter. They's lemon drops on the left, gumdrops in the middle, and licorice on the right. Them's always been sittin' the same place ever since you and George started the mercantile. Milk pails hang third nail on the left. Iffen I be needin' a blanket, I walk in and yank me one off the first table on the right. Iffen I be—"

"Stop. It's good marketing, not because of George. It's...it's convenient for customers to know—"

"Yeah, convenient, but it ain't good marketing." He didn't want no argument. He knowed a long time ago Emma didn't never lose. George told him that nugget of wisdom long 'bout two weeks after they said their I dos. "Iffen you'd make 'em look for stuff, they might see somethin' they didn't knowed they needed. But, Emma-girl, we's gettin' on the wrong road."

She moved her hands to her lap. "So, if you move to town, you think you will be compared to George? John, we've known one another for years. The three of us were good friends. Yes, I loved

George…very much. But now I—"

John stood, and once again put his finger over her lips. "Don't say it, Emma. Don't say words what you don't mean. Anyways don't mean yet. Could be one day, but not now."

She pulled his hand away from her mouth. "But I do—"

He shook his head. "I ain't hankerin' to hear them words 'til I'm ready to say 'em back at ya."

"You're not ready? You asked me to marry you, John, but you're not ready?"

"I ain't never done this b'fore, Emma. I ain't sperienced like you. I know I done liked you a whole lot for a long time, even b'fore ya choosed George. I just ain't sure if it's that word, you know."

"You mean the love word? John, George never told me he loved me until our— Until the first night we were married."

He ran his hand through his hair. "That there is what I mean. I ain't George. Movin' into the mercantile won't never make me George. You'd be plumb disappointed with me, and I ain't at all sure I could stand that. I reckon I be needin' some time to put some thinkin' on it a bit longer."

Emma's eyes puddled. "Then you're saying you don't want to marry me after all?"

John pulled her to her feet and cradled her head against his chest. "Oh, Emma-girl. I wanna marry you worser'n I ever wanted anything in all my borned days. But I can't do it 'til I know I won't never wonder iffen it's me or George you're a-lookin' at across the table or layin' aside at nighttime." He kissed the top of her head. "Ya better go home. I'll saddle up and ride with ya to make sure ya don't come on any trouble."

She stepped away. "No, I'll be fine. I guess there's nothing else I can say for now. You know where I am if you decide to change your mind."

John watched her shuffle to the door, then climb into her buggy. Not the usual spry Emma he'd known for so long. No, this were more like her feet was in a sack full've big ole rocks. He leaned against a porch pillar as she drove away, his heart so heavy he were gonna need a winch to hoist it back in place.

Emma poked another log onto the fire in the fireplace, settled into her chair, and lifted George's precious book, *Sonnets from the Portuguese*, from the side table between their two chairs. Two chairs. John was right. She'd kept things just the same ever since George died—his chair beside hers, the Browning's sonnets with the hank of yarn marking George's favorite number forty-three. The sameness gave her comfort, the same as the familiar arrangement in the mercantile. She never realized others thought it strange, or that John Wenghold was intimidated by it. Was she holding on too tight? Was she afraid of the changes a life with John would mean? Was she being unrealistic to want him to move to town?

John suggested she take time—that *they* take time—to think about their relationship. Perhaps she should accept Florence's invitation to accompany her to Penn-sylvania. She'd apprise her of that very thing in church tomorrow.

Two weeks later

A shaft of morning sun speared through the cloud cover overhead and set the frost covered bushes along the road to Cedar Bluff aglow. The wheels of John's buggy crunched and bumped over the frozen ground, while his rear slapped the hard seat with every jolt like a beaver's tail warnin' of danger. Iffen he had a lick of good sense, he'd've stayed cozied up to the fire, but what teensy bit of smarts he could claim had done disappeared when he told Emma he needed time to figger things out. Well, by gum, he got it all figgered, and if that good woman would still have him, he'd be movin' to town. Ty and Sam could take care of things at the Feather during the winter. Might be right nice to not have to worry about huntin' strays and feedin' critters when the snow was a- blowin'. Maybe come spring, Emma might give a thought to movin' to the ranch. He hunched his shoulders against the bitter wind. Yes, siree. He done had things figgered real fine. Doggone, he'd plumb up and whistle a tune if it weren't too cold to pucker.

John wrapped the reins around the brake handle, then climbed from the buggy and stomped his feet to get the feeling back into them. There weren't no other horses hitched to the rail in front of the mercantile, and he was right glad of it. Now, if only there'd be no womenfolk gossipin' and gigglin' inside. Hard tellin' what peoples were thinkin' with him not comin' to town for so long. He hobbled to the door. If Emma were alone, he'd hustle right in and not give a worry to the bell clangin'. Weren't no use a-sneakin'.

Once inside, he removed his hat and smoothed his mustache before steppin' to the front counter. His feet were so cold they felt like stumps, and prickles shot clean up his leg with ever' step. It were a good thing Emma weren't standin' there watchin' him totter, but where was she?

"Emma-girl? You in here?" He lifted the lid of the gumdrop jar and it pealed like a bell when he glass hit glass. He chortled. That'd bring her a-runnin'.

Footsteps approached from behind the curtain, and he pulled his shoulders back so he'd be standin' straighter. Only problem were, now he couldn't tell if the buzzy feelin' in his legs was because his toes were 'bout froze off, or if thinkin' of proposin'...again...was makin' him shiver.

"Is that you, John Wenghold?" Albert Harvey stepped from behind the curtain. "Emma said if I heard a candy jar lid clang it would be you trying to steal gumdrops."

Well, now, if that wouldn't take the chirp out of a cricket. Albert didn't fit nowhere in the plans he'd made. "Good to see ya, Albert, but I was hopin' to have me some time with Emma."

Albert shook his head. "Afraid that won't be possible. Emma's gone."

John's legs wobbled and his chest went as tight as if someone throwed a lariat around him and pulled tight. He placed both palms on the counter to steady himself and leaned toward Albert. "What do ya mean, 'Emma's gone'?" If he coulda stood on one leg without fallin' to the floor in a heap, he'd be kickin' hisself for takin' so long to figger stuff out. He wiped at his eyes with the back of his wrist. "Ya don't mean—"

Understanding swept across Albert's face and he grabbed John's hands. "Oh, no, John. She's not *gone* gone. Florence Blair returned to Philadelphia and asked Emma to accompany her, that's all. She'll be back."

"When?"

A wrinkle of question puckered between Albert's bushy eyebrows. "When did they leave, or when will she return?"

"Both, I reckon." If he were a gamblin' man, he'd bet his ranch it were soon after he uttered them things 'bout needin' time to think. What was worser than her leavin' was thinkin' of that slick-faced cousin of Florence's swoopin' in like a hawk.

Albert twisted his mouth to one side and scratched his head. "Going on two weeks ago, I think. Yes, for sure it was two weeks today when she asked if I could take care of the mercantile while she was gone."

John plopped his hat on his head. "I shore would like to yap at ya 'bout how you be likin' measurin' out dress goods and sellin' lady's pretties, but I don't got the time now."

"There's a whole lot more to it than selling lady's pretties." Albert laughed. "Where you going in such a hurry, anyway?"

John turned in the middle of the aisle. "Gonna see Carl Rempel 'bout a ticket on the first train to Philadelphia, that's where!"

TWELVE

Emma rubbed her temples in an attempt to stop the whirl of so many thoughts—each one pounding for attention. Whatever made her think she could forget her problems if she accompanied Florence to this busy, noisy part of the world? Her hostess was gracious and the accommodations beyond anything she'd ever experienced. While the food was not the simple fare she was accustomed to, it was wonderful and—best of all—she didn't have to prepare it.

Yet she was homesick for her hills and the prairie they embraced. She missed the daily gathering of Cedar Bluff women who made sure she knew all the news from around the area. And she missed John Wenghold. Her hands stopped the circular motions against her temples. Like finding a tiny speck of gold in an otherwise nondescript rock, she'd just admitted to herself what she'd never voiced aloud. She missed John.

Oh, not in the way she missed George after he left her, though her grief had been long and so very painful. But she knew his leaving was not his choice. Now, the realization of her separation from John took on a new insight. They were apart, not because John chose to leave her, but because she—Emma Ledbetter—allowed four walls full of merchandise to come between them. Had she not made changes because of George? Or was it because she was afraid of change? Had she sought comfort in memories rather than in the open arms of Jesus?

She leaned her head against the back of the chair. "Lord, what have I done?" She'd advised others, over and over again, to look to God's Word for the answers to what was bothering them. She'd quoted scripture to young wives, admonishing them to honor their husbands, to love them and never try to change them. Yet that's what she'd attempted to do with John.

Now she'd possibly alienated the person she missed so much she could see his face in her mind's eye—his sun baked-face with the boyish dimples and eyes that could melt her into a puddle of— She gasped. Of *love*.

Emma bolted to her feet. There it was. She loved him. She loved John Wenghold. But what if he never got things "figgered out"? Would they still be close friends? Oh, how she would miss their comfortable friendship, their companionable silence, and their heated arguments. How much different would it be should they marry? What if this entire incident left them stranded on opposite sides of a chasm that neither were willing to cross?

She'd been in too big a hurry to leave Cedar Bluff, and too hurt and confused to stay. Even before she boarded the train with Florence, she knew she'd been wrong to ask John to move to town. It would be like asking George to ride the hills looking for strays day after day. It was never in either of them to be anything but who they were, and she was wrong to think it. Would he give her a chance to tell him she'd live on his ranch? Would he listen to her voice her love and believe she'd live anywhere with him, as long as they could be together? Or would her departure without telling him only widen the gap between them?

Emma parted the lace curtains beside her chair and looked out over Florence's spacious backyard. Though still wearing its brown winter garb, it was beautiful to her. The prairie was brown in winter, too, although it held so many different shades of brown its expanse never grew old.

A soft pad of footsteps approaching signaled she wasn't alone. She'd left her door open purposely so Florence would know she was welcome to enter. Emma had spent too many days holed up and aloof, and her kind friend would never think of intruding on her privacy.

"Miz Ledbetter, ma'am." Colleen, the sweet Irish girl Florence employed, stood at the doorway. Not the voice Emma had expected, but Emma couldn't hold back a smile. Even from a distance, Emma could see the twinkle in Colleen's eyes, and her freckles almost popped with excitement.

Emma beckoned her to step into the room. "My goodness, what has turned your face as red as your hair?"

Colleen giggled and stepped closer. "Ya have a visitor, ma'am." She leaned to whisper. "It's—"

"No, don't tell her. I want it to be a surprise."

Wynston Alexander. Another voice she hadn't expected to hear. Hadn't Florence said he'd gone to Chicago on business? Yet, here he stood, nearly filling the doorway.

She folded her hands in her lap in hopes he wouldn't see them shaking. "It is a surprise, Mr. Alexander. I…I thought you were in Chicago."

Though uninvited, he stepped into the room and leaned against the wall on the other side of the window beside her chair. "I was, but when Florence apprised me of your presence in her home, I decided Philadelphia held more urgent business than Chicago. And, by the way, you called me *Mister* again. I thought we were past that." He turned to the young girl who remained near, her eyes beaming and face as pink as ever. "You're dismissed, Colleen. Next time you needn't spoil the surprise."

The girl ducked her head, but not before Emma observed her water filled eyes. Emma rose. "Never you mind him, Colleen. I'd much rather have the visitor announced than to be caught by surprise." There, that should soften the blow a bit.

Colleen scurried out, then Emma turned to Wynston. "That was an unnecessary rebuke. I imagine she did exactly what Florence has trained her to do. If you wanted it to be a surprise, then you should have told her so in the first place. Colleen would never have gone against a direct order."

Wynston raised one eyebrow. "You're scolding me?"

"Someone needs to. You embarrassed the poor girl for doing her job."

He shouldered away from the wall. "Clearly are not accustomed to dealing with hired help."

"And clearly you are not accustomed to following rules of propriety. Even in our humble, simplistic, uneducated society in Kansas where we don't deal with hired help, a man would never enter a woman's bedroom without an invitation. Does Florence know you're here?"

He shrugged. "I can't answer that question. I didn't see Florence when I came in."

"Really? And yet I remember you insinuating concern for my reputation as well as my safety when you observed John Wenghold's horse tied to the hitching rail in front of my mercantile on New Year's Day."

"That was an entirely different situation. You were alone with him."

"As I am now, with you." She pointed to the doorway. "I would feel much more at ease if you were to leave, at least until Florence returns and is aware of your presence."

He exaggerated a bow. "I will take my leave, as you suggested. But do remember, Emma Ledbetter, I don't give up easily. Had I not acted so impulsively and assumed you'd be as pleased to see me as I was to learn you were here, perhaps this conversation would have taken a different turn. I have errands to run, but I'll be back. I'll instruct Coleen to tell Florence I shall join you for dinner." He departed.

Relieved that he left without further argument, Emma leaned her head against the crocheted antimacassar that covered the rose tapestry covered chair. She was so very tired and longed to be back in her small living quarters behind the mercantile. If only she knew how John would react upon her return.

She'd just closed her eyes when she sensed the presence of someone near her, and she prayed it wasn't Wynston. With her eyes open just enough to peer through slits, she tried to focus without turning her head. It was Colleen, leaning close enough it caused them both to jump when she opened her eyes wide.

"I'm so sorry, ma'am." She looked behind her then leaned even closer "You have another visitor, ma'am." She straightened, a smile beaming across her cheeks.

"Another visitor?" Emma sat up and smoothed the sides of her hair. "Gracious, dear, I don't know anyone else in this town. Did they give you a name?"

Colleen bobbed her head. "It's a mister. But he doesn't want to come in unless you invite him."

Emma scowled. "Please don't tell me it's Mr. Alexander."

"Oh, no, ma'am. He says his name is John...John—"

Her breath caught. Surely not. "Wenghold? Is his name John Wenghold?"

"Yes, that's it. It's a hard name, isn't it?"

"And you say he's downstairs? In this house?" Oh, my. Now what should she do?

The girl shook her head. "No, ma'am. He's downstairs, but he's not *in* the house. He's standing on the step with his hands in his pockets. He says he won't 'darken no door' 'til you say. I don't know what he means, but he won't come in. I'm afraid Miz Blair will find him standing out there and think I've not—"

Emma pushed herself to her feet and put her arms around the girl. "I'll take care of Florence Blair. You go down and tell him I said he's to meet me in the parlor in fifteen minutes. Show him to the parlor, then you come right back up here and help me pick out something to wear."

Colleen rolled her eyes. "Is he your beau?" She giggled.

Before Emma could answer, a breathless Florence bustled into the room.

"Emma, I found John Wenghold standing on the front steps. I've asked him to wait in the parlor. I hope that meets with your approval." Florence removed her hat and laid it on Emma's bed. "Of course, you will invite him for dinner."

Colleen wrung her hands "I told him he could—"

"Don't you worry." Florence put her arms around the girl's shoulders. "I know this man and I'm quite sure he told you he wouldn't even enter the house until Emma gave him permission."

"Yes, ma'am. Is that what it means to 'darken no door'."

"Exactly. Now you hurry back down and assure him that Emma will join him shortly. Oh, and you might suggest he sit. Knowing John, he won't make a move until invited."

Colleen curtsied. "Yes ma'am." She grinned at Emma. "I like your brown dress, Miz Emma. The one with the blue edging." She turned to Florence. "She asked me to help her, Miz Blair."

"Of course, dear. Now you do as I asked, and I'll make sure Emma gets dressed."

When the young girl left, Emma motioned for Florence to step closer. "Wynston was here. He said to tell you he'd return for dinner."

Florence's eyes snapped. "You leave him to me. I guarantee you, he'll not bother you again. Now, let's get you dressed. However, you'll not wear that dreary brown dress. I have a feeling this visitation calls for something a bit happier." She searched through the wardrobe, then pulled a cobalt blue garment from its hanger and held it against Emma. "I knew it. This will fit you just fine, and I have a lovely shawl to go with it."

Emma entered the parlor with hesitation. Would she face an angry John? Would he give her an opportunity to declare her feelings and assure him she'd live on the Feather with him with no regrets? She stood for a brief moment, peering at the back of the man she now knew she loved, while he stood with his hands clasped behind him, peering out the window.

"I can't believe you're here." Her words broke the silence as though she had shouted from the rooftop.

He turned, his gaze moving from head to foot then up to her own eyes. Without a word, he took three long strides and gathered her to him. "I ain't never said these words 'cept to my ma, but Emma

Ledbetter, I done love you even more than my ranch, and I'll live wherever you want as long as it's with you."

Emma squirmed away from him just enough she could see his face. "No, John. You were right. I *was* hanging on to George. But being here, away from you, made me realize how much I truly love you. I was wrong to even suggest you give up your ranch, and I'll declare before God and all of Cedar Bluff that I will be honored to be the wife of John Wenghold, and *where thou lodgest, I will lodge.*"

John cradled her face in his hands. "You tellin' me you'll give up the mercantile and move out to the Feather with me?"

"The minute they pronounce us man and wife, John Wenghold."

He winked and then lowered his face to hers, stopping just inches from her lips. "Ya tell me iffen I don't get this right, you hear?"

Emma smiled at him as they finally drew apart. "John Wenghold— that was the most 'right' thing ever."

EPILOGUE

Late March, 1880

Emma leaned to peer into the mirror of the small room that at one time served as the pastor's office. Instead of the gray hair and wrinkles she was accustomed to seeing, she beheld the face of a bride. It was different this time, not in a bad way, just...different.

Emma's Mercantile was no longer hers. Albert and Lark had approached her with an offer to buy the establishment, and she was happy to oblige them. The mercantile she and George so lovingly maintained would continue as a hub for trade, and—best yet—her soon-to-be niece-in-law was taking Emma's place. So it was staying in the family.

The weeks since returning from Philadelphia had been busy ones. Yet, in the dark of night, when all was quiet, she'd prayed and sought the Lord's help in saying goodbye to George. While she never wanted to forget him, and he would always be her first love, she didn't want his presence to remain between her and John. It had come slowly— this last farewell of a sort. And not until she was able to pack away the Sonnets of the Portuguese did she realize she'd finally released him. John never mentioned him again since that day in the mercantile, and neither had she pursued the subject.

Now, today was their wedding day, and she could embrace the

difference. The reality of life that comes with age, knowing that it was okay to dream, but better to take each day as a gift with grateful acceptance. Being certain she had the love of a good man, and that her love for him held hope, free of expectations.

She took one last look to make sure the wisps of hair were loose and lay against her cheek the way John requested, then smoothed the front of the red dress she'd worn to Henrietta's soiree—again, at John's request.

"Emma, you ready? The church is full and waiting." Ty Morgan slipped into the room and strode to her. "You have no idea how beautiful you look, dear Emma. You will take John's breath away."

She sighed. "And you have no idea how much I appreciate those kind words, my boy. You know what? I feel beautiful, and so blessed." She hooked her arm through his crooked elbow. "Thank you for being my escort."

He kissed her cheek. "I'm honored. Now, wait until you see what my wife and her sisters have done for you. Promise me you won't cry. Even after these past few years with Robin, I have no idea what to do with tears."

As soon as they stepped into the back of the church, tears began to flow. Between each window hung a swag of red and white paper hearts strung on twine. On each window sill was a nest structured of small twigs, and nestled in each nest was a glass open top dome which protected the flame of the white candle within. There was an expectant hush, then John stepped toward her. What was he doing? Wasn't he supposed to wait for her.

"Here we go, Emma. Meet him."

"What?"

"Trust me."

Why was everyone so quiet?

As they reached the middle of the aisle, John grasped her hands. His arms shook, but his gaze never wavered.

"Emma-girl. I never knowed how full a heart could get without bustin'. I never knowed I would one day lay awake all night thinkin' of a woman the way I figger a man thinks of his love. I never knowed lovin' a woman would be so hard, and so easy all at the same time. And I never figgered that I'd ever be standin' here like this, pledgin' to love you till I ain't got breath. I wanna learn all the words you wanna hear. I wanna be the man what never makes ya cry, but who'll wipe them tears away if ya do. I knowed I could utter all this when we was alone, but I reckon ever'body here oughta know my feelin's for ya. I love ya, Emma-girl. Reckon I always have, ever since ya was in pigtails, and I know for right certain I always will."

He turned to Obed. "I reckon ya oughta say the words what makes us married, so I can kiss her, b'cause iffen ya don't hurry, I'm gonna do it anyway."

A titter ran through the audience, but was soon drowned out by the organ. Not until Obed introduced them as Mr. and Mrs. John Wenghold, did Emma's legs stop shaking, and she welcomed John's lips on hers.

Emma awoke the next morning with her head cradled on John's arm. He lifted a wisp of hair from her cheek and tucked it behind her ear, then kissed her forehead. "I never knowed, Emma-girl. I never knowed b'fore now what it were like to love somebody so much it hurts."

She turned to him and pulled his face to her. "You hurt? Where? Here?" She kissed the tip of his nose. "Here?" She kissed his eyes. "Or here?" She leaned on her elbow and kissed his ear."

He laughed and pointed to his lips. "No, ma'am. Here."

"Well, I have just the cure for that." She kissed him soundly.

T'was true. Like fine wine, love sweetened with age.

The end.

MOM HIEBERT'S
Niejoash Kokae

2 ¼ teaspoons dry yeast
½ cups warm water
2 cups milk
3 eggs, beaten
¼ cup butter
¼ cup sugar
2 cups raisins
4-5 cups flour

Dissolve yeast in warm water, along with 1 tsp of the sugar.

Add butter and the rest of the sugar to the milk and scald, stirring to make sure sugar is dissolved.

Cool to lukewarm and add the yeast mixture, eggs, raisins, and enough flour to make a soft dough.

Let rise.

Drop by spoonful into hot deep fat and fry until golden brown.

Roll in sugar.

OTHER TITLES
in the Brides of a Feather trilogy by Julane Hiebert

Robin
BOOK ONE

Lark
BOOK TWO

Wren
BOOK THREE

STORIES IN OTHER COLLECTIONS

"Doctor Kat" in *Unlikely Pursuits*

"A Shelter in a Weary Land" in *Destination: Romance*

Learn more:
www.WingsofHopePublishing.com
www.JulaneHiebertAuthor.com

Est. 2013

Wings of Hope Publishing is committed to providing quality Christian
reading material in both the fiction and non-fiction markets.

Made in the USA
Columbia, SC
06 March 2018